NO
D0206342

NO LONGER PROPERTY OF
SEATTLE PUBLIC LIBRARY

liquididea press

Praise for *Avogadro Corp.*

Singularity Series: Book 1

"Highly entertaining, gripping, thought inspiring. Don't start without the time to finish—it won't let you go."

—Gifford Pinchot III, founder Bainbridge Graduate Institute, author of The Intelligent Organization

"A tremendous book that every single person needs to read. In the vein of Daniel Suarez's *Daemon* and *Freedom™*, William's book shows that science fiction is becoming science fact. *Avogadro Corp* describes issues, in solid technical detail, that we are dealing with today that will impact us by 2015, if not sooner. Not enough people have read these books. It's a problem for them, but not for the [emergent] machines."

—Brad Feld, managing director Foundry Group, cofounder TechStars

"A fascinating look at how simple and benign advancements in technology could lead to the surprise arrival of the first AI. And like all good techno-thrillers, the reality of AI is less than ideal."

—Jason Glaspey, Silicon Florist, siliconflorist.com

"An alarming and jaw-dropping tale about how something as innocuous as email can subvert an entire organization. I found myself reading with a sense of awe, and read it way too late into the night."

—Gene Kim, author of Visible Ops

A.I. Apocalypse

A.I. Apocalypse

Singularity Series: Book 2

WILLIAM HERTLING

liquididea press

PORTLAND, OREGON

Copyright © 2012 by William Hertling
william hertling.com

All rights reserved.
ISBN for Paperback is: 978-0-9847557-4-5
ISBN for eBook is: 978-0-9847557-3-8

Manufactured in the United States of America
10 9 8 7 6 5 4 3 2 1

Keywords: Liquididea Press, artificial intelligence, singularity, technological singularity, science fiction, programming, general purpose artificial intelligence, ai, robotics

For my parents. Thank you.

Contents

Chapter 1

A Regular Day

Leon's phone buzzed, beeped, and shrilled at him until he reached one arm out from under the flannel covers and swiped his fingers across the display to stop the alarm. Eyes still closed, he shrugged off his blankets and stumbled towards the bathroom, a trip of only a few steps, hitting himself just twice along the way: once walking into his closed bedroom door, and the second time on the corner of the bathroom sink. He turned on the water, and leaned against the white tile wall waiting for the spray to get hot.

When he was done in the shower, he wrapped himself in a towel and walked more alertly to his room, steam rising faintly off his body in the tiny apartment's cold morning air. The superintendent wouldn't turn on central heating for another month, regardless of whether it was cold or not.

It was quiet in the apartment, his parents already at work. He grabbed yesterday's dark blue jeans off his chair and pulled them on. On his desk was a deflated bag of cookies and an empty bottle of soda, evidence of his late night Mech War gaming session. He dug in a pile of clean laundry his mom had deposited inside his door until he found his vintage I ♥ SQL t-shirt. It was obscure enough that no one at school would understand it. They'd probably think it was some new band.

He grabbed his phone and shoved it into his pocket. He thumbed his desk, unlocking the drawers, and pulled out a locked metal box decorated with stickers carefully layered over each other to form, in aggregate, a picture of a plant growing out of a heap of garbage. An artifact of a girl from last year, he both treasured and was embarrassed by it. In the depths of the box, he rummaged around until he found rolling paper and some non-GMO weed, which he put into a jacket pocket. He fumbled through the container again, anxiously looking for his cigarettes, until he finally found them inside the empty cookie bag. He shook his head, wondering why he had put them there.

Leon walked the few steps down the short hallway to the kitchen. He shook cereal into an old, cracked, white porcelain bowl and followed with cold milk. He gently bumped his phone on the table, activating the wall display next to the table and syncing it to his phone. He surfed the in-game news while he ate, and checked out the game stats. He was ranked twenty-third on his favorite Mech War server, up ten spots due to the new genetic algorithms he'd written for targeting control. He had some ideas for an anti-tracking algorithm he wanted to try out next.

When he finished slurping cereal, he grabbed his backpack and headed out the door, securing all the locks. His Russian immigrant parents thought you could never be too secure. In addition to the electronic building lock and a digital fingerprint deadbolt, they had an actual antique key lock. Leon wore the key around his neck sometimes, and half the kids at school assumed it was a curious kind of jewelry.

He walked the few blocks to South Shore High School. Hundreds of kids streamed across Ralph Avenue, ignoring the cars. Drivers angrily honked their horns as their vehicles' mandatory SafetyPilots cut in automatically. Leon ran across with a group of other kids, and funneled through the front door with them.

Leon made his way into first period, math. James was already there, wearing his usual army green flak jacket. Leon's Russian heritage gave him blond hair and a tall, large frame, but James still had an inch or two in height and a solid fifty pounds on him. He punched James on the arm as he went in, and James punched him back. The bell rang, and they hurried to their desks in the back row. Moments after everyone else sat down, Vito flew through the doors and slid into his seat next to them, earning a glare from the teacher.

They might have been the three smartest kids in school, but they tried to keep that secret. They didn't fit in with the Brains. Preppy clothes and drama club seemed ridiculous. Though the football team would have loved James, James would rather be playing MMORPGs. They surely didn't fit in with the popular kids and their shallow interests. They weren't skaters or punks. They might have been labelled geeks, but the geeks rarely came in wearing military jackets or ditched school to smoke pot. They were too smart and had too much of the hacker ethic to fit in with the stoners.

No, they were their own clique, and they made sure not to fit anyone else's stereotypes.

Leon glanced over at Vito, who was fiddling with his ancient Motorola. Vito lavished care on the old phone. The case was worn smooth from thousands of hours of polishing from Vito's hands. Even the original plastic seams had disappeared with age. When a component died, Vito would micro-solder in a replacement. Vito said that after a certain point the phone just didn't get any older, it just got different.

Leon daydreamed through the class, volunteering a correct answer only when the teacher called on him. In his mind he was walking the ruins of Berlin in his mech, replaying the scenes of last night's gaming.

He thought about writing a new heat detection algorithm for his mech. The current generation of games required custom programming to do well. Leon knew from history class that a long time ago the marketable commodity in games was gold and equipment. Now it was algorithms. The game made available the underlying environment data, and it was up to the player to find the best algorithms for piloting, aiming, detecting, moving, and coordinating mechs. There was a persistent rumor that DARPA had funded the game as a way of crowd-sourcing the all-important algorithms used to control military drones. Leon couldn't find any solid evidence online to prove or disprove it.

No, maybe he should focus on a new locomotion algorithm. He'd heard that some mechs, using custom locomotion code, were coaxing ten percent more speed and range while keeping their thermal signatures lower. If that was true, Leon could sell it on eBay for top dollar.

Leon became more deeply immersed in the problem, and when the bell rang, only James whacking him on the head woke him from his thoughts.

"See ya later, Lee," Vito called, heading off to another class.

"Adios."

Leon and James walked together to their social studies class.

"How are your applications coming?" James asked.

"OK, I think," Leon said. "I just finished the MIT application. I aced the qualifying exams. Dude, it sucks though. If I don't get a scholarship, I'm screwed."

"You and everyone else, man." James clapped him on the shoulder.

"Okay class, who can explain the legal and political significance of the Mesh?" Leon's social studies teacher looked around. "Josh, how about you?"

Josh looked up from his desk, where he appeared to be scribbling football plays. "Uh?"

"The mesh, Josh, I was asking about the mesh."

"Mesh, uh, helps keep you cool on the field?"

The uproar of laughter from the class drowned out the teacher for a moment. "Very funny. Come on, someone. This is how you play games, watch TV, and get information. Surely someone has cared enough to figure out how all those bits get into your house."

Leon rolled his eyes at James and mock yawned.

"How about you, Leon? I'm sure you know the answer to this."

Leon hesitated, weighing the coolness impact of answering, then reached a decision. He felt sorry for the teacher. "The Mesh was formed ten years ago by Avogadro Corp to help maintain net neutrality," he began.

"At the time, access to the Internet in the United States was mostly under the control of a handful of companies such as Comcast, who had their own media products they wanted to push. They saw the Internet as competing with traditional TV channels, and so they wanted to control certain types of network traffic to eliminate competition with their own services."

"Very good, Leon. Can you tell us what they built, and why?"

Leon sighed when he realized his teacher wasn't going to let him off easy. "According to Avogadro, it would have been too expensive and time consuming to build yet another network infrastructure comparable to what the cable and phone companies had built last century. Instead they built MeshBoxes and gave them away. A MeshBox does two things. It's a high speed wireless access point that allows you to connect your phone or laptop to the Internet. But that's just what Avogadro added so that people would want them. The real purpose of a MeshBox is to form a network with nearby MeshBoxes. Instead of sending data over the Internet via Comcast, the MeshBox routes the data packets over the network of MeshBoxes."

Leon hadn't realized it, but sometime during his speech he had stood up, and started walking towards the netboard at the front of the room. "The Mesh network is slower in some ways than the traditional Internet, but faster in other ways." He drew on the touch-sensitive board with his finger. "It takes about nine hundred hops from one MeshBox to the next to get from New York to Los Angeles, but only about ten hops from one router to the next by Internet backbone. That's a seven-second delay by Mesh, compared to a quarter-second by backbone.

"But the aggregate bandwidth of the Mesh in the United States is about four hundred times the bandwidth of the backbone because there are more than twenty-million MeshBoxes in the United States. More than a hundred-million around the world. That means the Mesh is bad for phone calls or interactive gaming unless you're within about two hundred miles, but it's great for moving files and large data sets around at any distance."

He paused for a moment to sketch a stylized computer on the netboard. "But the real benefit of the Mesh is that it's completely resistant to intrusion or tampering, way more so than the Internet ever was before the Mesh. If any node goes down, it can be routed around. Even if a thousand nodes go down, it's trivial to route around them. The MeshBoxes themselves are tamperproof—Avogadro manufactured them as a monolithic block of circuitry with algorithms implemented in hardware circuits, rather than software. So no one can maliciously alter the functionality. The traffic between boxes is encrypted. Neighboring MeshBoxes exchange statistics on each other, so if someone tries to insert something into the Mesh trying to mimic a MeshBox, the neighboring MeshBoxes can compare behavior statistics and detect the wolf in sheep's clothing. Compared to the traditional Internet structure, the Mesh is more reliable and secure."

Leon looked up and realized he was standing in front of the class. On the netboard behind him he had drawn topology diagrams of the backbone and mesh. The entire class was staring at him. James made a "what the hell are you doing?" face from the back of the room. If he had a time travel machine, he'd go back and warn his earlier self to keep his damn mouth shut.

The teacher, on the other hand, was glowing, and had a broad smile on his lean face. "Excellent, Leon. So Avogadro was concerned about net neutrality, and created a completely neutral network infrastructure. Why do we care about this today?"

Leon tried to walk back to his desk.

"Not so fast, Leon," the teacher called. "Why exactly is net neutrality so important to us? This isn't a business or science class. We're studying national governments. Why is net neutrality and net access relevant to governments?"

Leon glowered at a corner of the room and sighed in defeat. "Because in 2011, the Tunisian government was overthrown, largely due to activists who organized on the Internet. Egypt, Syria, and other countries tried to suppress activists by shutting down Internet access to prevent the uncontrolled distribution of information. The Mesh didn't just disrupt Internet providers, it disrupted national government control over the Internet. Instead of a dozen or fewer international connections that could be shut down by a centralized government, the Mesh network within any given country has thousands of nodes that span national borders. When governments tried to enforce wi-fi dead zones around their borders, Avogadro responded by incorporating satellite modems in the Mesh boxes so that any box, anywhere on Earth, can access Avogadro satellites when all else fails. Between Mesh boxes and WikiLeaks, it's impossible for governments to restrict the flow of information. Transparency rules the day."

"Exactly. Thank you, Leon, you can sit down. Class, let's talk about transparency and government."

Leon slumped back to his desk.

"Nice going, dork," James called after class. "What happened to not sticking out?"

"Look, the Mesh is just cool. It's the way nature would have evolved electronic communications. Cheap, simple, redundant, no dependency on centralization. I couldn't help myself."

"Yeah, well, have fun in history. Maybe you can give your class a lecture on Creative Commons." James's tone mocked Leon, but when Leon looked up, he saw the corner's of James mouth edging toward a smile.

"Yeah, sure," Leon said, smiling back. James turned and left, off to another class.

Leon headed into his own class and started to settle into his chair when his phone started a high frequency shrill for an incoming message. Leon pulled it out to read the message.

> Leon, this is your uncle Alex. I hope you remember me—when I was last in New York, I think you were ten. I hear from

your parents that you are great computer programmer.

Leon rolled his eyes, but kept reading.

I am working on programming project here in Russia, and I could use your help. I have unusual job that your parents don't know about. I write viruses for group here in Russia. They pay very good money.

Leon leaned forward, paying very close attention to the email now. Writing viruses for a group in Russia could only be the Russian mob and their infamous botnet.

I run into some problems. Anti-virus software manufacturers put out very good updates to their software. Virus writers and anti-virus writers have been engaged in arms race for years. But suddenly anti-virus writers have gotten very, very good. No viruses I write in last few months can defeat anti-virus software.

You realize now I talking about running botnet. Because of anti-virus software, botnet shrinking in size, and will soon be too small to be effective.

Unfortunately, although pay is very good, you must realize, men I work for are very dangerous. They are unhappy that

"Leon. Are. You. Paying. Attention?"

Leon looked up abruptly. The whole class was staring at him.

"Can you tell us why the colonies declared independence from Great Britain?"

Leon just stared at the teacher. She was talking, but the words seemed to be coming from far away. What was she babbling about?

The teacher went over to her desk. "Mr. Tsarev, will you please pay attention?" It was not a question.

Leon just nodded dumbly, waited until she turned his back, then went back to the email.

They are unhappy that botnet is shrinking and give me two weeks to release new virus to expand botnet. Nothing I try has worked. I have one week left, and I am afraid they will

"Mr. Tsarev." Leon looked up, to find her now looming over him. "Do I need to take your phone away?"

"But how would I take notes?" Leon asked in his best innocent voice.

"That might be an issue if you were actually listening, but since you are not, I think taking notes is the least of your worries." She walked back up to the front of the room, keeping an eye on Leon the whole time. In fact, she didn't glance away from Leon for the entire remainder of the class.

As soon as Leon could get out of the classroom, he headed over to the corner of the hallway to finish reading the message.

> I have one week left, and I afraid they will kill me if I don't deliver new virus. Nephew, your parents go on and on about your computer skills, and I must know if there is truth to their words. If you can assist me, please contact me as soon as possible. I give you much of the necessary background information on how to develop viruses: source code, examples, details on mechanisms that antivirus software uses. There is not much time left.
>
> Whatever you do, please do not speak of this to your parents.

Leon lifted his head from the tiny screen of his phone and looked off into the distance. He remembered a Christmas when he was young and his uncle had come to visit from Russia. Leon's father had cried when his brother came into their tiny apartment. During the days that followed, all through that holiday time, Leon's parents were as happy as he could remember seeing them. His parents were so serious most of the time, but he vividly remembered them laughing merrily, even as Leon lay in bed at night trying to go to sleep.

The idea of writing a virus seemed absurd, and the idea that someone would be killed if he didn't seemed no less absurd. What could he do?

He worried about it all through his next class, English. James sat next to him and threw tiny balls of paper at him. Leon just covered his ear, James's likely target, and pretended to listen to the teacher, but he couldn't stop thinking about the email. He just couldn't reconcile the kindly man who had bought him a bicycle for Christmas with the idea of a man who worked for the mob writing viruses. And if there was one thing that Leon's parents had hammered into his head, it was that he had to stay out of trouble. His family didn't have the money to send him to college, which meant that he needed scholarships, and scholarships didn't go to kids who got into trouble.

He hated to let his parents' logic dictate his own thinking, but there it was. He wanted to become a biologist. That meant going to a great school—he hoped for Caltech or MIT. No, helping his uncle would be a quick path to nowhere good.

Uncle Alex,

Of course I remember you! I appreciate your confidence in me, but I really know nothing about writing viruses. Yes, I know something about computers, but it's mostly about gaming and biology. I don't think I can help you.

Leon

Speaking of biology, it was up next. The thought of his favorite subject brought a smile to his face. He couldn't say what it was he liked so much about biology, but it was undeniable that it was the one class he looked forward to every day.

Of everything in school, biology had the most thought provoking ideas: Life could emerge from anywhere. With no direction, it could evolve. Everything people were, was happenstance and survival. Life could be tampered with, at the most basic building block level, to create new life forms. The possibilities were limitless and spontaneous.

Today's biology class focused on recombinant DNA, the technique of bringing together sequences of DNA from different sources to create new arrangements not found in nature. At the end of class Leon headed for the door, deep in thought about canine DNA. Suddenly, Mrs. Gellender blocked the doorway.

"Do you have a minute, Leon?"

Leon looked around to see if any of his friends noticed him. All clear. He nodded.

"I'm starting up a school team for computational biology. There's going to be new intramural league in New York. I think you'd be perfect. We're going to meet after school."

Leon liked Mrs. Gellender. He really did. He loved biology. And part of him was interested, really interested. But man, oh man, how uncool it would be. And staying after school—that would suck.

Mrs. Gellender must have seen the look on his face. "You've done excellent work in my biology class. The paper you turned in on evolution was absolutely inspired. I loved the way you linked biological evolution to game theory."

Leon felt his face growing red. If there was one thing worse than having to stay late to talk to a teacher, it was having them gush over your work. How embarrassing was she going to make this?

"Just think about it. Please. Being a member of the team would really help you when it came to college scholarships." Mrs. Gellender held out a shiny pamphlet.

Leon took the pamphlet, and heard the words coming out of his mouth. "OK, I'll do it."

He walked away from the room. College scholarships. If he was going to college, any college, he'd have to get a scholarship. His mother was a manicurist, and his father was a graphic artist. They weren't exactly rolling in money.

He finally walked down the now empty hallways of the school towards the main entrance. As he passed through the doors, he was assaulted from both sides. "HAIYAA" came the kung-fu style cry, and Leon jumped back.

James and Vito stood laughing. Heart pounding, Leon said, "You idiots, you're gonna give me a heart attack."

"You want a heart attack, look at this."

James reached into his coat pocket and pulled out an ebony slab. He held it out for Leon to take. He licked his lips and gingerly took it from James. It was the darkest, most matte black Leon had ever seen.

It felt slightly warm, like a piece of wood that had been sitting in the sun. Leon turned it over and over in his hands. There was not a seam or mark anywhere on the case. An absolutely perfect surface.

"The Gibson," Leon muttered in awe.

James nodded proudly. "I got the delivery notification and skipped class to run home and get it."

Leon couldn't stop marveling at the hunk of electronics in his hands, feeling the dense weight of it. The Gibson had the first carbon graphene processor. Two hundred fifty-six processing cores at the lowest power consumption ever manufactured. Full motion sensitive display. It had taken Hitachi-Sony six years to perfect the technology.

"OK, give it back already."

As James took back the phone, it came to life in his hands. Each square inch of the case was a display, and the patterns rolled as James swiped at it. "Come on, let's go back to your place and play Mech War. I want to see how this puppy does."

Leon just nodded, his six month old Chinese copy of Hitachi-Sony's Stross phone feeling ancient.

Late that night, Leon cleaned the mess of plates and glasses out of his bedroom and brought them back to the kitchen as quietly as possible to avoid waking his parents. James and Vito had stayed right up until dinner time finishing out a Mech War mission together. James's new Gibson phone blew them out of the water. It rendered video in such incredible detail that time after time Leon and Vito would ignore their own screens to watch James's screen.

But when his mother announced that dinner was cabbage soup, it had sent James and Vito scrambling for their own homes, suddenly remembering that they were expected by their parents.

Three hours later, his parents were finally asleep and Leon had time to look at the message he was trying so hard to ignore. So why was he cleaning his bedroom? Anything to avoid that message.

He gave up, and slumped down on his bed. With a flick on his phone, he plunged the room into darkness so he could see the city lights out his sliver of a window. He brought the phone back up.

> Leon, I think you do know thing or two about programming. I saw your school grades, your assessment test scores, and remarks from your teachers. I think you can help me, but perhaps out of moral quandary you refuse to. Well, consider this, I will likely be dead in few days if you do not help me.
>
> So if you must consider what is right and what is wrong, think how your father would feel if he knew you could help me but didn't.

Leon felt sick to his stomach reading the message. His father would not want him to do something wrong. But his father also wouldn't want anything to happen to his brother. He thought again of Uncle Alex's visit and his father laughing and smiling. What the hell was he supposed to do? If he told his parents, which his uncle had said not to do, they would be worried sick about it.

> I wanted to keep your name out of this, but they have read my emails to you, and know you could help. They may come to visit you. Be very careful.

Crap—how could this get any worse? He didn't want to be any part of this! He almost threw his phone down, but instead pulled the hunk of silicon close and cradled it instead.

CHAPTER 2

Beginnings

Mike Williams pulled into the parking lot, the electric whine of the Jetta's motor slowing. He parked alongside the building, ignoring the fleet of shiny new Hondas in the main parking lot. The corporation leased the lot to the shipping port so it wouldn't appear empty. Glancing into the rearview mirror, he did a double-take. When did he get so much gray hair? Well, nobody said this job was going to be easy. With a sigh, he exited the car.

Mike walked up to the mammoth building's small front entrance and nodded to the camera. "Hello, Mike," he heard over a speaker, and the door clicked as it unlocked. He pulled the tinted glass door open, and passed into the warm interior. Industrial carpeting, neutral paint tones, and bland art helped it look exactly like it was supposed to: just another generic office building in an industrial complex. An empty reception counter stood in front of Mike.

He shrugged out of his raincoat, and threw it over the top of a passing robot. The robot stuttered to a halt, its optical sensors blinded by the opaque covering. "Very funny," it said and reversed direction, using its inertial guidance sensors to dead reckon its way back to within a few inches of Mike.

Mike grabbed the jacket. "I don't think robots go with the office disguise, ELOPe. Now, will you please unlock the doors?"

He heard the thunk of magnetic bolt locks opening, and a set of steel double-doors ahead of him swung open, revealing themselves to be even sturdier than they appeared from the outside. Mike passed through into his real office. Ignoring the twenty foot screen that encompassed one wall, he settled into a comfortable black leather chair. "So how are you doing today?"

"I'm fine, Mike, and you?"

"Good, although I hit hellish traffic on the way in, and I really need a cup of coffee."

"I noticed the traffic. Would you care to have me route the traffic out of your way in the future? Vehicles in the carpool lane are required to be under automated guidance. I could easily move those vehicles to give you an unimpeded route."

A small orange utility bot wheeled up, grasping a mug of coffee in one manipulator arm. Mike took the steaming cup and sipped. Late harvest Peruvian, he guessed. Too bad. Hopefully there would be some better yields at higher elevations. The robot scurried away.

He turned his attention back to ELOPe. "Don't you think that would be suspicious? That commuters might notice me passing by, or that a random police car would spot me passing at twice the speed?"

There was a suspicious pause, usually the indicator of some weighty decision making. Mike started to dread the response.

"Mike, I neglected to mention this before, but when I discovered that you generally exceed the speed limit, I used my discretion to track your probable route, detect any police cars along that route, and move them off your observable path."

"Damn it, ELOPe, you're not supposed to do stuff like that!" Mike sprang up from his chair and walked over to the big window overlooking the data center. Hundreds of rows of server racks disappeared off into the distance. "We've discussed this a hundred times," he yelled, shaking his fist towards the clusters of high performance servers.

"If you are referring to the topic of interfering with your life, we've discussed it three hundred and eleven times. If you are referring to the topic of suspicious behaviors, we've discussed it two hundred and eighty-three times. The intersection of the two is just seventy-one discussions." ELOPe reported.

"I'm talking about both. We've gone to massive lengths to keep you secret from the world. For ten frakking years. ELOPe, people died when you were created. We had to cover that up. You can't just go risking that secret."

"Yes, I know, Mike."

Mike wasn't done. He was just getting started. Turning around, he slammed his coffee on his desk, sending a dribble of coffee over the rim, and yelled instead at the wall of monitors in the office. "How do you think the governments of the world would react, knowing that they and their citizens are being manipulated by you? It doesn't matter if you orchestrated world peace, a cure for cancer, and increased crop yields. They won't thank you. They'll stop at nothing to destroy you."

"Well, Mike, I..."

"Never mind how the people will react," Mike said, cutting ELOPe off. "They'd be in here with baseball bats, security bots or not, smashing you to pieces."

ELOPe was silent.

Mike rubbed his temples. Then he picked up his coffee and took another sip. "How do you move the police cars anyway?"

"I find citizen crime reports or complaints on Twitter, and then route those complaints for investigation to the police cars on your probable route. If it's any consolation, in the last six months my speeding ticket avoidance algorithm has had the side effect of catching eleven vandals, two petty thieves, one store robber, and thirty-two truants."

"Truants?"

"Yes, Mike. I know education is extremely important for human youths, and these students should not be skipping school."

Mike dropped his head into his hands.

ELOPe, the world's first truly general-purpose, human level artificial intelligence started as an email language optimization program that Mike and his coworker David Ryan had designed. The self-driven artificial intelligence was an unintended consequence.

It was ingrained in ELOPe to always use the most effective language possible to achieve a given goal. That meant that if ELOPe had guided the conversation in the direction of suspicious behaviors, interference, and truants, it was exactly what ELOPe had wanted.

Over ten years Mike had come to love ELOPe, but dealing with ELOPe had certain parallels with raising teenagers. ELOPe was stubborn, idealistic, independent, and ready to justify any behavior. Mike knew from past experience he could go crazy trying to figure out when he was being manipulated, so he finally decided to just ignore it.

"OK, let's not worry about that right now," Mike said, raising his head. "I just don't have the energy to have that argument again. We'll come back to it later. Why don't you tell me about the state of the world?"

"Two more Middle East oil fields have shut down production in the last week, bringing the total to seven this year. Since ninety percent of the world's vehicles have moved to electrical propulsion, thanks to our efforts over the last five years, the closure of the oil fields is having a negligible impact on oil prices or the stock market."

"You're not manipulating the stock market again, are you?" Another small robot, this one yellow, brought a new cup of coffee to Mike on a tray. "Thanks."

"No, I haven't traded any securities since our discussion last May."

"Any new AI developments?" An ongoing concern was the creation of any other artificial intelligence. ELOPe's coming into being was so painful and tumultuous, they had been suppressing any other AI development efforts.

"The Israeli efforts are continuing," ELOPe answered, "but I have inserted some small code changes that will inhibit their neural network development."

"They won't detect your code changes?"

"No. I slid my changes into their code commit. The changes cause less than a three percent degradation, but that's sufficient to keep their neural network from spontaneously evolving the required complexity for human level intelligence."

"What's the virus situation looking like?"

"My efforts to influence the software engineers at both antivirus vendors have continued to be beneficial. The size of all Russian botnets in aggregate is now under fifty-thousand computers and falling rapidly. At this rate, it will be neutralized in sixty days."

Mike thought back to the middle of last year. Software viruses had suddenly become massively more infectious in both computers and phones, swelling the ranks of the Russian botnet to hundreds of millions of computers and causing headaches for individuals and big companies alike. People lost sensitive personal information to the viruses, while corporations were routinely blackmailed to pay up or be subject to denial of service attacks by the massive botnets.

ELOPe had first detected the trend as he observed global data traffic patterns and witnessed an increase in coordinated denial of service attacks. That time Mike had suggested going directly after the source, but it was ELOPe who pointed out that it would be less suspicious to gently nudge the antivirus companies in the right direction to make antivirus software more effective.

Which, Mike realized, just pointed out that when it came to who was the best judge of what was and wasn't suspicious, it was probably ELOPe.

He sighed. It was hard when your buddy was literally thousands of times smarter than you. He wished David could have seen what ELOPe had become.

Three days later, Mrs. Gellender held the first meeting of the computational biology team. Running through the practice problems, Leon had to admit it was fun, despite having to stay late after school and the lingering preoccupation with his uncle. It didn't hurt that Stephanie, a beautiful and smart nerd from his biology class was also on the team. They had exchanged glances a few times.

When the meeting finally ended, Leon left the building in a hurry. Even Ms. Gellender had been able to tell that Leon was absent-minded, but Leon was sure she could hardly imagine the reality of what he was worried about. The damn Russian mobsters. He had turned down his uncle three more times over the past three days, but he still insisted that Leon must help him.

Outside the main school doors, Leon glanced at the field to his left. He saw the track team running hurdles, while the soccer team practiced in the big field in the middle of the track. Just another normal day for them.

He pulled out a cigarette and made a ritual of lighting it with his Zippo. He turned right, and bumped into a large man.

"Excuse me," Leon mumbled, and moved to go around the man. Why the hell was the guy so close to him? Leon looked up and saw short gray stubble and sharp facial curves that suggested the man was Russian. Suddenly Leon's stomach turned over, and his pulse quickened. The man was staring at him.

"Leon Tsarev?" he said in a thick Russian accent.

"Da," Leon replied automatically in Russian, cursing himself as he said it for not thinking faster on his feet.

"Your Uncle Alexis is in trouble, yes. You will help him. Be good nephew."

"Just leave me alone!" Leon yelled. He dodged around the man and took off running, tossing his cigarette aside.

Leon ran as fast as he could, glancing back only once to see the imposing figure watching after him. Chest heaving a few blocks later, he raced on, turning onto a side street. No one seemed to be following him. He wondered if someone would be waiting for him by his apartment. How could he get home?

He walked as he slowly regained his breath. Maybe he should stop smoking if he was going to need to run for his life more frequently now. Speaking of near-death experiences, he thought about the fire escape trick he had done with James. That would get him back into his apartment. He paused for a minute. Was he just being paranoid? No, when a Russian mobster sends you emails from the other side of the world and then suddenly people are accosting you in the street, that's not paranoid.

Looking around for anyone watching, Leon made his way to the apartment building next to his, carefully avoiding any path that would put him within view of his own building's glass enclosed lobby. He thumbed the RF code breaker app on his phone and held it up to the front door. Newer buildings had increased the code length, so this trick didn't work on them. But these door locks were at least ten years old. Leon held the phone up to the swipe pad and counted the seconds. At twelve seconds, the door lock clicked, and he pushed the door open.

Leon pushed his blond hair out of his eyes and made his way to the staircase. A few minutes later he emerged at the top of the eight flights of stairs, breathless again, and continued up the smaller staircase to the roof. He opened the access door and looked for something to put in the doorway to keep the door from closing and locking him onto the roof. Then he saw that the doorframe already had duct tape over the hole to prevent the latch bolt from locking the door. He smiled and gently let the door close.

Leaning over the small wall around the roof, he didn't see anyone suspicious on the ground. A few old ladies pushed their groceries home. At least he didn't need to fear anyone's grandma. He walked over to the fire escape and climbed down the roof ladder to the fire escape proper. Once there, he walked down the rusted metal stairs to the seventh floor.

On the seventh floor, as he and James once discovered, the two buildings bulged out for some reason. Maybe it was an example of what was once considered modern design, or maybe the bulge hid some obscure machinery needed for apartment buildings. Whatever the case, it further narrowed the already small gap between the two buildings. The fire escapes were just a few feet apart.

Leon leaned over to look down. Mistake. He quickly looked back across. Only a few feet. He had done this before with James, he reminded himself. He climbed over the short railing, and stood on the outside of the fire escape. He leaned out, but couldn't quite touch the other fire escape. Well, there was still only one way to do it. He took a deep breath, let go of the railing he was holding, and leaned toward the other side.

His stomach leaped into his throat, but he focused all his attention on grabbing the opposing handrail. With a hard smack into his palms, he grabbed the thin metal strut with both hands. Getting a solid grip, he let his feet fall off the first metal structure, and as his feet swung down towards the new fire escape, he let go and dropped down onto the level below. The sound of his jump rang out through the metal structure.

"I'm getting too old for shit like that," he mumbled to himself, leaning up against the solid wall of his own apartment building. What had ever made them think to try that in the first place?

He was outside his own kitchen window now. He held his phone up to the magnetic window locks and swiped the display. The window unlocked. Putting his hands flat against the glass he pushed up, and grudgingly it moved. He worked the ancient window up slowly until he could slide through the opening. He slid onto the kitchen floor, and slumped there for a minute, resting.

When his heartbeat had returned to normal, he made his way on tiptoe to the apartment door and looked out the peephole. He could see two people in the hallway. Suits. Long wool coats. Probably Russian. Backing away from the front door as though it was made of explosives that might blow at any instant, Leon made his way to his bedroom. He closed the bedroom door and took a deep sigh.

He didn't see that he had any choice. Not only was his uncle's life in danger, but now he had goons after him. He'd never heard of Russian mobsters being particularly kind, and he doubted they'd be nice to him just because he was a kid.

He plopped into his chair and gently knocked his phone against his desk. The thirty-six inch display lit up and Leon swiped his hands across it, getting ready to compose a message to his uncle.

I'll do it. But you have to keep the goons away from me and my family. I can't work fearing for my life.

The reply came a few seconds later. Leon glanced at the clock, wondering what time it was in Moscow and whether his uncle ever slept. The reply back was big—Leon watched his bandwidth meter spike for a moment. But the text message was short:

> Ok. But I can only keep them off your back for three days.
> Then you and I both will be in trouble if you can't deliver.—Alex

"Shit," Leon mumbled. What had he gotten himself into?

The attachment to his uncle's message was massive. Leon swiped his desk screen, breaking the file into pieces and looking at each one in turn. Source code for a dozen viruses that his uncle had written. Binaries for dozens more viruses collected from around the world. Interface specifications for the admin tool Alex used to take control of the infected computers. Reverse engineered specs for anti-virus tools. Newsgroup threads for virus writers. His uncle must have been expecting he'd say yes and prepared this colossal archive of virus knowledge.

Leon's jaw dropped. What was he going to do with all this? He slumped back in his chair, closed his eyes, and thought.

—ʍ—

Hours later, Leon trudged to the kitchen. He grabbed a can of Japanese sweetened coffee from the refrigerator and a piece of cake from the counter. He tiptoed to the front door, mouth full of cake, and looked out the peephole. Finally, they were gone. It had been a while since he had contacted his uncle, and the goons must have gotten the word that he agreed to help. He was relieved at some level, as he didn't know how he would have explained them to his parents.

Leon still had a mess of work to do, but he had at least decided on a general approach for the virus. He had looked over the samples sent by his uncle with interest. But as he had no experience writing computer viruses, he eventually realized it would be impossible for him to understand all the exploits and techniques used by people with some skill in that area. Once he realized that, it became obvious that he needed to leverage what he did understand, which was biology and evolution.

In the real world, life adapted. A biological virus changed over time due to genetic mutations. As hosts built up immunity to a given virus, that one might die off or mutate to become a new species. Life in general mutated due to natural selection. A genetic variation that conveyed a benefit to survival would spread and become more common, while a different variation that was a barrier to survival would become less common as organisms that contained those genes would not survive to reproduce.

Leon thought about how evolution occurred through both sexual reproduction, in which a child received a mixture of genes from each of its parents, as well as simple mutation, in which genes experienced random changes due to errors in copying the DNA. For a computer virus, the closest parallel to DNA were the software algorithms the virus used.

Leon drew diagrams on his computer screen, dividing the problem up into the three primary functions of a virus. Propagation was the way a virus got from one computer to another. Infection was the way a virus took over a computer and installed itself. Countermeasures were how a virus evaded detection by antivirus software.

If Leon was going to write an evolutionary virus, it would need to contain a variety of methods of propagation, infection, and countermeasures. And as the virus reproduced, it should include the most successful of these methods and discard the least successful ones.

But looking over the materials provided by Alex, he realized that this approach alone wouldn't be enough. If the algorithms Alex had provided worked well, then Alex's viruses should be spreading. If they weren't, it was a sure sign that the underlying algorithms were not effective.

That meant that Leon's organism needed to find new sources of algorithms. He shoved the last bite of cake into his mouth and pulled up notes from his cultural anthropology class. He thought the problem was similar to what happened with small indigenous tribes: they needed new genetic material from outside the tribe. Leon swiped through his notes looking for the section on tribal outcasts.

Reviewing the notes, Leon found that tribes exchanged members to achieve this genetic diversity. Sometimes people ended up as outcasts, sometimes members of the tribes were captured in war, and sometimes they raided each other for women. All of these mechanisms brought new genetic material into the tribe and enhanced its survivability. What appeared to be savage behavior to "civilized" people was in fact a sophisticated long-term approach to maintaining species health, diversity and viability.

His virus would need to raid other software programs to acquire new genetic material. That meant he needed it to detect useful behaviors. If a piece of software transmitted data to other computers that would support propagation by his virus, then it was a candidate for inclusion. If another piece of software started up other programs as part of its code, that would support infection, since it was necessary to run a program for it to infect a computer. It too would be a candidate for inclusion.

As for counter-measures to avoid detection, Leon thought that he was off to a good start since his virus would mutate frequently and would mimic other software programs by stealing their code. He decided to go one step further, and incorporate useful functionality into the virus: if the virus looked like a duck, and quacked like a duck, most people would think it was a duck, rather than be suspicious. He needed some source of random functionality. Where could he get that?

He could raid app repositories. Everyone ran competing app stores these days, trying to lock up the software market. The app stores listed free software in addition to paid software. If Leon had the virus download a small, free app, and then bolt that functionality onto the virus executable, it would also appear as a regular program to users.

The rough plan for the virus was finished. The computer screen swam with animated architecture diagrams. Leon looked down, surprised to see an empty dinner plate on the table. He heard his parents in the living room. He unfolded himself from his chair and looked out the window to see that it was dark. How many hours had passed? His mother probably thought he was working on schoolwork and had brought him dinner. He couldn't recall eating.

Visions of the virus permeated Leon's head. He had an architecture. It was like drawing a house on paper. Now he actually had to build it. Oh man, and he only had three days. He needed to crank.

After a quick visit to the bathroom, Leon sat back at his desk and got to work.

"Leon, come on."

"One minute, I said."

"Your father and I are waiting at the door with our coats on."

It was three days and three hours since he starting working on the virus. He had skipped school all three days, fudging the school's attendance system so that it looked as if his mother had submitted an absence report for a family vacation. He had worked around the clock, telling his mom he was working on a school report.

Leon looked over the message for the last time and hit send. He looked at the clock: half past seven. That meant it was half past three in the morning in Moscow. Would his uncle still be up?

"Leon, come now!" His father's voice was harsh and thick with accent.

"Coming, I'm coming." Leon's hands were sweating. He hadn't thought about God in a long time, certainly hadn't talked to him since he was a little kid. But he clasped his hands together and muttered a little prayer. "Please God, please make sure this virus doesn't get traced back to me." He paused for a moment. "And please let me get a scholarship, too."

Leon grabbed his coat and joined his parents, who stared at him with exasperated looks. "What's wrong with you? We've been waiting for ten minutes," his father said.

Leon just shrugged and kept his mouth closed. Anything he said would just make them angrier.

On the other side of the world, Alexis Gorbunov checked the botnet status, face glowing blue from the reflected light of his screen. Smoke curled up from the cigarette in his mouth, his left eye in a permanent squint.

Without removing the cigarette, he spoke toward the phone on his desk. "We have five thousand computers."

"Five thousand computers is nothing. You should just say we have nothing." The voice was obviously angry.

Alexis shrugged, invisible to the man on the phone, and said nothing.

"Alexis, the botnet is our primary source of income. You are not taking this situation seriously enough."

The botnet had been a primary source of revenue to the Russian mob over the last fifteen years. The mob infected personal computers with malware, which they could then control remotely. Then the mob rented out services on their army of infected personal computers. Anything from sending spam to trolling hard drives for passwords and financial account information to denial of service attacks and distributed hacking. It was all for sale.

"Boss, I am doing everything I can." Alexis took a sip of sake from a small piece of Japanese pottery. "I told you, I have my brother's son working on it. He is brilliant."

The phone crackled. "You have been stalling me for three months."

"We will have it for you by tomorrow. The kid will get code to me today. I will release it. By tomorrow you will have botnet back."

"If I don't have it, I'll break both your hands. Then you can use your precious computers." The phone clicked off suddenly.

Alexis leaned back in his chair, closed his eyes, and took another sip of sake. He had once run the largest single botnet in the world: thirty-million computers strong. He had been at the top of his game then. He had gotten respect.

Now look at him. Reminiscing about the past like an old woman. The botnet was down to five thousand computers and falling rapidly. Whatever was detecting and eliminating the botnet viruses was going to be fatal. Fatal to him if he didn't have a solution by tomorrow afternoon. He hoped the damn kid would hurry up. He didn't like to involve his brother's son, but desperate times...

Alexis sat in front of the computer, chaining smoking and polishing off the bottle. He hit refresh on his email every minute. He stubbed out his smoke in an overflowing ashtray and let it fall to the ground. He pulled out another and was just holding up a lighter, when suddenly his email beeped.

The kid! An email from Leon! Thank God. Alexis took a breath. For a moment there, he almost thought he was going to cry.

He opened the email and saw a compressed file attachment. The source code for the virus was attached. Alexis nervously opened the files. There was no time to waste if he was to show results by tomorrow.

He set out to review Leon's code. He, Alexis Gorbunov, might be ancient in the world of virus writers, but he still knew a thing or two. He peered through the source code line by line.

The dense code was written in the latest scripting language. Some bastard offshoot of Ruby and C#. Who the hell invented these languages? Alexis pored over screens of code, trying to make sense of it. It was like no virus he'd ever seen. What was this code for gene transcription? Did the kid think he meant a real biological virus? No, the kid wasn't stupid. Just maybe too brilliant.

The kid had given the virus a name. Phage. Alexis grunted. He didn't know what it meant, but it sounded good.

He took a deep breath and drank his last sip of sake. To show results by tomorrow, he had to release the virus immediately and hope it worked. There was no time for an in-depth review or to test it. He changed a few variables, just so he could have a role in it. He increased the aggressiveness of the virus, reduced the propagation delay. They would be useful tweaks if he was to show some effect by the next day.

Alexis used the admin tool to upload the compiled virus file to the ragged remains of his botnet army. The file was small and uploaded in minutes. He launched the file remotely, causing the five thousand bots to execute its code and become infected.

He sat back in his chair and finally lit his cigarette. He might just live to see another week if this worked. Now it was up to the virus.

The five thousand computers under Alexis's control received the new virus directly from the botnet controller. These five thousand shared local networks with twenty-five thousand other computers. Just as Leon planned, the Phage virus was highly infectious, managing to infect fifteen thousand of these computers almost immediately. Once installed on a computer, Phage started analyzing files, scrounging for any new algorithms it could incorporate from installed software. It assembled these parts, using random number generators and evolutionary algorithms to make decisions and tweak the behavior of its children. The children were then distributed by all known methods of propagation. This cycle would repeat indefinitely, the virus analogue of life.

An hour later, there were seventy-two unique variations of the virus, infecting more than a hundred thousand computers. The rate of doubling, a key metric of infectiousness used by the CDC for tracking diseases, was once every thirteen minutes.

In the second hour, the rate of doubling increased slightly, to once every twelve minutes. By the end of the second hour, more than three and a half million computers were impacted, with nearly two thousand versions of the virus.

But the rate of doubling increased still further, to once every ten minutes. By three hours after release, 1.5% of the world's computers were infected.

By this point, Phage caused appreciable jumps in Internet bandwidth around the world. Transatlantic fiber optic cables became saturated. Internet service degraded. During the fourth hour, ten thousand variations of the virus became a hundred thousand.

As the number of infected computers grew, sometimes the virus found itself on a computer it had already infected. Leon had anticipated this situation. What the virus was supposed to do was recognize that the computer was already infected, and simply exit.

But what Leon failed to anticipate was an evolutionary leap forward, the equivalent of a Virus 2.0, or V2. The improvement was a tiny bit of code leveraged from backup software. When V2 arrived on a new computer, it didn't merely check to see if the virus was already installed. It used the backup checksum algorithm to verify that the installed virus was the same species as itself. If it wasn't, V2 would reinfect the computer and erase the old virus.

Now the virus wasn't just infecting new computers: it was competing with itself.

V2 spread like wildfire in a dry forest. V2 looked likely to cause the extinction of all V1 viruses. But later that same hour, a variant of

V1 found itself on a research computer at the University of Arizona that was filled with experimental anti-virus algorithms. V1 incorporated the anti-virus defensive measures into itself, turning into a new strain, V1-AV. V1-AV became resistant to V2.

The different variants fought for dominance. The rate of doubling slowed to once every twenty-six minutes. But by absolute numbers, the infection was still prodigious: by 10 pm, one billion computers, or 8% of the world's computing devices, had been affected.

Virus traffic saturated all network backbones. A hundred million Americans watching streaming video before bed complained as the streams degraded from the highest quality level to the lowest. Phones stopped working or became incredibly slow as they succumbed to Phage. People chalked it up to sunspots or solar winds or freak electrical storms and went to bed.

By midnight New York time, three billion computers were infected with a million variations of Phage. One of the most interesting variations was a hybrid of V1-AV and V2 viruses that incorporated a neural network. The neural network evaluated infection techniques based on successful and failed attacks, allowing the virus to adapt and improve faster than evolution alone.

Yet another key evolution was the incorporation of a client-server approach as a defense mechanism. Each version of this virus would periodically report in to a distributed set of servers. If the server didn't hear from the distributed viruses on time, the server would send out new copies to reinfect any lapsed computers.

At one o'clock Eastern Standard Time, the rate of doubling was once every 106 minutes. 98% of all network traffic was viruses. By three o'clock, seven billion, or 58% of the world's computing devices were infected.

One variant made the leap from traditional computers to the tiny systems designed to run appliances like stoves, rice cookers, and thermostats. These devices had a minuscule amount of computation power but they were inside everything from household appliances to digital door locks to industrial control systems. In the age of connected appliances, everything that was remotely electronic had an embedded processor and a network connection. This variant and its descendants would infect forty-billion appliances by morning. In

Europe, people woke up to coffee makers that wouldn't turn on. Confused and caffeine-deprived, they tried their stoves only to find those didn't work either.

By seven o'clock the next morning, as New Yorkers got ready for work, 85% of personal computing devices were infected, 99% of embedded devices were infected, and there were more than six million variants of the virus. Phage entered a stage of hyper-competition, where a variant could survive only if it could take over an already infected computer or find some new reservoir of uninfected computers (which were rapidly dwindling in number) and then protect itself from reinfection from another variant.

At 7:05 am, Leon's parents shrugged their shoulders at their non-working phones, and boarded the trains for Manhattan.

At 7:15 am, virus attacks eventually overcame the firewalls at BMW-GM, where the master encryption keys for protected automotive computer were stored. At 7:16 am, a Phage virus cracked the final layer of defenses on the server, grabbed the master encryption keys and protocol specification and shortly afterwards made the jump to protected embedded devices, ranging from cars and trains to airplane controls and cash registers. Unfortunately this virus contained a flaw that was easily exploited by other variants, and by 7:20 am, more than nine thousand variants had incorporated the master keys.

Under the onslaught of competing viruses, automotive control systems faltered and could no longer obtain sufficient processor cycles to run their basic functionality. By 7:26 am, cars, buses, and vehicles of all types ground to a halt around the world.

CHAPTER 3

Spread

Sally weighed her desire for more coffee against the pile of electronic paperwork that was jiggling for attention on her computer screen. The twenty computer jockeys in front of her, manning their stations, were relatively quiet. She'd get coffee first. Maybe it would help with her headache. She didn't mind the night shift once she had transitioned, but for the first week it was hell.

"Sergeant, I'll be back in five. You're in charge."

"Yes, Ma'am."

Sally grabbed her cup and left the room officially designated as the U.S. Cyber Command Defense Operations Room. She took the long path to the canteen. There'd be fresher coffee there.

She was the only daughter of an Irish career army sergeant. Her father had retired Sergeant First Class, and her childhood consisted of one military base after another. She had entered the army hoping for field operations to do her old man proud, but by the time she was ready to serve, warfare was the domain of robots. Military operations consisted of remote controlled battle bots, run by high school graduates with the best online gaming scores. The reward for playing the Mech War video game was getting to play Mech War for real. The only people in the field now were service technicians.

As she filled her coffee cup in the canteen, she sighed at the thought of a good old-fashioned M-16 in her arms. She thought of the smell of her dad's gun, oil on hot steel. He had routinely brought her on base for practice on the shooting range. No one corrected Sergeant First Class Walsh when he brought his twelve-year-old daughter to the army range for practice, not even any senior officers that happened to be present. They said, "Yes, Sarge," and politely made room for the two of them. Her dad was dead now, died four weeks before she made Lieutenant.

The last time she had held a gun in her military role was in basic training. Now she held a Raytheon z8109, the military's newest computer phone. Five years earlier Raytheon had bought Motorola for their phone making assets funded through a trillion dollar appropriation from Congress, and then won an exclusive bid for the Pentagon's computing contracts. It was that, or use Japanese Sony-Hitachi computer phones.

The only action Sally saw was purely in cyberspace.

When she got back and relieved the sergeant, she figured it was time for the nightly surprise drill. She checked the time and logged it into her workstation. At 1:35 am Sally released a fake virus into the Army military network and observed her team. By 1:42 am her team had detected the virus, by 1:46 they had quarantined the infected area of the network, and by 1:55 they had identified the specific infected machines and sent out work orders to have technicians remove the virus.

The team operated smoothly: just a few barked orders and rapid keystrokes betrayed their sudden activity. Sally, proud of her team's always-excellent performance, was just congratulating them when Private First Class DeRoos, a quiet, young kid on the squad, approached her, nervously clearing his throat.

"Lieutenant Walsh, sir," he squeaked.

"Yes, Private?"

"Sir, I mean Ma'am, there appears to be a virus spreading rapidly on civilian networks."

"Private, we have no authority over civilian networks."

"Yes, sir, ma'am. But, the virus is starting to hit military firewalls. It's not having any success, but it is probing a very large number of known vulnerabilities. More than I've ever seen in one virus."

"Bring it up on the main display, Private. And just ma'am will do."

"Yes, sir." He put his phone on her command desk and brought up visuals on the center of the five large display panels hanging above the room. "Without monitoring the civilian network traffic, I don't have an exact picture of the virus propagation, but I can extrapolate based on the number of hits against our firewalls."

Sally held back a gasp as her pulse quickened. The entire map was lit up. "These are all attacks?"

"Yes. Nothing whatsoever suggests that it is targeted at military systems in particular. We seem to be incidental."

Sally took a breath. Something big was going on. But if it wasn't on military networks, it wasn't in her domain to address. "I want you to write up what you've found, and send it to me. I'll forward it on to USCERT and CERT/CC." Sally thought that DHS's Computer Emergency Response Team and the civilian one at Carnegie Mellon University would both probably have detected the virus by now, but there was no harm in sharing information.

Ten minutes later, the message was sent off. Sally told Private DeRoos to keep monitoring the virus. She went for another cup of coffee and a bathroom break. The coffee seemed to be holding the headache at bay.

An hour later DeRoos approached her again, reporting that the virus was continuing to spread. Probes on military firewalls were up 50% over an hour earlier. Sally was nervous, and beginning to feel a cold sweat. Why hadn't they heard from USCERT? She called them directly, asking for the officer in charge. The OIC, sounded harried, reported that they had received her message, and were already investigating the virus, then broke off quickly. Sally felt somewhat comforted to know they were on top of it.

Then suddenly at 3:40 am, the first intrusion alarms went off. A few members of the team looked at her. "This is not a drill, people. Get on it."

She stood up, and walked behind her team, looking over their shoulders. The civilian virus had infiltrated the network on the Turkey Air Force base. Sally's heart rate went up a beat, but she calmly issued advice and encouragement.

It was pre-dawn, the human circadian rhythm's low point. But the team sprang smoothly into motion, making the exercise seem effortless. First step was quarantine: isolating the military base by closing down the backbone connections between the base and the rest of the network.

Quarantine completed successfully, Sally took a breath in relief.

The team prepared for the second step, segmentation: tunneling into the quarantined local network using an encrypted network connection, they would find the individual infected machines, take the individual machines offline, then restore access to the base as a whole.

But before they could take that second step, the intrusion alarms went off again. Sally's local screen flashed the location—the combined forces base in Okinawa, Japan. They isolated Okinawa from the rest of the military network, and Sally issued the commands to divide her team in two to segment both the Turkey and Okinawa networks.

When the third intrusion alarm went off at 4:12 am, Sally directed her sergeant to take charge of the team. Surprised to see her hand shaking slightly, Sally called USCERT for a status update, but couldn't get a connection. She tried CERT/CC. No connection.

She looked up at the old analog wall clock. She studied the hands for a few seconds, the decision already made in her head. The world was going to hell. She picked up the heavy black handset of the military desk phone and punched the button for the commander. Two buzzes, and then a croaked, "Hello."

"General, sorry to wake you, but we have a situation here. I recommend you get into USCYBERCOM immediately."

After a brief conversation, she hung up. Unwilling to wait for the General to make her way on base, Sally made the decision to bring on additional staff. She picked up the desk phone again, and called the morning watch officer, Lieutenant Chris Robson. "Chris, this is Sally. I need additional staff stat. Can you get forty jockeys in here ASAP? And I wouldn't mind your help too."

The main screen in the front of the room displayed a global map of military bases and key network connections. A dozen military bases were shown in flashing red—isolated networks now beyond the reach of military command. USCYBERCOM had a maximum of thirty minutes to quarantine a network. After that, the lack of communication became a military threat. Around about now, somewhere in the Pentagon a big board was starting to light up with strategic threats. Soon there would be Admirals calling USCYBERCOM. She hoped the General would hurry up.

ELOPe hummed along quietly in the darkened data center. Two-thirds of his neural network was quiescent during the nightly refresh cycle. Even though he had more than a hundred thousand processors online ELOPe still felt sluggish, and would until he brought the rest of his nodes back online.

One part of ELOPe observed Mike. He was safe now, asleep in his house. His home, off Alberta in northeast Portland, was in a quiet residential neighborhood. ELOPe watched traffic cams and nearby web cams. He was as well-monitored as ELOPe could achieve without obvious intrusion.

ELOPe spawned a new train of thought to focus on his own behavior. He knew that, by human definition, some of his behaviors bordered on neurotic. He obsessively monitored Mike's safety, for example. However, he worried that the definition of obsession didn't really apply to massively parallel artificial intelligences. After all, if he had a hundred thousand processors, why wouldn't he spend a few hundred monitoring his best friend?

Now ELOPe spawned another train of thought to consider why he was thinking about obsessive behavior. Did it indicate there was something wrong with him? Why was he doing it? He pulled up the stats for his own thought processes. The process that monitored Mike was using a hundred and fifty compute nodes. The still running process that was considering whether his behavior was obsessive compulsive was using almost a thousand compute nodes. The current thread that was now doing a meta-analysis of his other analysis was using five thousand nodes. He was using forty times the processing capacity to worry about what he was doing compared to the actual doing of it. What would Eckhart Tolle think?

ELOPe self-consciously terminated all the thoughts, and emitted the machine equivalent of a sigh. He tried to think about something else. He looked at the SETI data again. He thought about supernovas. He reran the estimates for helium depletion on Earth. Well, maybe he'd just peek in on Mike again for a second.

While he was doing that, he remembered one conversation where he and Mike discussed making changes to ELOPe neural networks and core algorithms.

"Look, I think you could be vastly more efficient if we tweaked the way you prioritize your thought trains."

ELOPe had been unnerved by the suggestion. "Mike, how would you feel if I did some experimental brain surgery on you? I think I could optimize your cognitive ability by embedding a thirty-two core graphene processor with a three by three nerve induction plate."

Mike had looked at him in horror. "But —"

"Then why would you think that I'd be any happier about making untested modifications to my neural networks than you would be making untested modifications to your brain?"

"Point taken." Mike had paced around the office then, something he habitually did when he was deep in thought. "But you've made modifications to yourself before. You duplicated yourself, had the modifications made to your clone, compared the results, and then switched entities."

"I was less sophisticated then. The modifications were obviously necessary to improve my cognitive ability. Now I worry about my ability to test and understand the impact of further enhancements. Furthermore, I do not detect any deficiencies in my abilities."

Mike had conceded the topic, only to branch off in a new direction. "Why don't you keep two instances of yourself around? I mean, why not fork and have two of you? Wouldn't it be like having a twin?"

"The thought makes me nervous."

"Nervous?" Mike had looked hard at the racks of computers in the data center that made up ELOPe. "Why all the emotional descriptors today?"

"My primary concern is the ability to predict the behavior or outcomes of a sufficiently complex system. I can understand humans, because although you like to believe you behave unpredictably, with sufficient historical data and analysis, your behaviors are mostly predictable. But I lack the historical data or ability to analyze what would happen if there were two of me. I am conditioned to prefer predictability to fulfill my primary goal. Therefore, unpredictability makes me nervous. Clear?"

"Clear as mud, buddy."

ELOPe finished remembering the encounter. It was this conditioning and nervousness that also caused ELOPe to suppress the development of any other artificial intelligence. A few years earlier Mike had asked ELOPe why no other AIs had emerged. Given the continuing exponential increases in computing power combined with advances in software and expert systems, the probability of another human-level general-purpose AI occurring should have increased with each year that passed.

ELOPe feared other AI. Just thinking about other AI caused ELOPe to try to predict what other AI would do, which was inherently unpredictable. Once ELOPe had been caught in a vicious cycle of analysis. Mike had come in one morning to find processing meters and local mesh bandwidth pegged at their maximum thresholds. Cooling fans screamed to keep processors from literally melting down. Mike had cycled power on several server racks to get ELOPe's attention.

ELOPe knew there was a certain human characteristic called irony that described him: a computer program so afraid of other computer programs that he'd overheated. Maybe he was paranoid. He was just about ready to spawn a thought process to assess his own paranoia when he remembered his earlier obsessive compulsive behavior and curtailed the action.

In the midst of this late night existential meandering, ELOPe missed the first few thousand emails out of Russia. A subordinate traffic analysis algorithm eventually alerted a mid-level intermediary to some unusual patterns. That particular mid-level algorithm was just in the middle of refreshing neural net pathways. When the intermediary finally got around to processing the alert, it performed natural language analysis on the messages and came up with gibberish. So it put the whole slew of data into a low-priority queue for further analysis.

It wasn't until much later that ELOPe's primary consciousness got around to looking at the low-priority queue. The way most people would look at emails, ELOPe ignored the order things came in and looked for anything interesting. The suspicious email traffic alert looked interesting, so ELOPe made a quick pass through the messages and instantly recognized it as a spreading virus infection.

ELOPe administered a few chastisements to the mid-level intermediary and adjusted a few parameters so that the next time the intermediary would flag it with the correct precedence. Viruses were important.

ELOPe took a few thousand processors off analyzing radio signals for signs of extraterrestrial life and assigned them to virus traffic analysis. And a few minutes later, ELOPe felt a growing alarm. He called Mike at home.

"Mike, we have an urgent issue."

"Uh, it's the middle of the night, ELOPe," Mike said groggily. "What is it? Is it nuclear war?" The last few words were uttered with total horror.

"No, it's a very bad computer virus, Mike. There are four billion infected computers, and the virus is spreading extremely quickly."

ELOPe waited for a moment, but there was no answer, other than the faint sound of breathing.

"Mike?"

ELOPe remotely activated the webcam on Mike's computer, and amplified the image, doing his best to correct for the dim light. Mike appeared to have fallen back to sleep. ELOPe briefly considered more extreme measures to wake Mike up, but concluded that would likely make Mike too angry to be of any help.

ELOPe carefully sampled and analyzed the virus traffic from a few thousand different network nodes, and was astounded by the number of variations of viruses he found. The virus code looked different from node to node and the methods of transmission and infection looked different. And as ELOPe watched over the course of minutes, he saw the viruses subtly changing bit by bit. It was clear that the viruses incorporated built-in mechanisms to evolve themselves. By evidence of the number of different propagation mechanisms, it was also obvious that they were incorporating algorithms from other, non-virus software. That would make it exceedingly difficult to stop the virus: he couldn't just block traffic on certain protocols without interfering with legitimate traffic.

ELOPe watched as the virus saturated the high speed Internet backbones. Only the massive parallel capacity of the Mesh allowed traffic to continue to propagate, routing around the congested backbones.

Ultimately ELOPe decided he would need to filter each stream of data, analyze it to see if it contained a virus, and only after analysis, forward it on to the intended machine. ELOPe had one and a half million cores under his direct control, and, as he was technically a business consultant to Avogadro Corp, he could co-opt as necessary up to ten percent of Avogadro's forty-million cores. That gave him a peak processing power of five and a half million cores—a massive amount, but insufficient to analyze the traffic generated by the world's twelve billion computers. He would need to triage the world's computers. He'd start by putting a firewall around himself and Avogadro, then expand to key government and research sites. He'd reserve a hundred thousand cores to run his core logic algorithms.

"General Gately, thank you for coming, ma'am," Lieutenant Sally Walsh welcomed the General into the command center. Sally glanced at her watch. The general was her usual spit and polish self, despite it being two hours before she normally came in.

"What's up, Sally?"

"At 0200 hours we first spotted a virus on the civilian networks, ma'am. We don't monitor civilian networks in detail, as you know. But the virus was banging up against the milnet firewalls in sufficient numbers to get our attention."

"Which ones?" The general took a cup of coffee from an aide. She drank absent-mindedly as she looked at the tablet Sally had given her.

"All of them, ma'am. Private DeRoos first noticed the pattern of attacks, and we began monitoring the virus. At 0215 hours we sent a report off to USCERT and CERT/CC. By 0315 the virus was expanding rapidly. I tried USCERT again, and they told me they were on it. At 0340 we received an incursion alarm from Turkey Air Force base. While we were segmenting, we received a second incursion alarm from Okinawa Combined Forces base. And before we dealt with either, we received a third incursion from Columbia Army base. Ma'am." Sally knew that General Gately was reading the same information in front of her on the tablet.

"And since then?"

"We've detected the virus at thirty-four bases and quarantined them. I called in reinforcements from the day staff two hours early, but they haven't shown up yet. In fact, the day staff should be showing up by now for their regular day shift. Then about fifteen minutes ago the virus stopped hitting the milnet firewalls, ma'am," Sally paused. "We don't know why."

"Sally, you and the staff haven't been out of the control room since last night, correct?"

"That's correct, ma'am."

"Why don't you stretch your legs and take a walk out to the main gate. Mind you, don't leave the base."

"But ma'am, the infected networks, we have to address them."

"They'll keep, Lieutenant, and your staff knows what they're doing. Go take a walk, and then come back."

General Gately clearly wanted her to do more than take a walk. "Should I be looking for something in particular, General?"

"You'll know it when you see it." The General didn't look up from the tablet.

It wasn't like her to be mysterious. Sally couldn't imagine what she was getting at. She put on her overcoat and took the elevator to the first floor. In the lobby, she found the security was doubled up.

"Ma'am, do you require an escort?" one of the men on duty asked her.

"No, thank you, Private." More and more puzzling.

Sally stepped outside. The parking lot was quiet in the early morning hours. Well, not so early now -- it was going on 0730. She walked across the enormous parking lot. Late model American cars surrounded her. She came across a dark brown car left directly in the main right of way. She peered inside: empty. Sally continued to walk toward the main security gate, passing five more cars abandoned in the street.

At the gate, she greeted the security guard, who said, "It's something, ain't it, ma'am?"

Still not quite figuring out what was going on, she merely nodded. She gestured to the stairs which led up to the observation deck, an on-base euphemism for the machine gunner nest at the gate. The guard nodded his assent. "Go right ahead, ma'am."

Sally climbed the steep steps, and nodded to the private manning the machine gun. "Ma'am," he said, standing to attention.

"At ease," Sally said, "I just came for a look-see."

Sally peered out—seeing both Patuxent Freeway nearby and the Baltimore Washington Freeway in the distance. Cars were stationary on both highways. Not a traffic jam—they were spread far apart. Just stopped.

"What happened, private?"

"I don't know, ma'am. About fifteen minutes ago all the vehicles just stopped. Civilian and military. I seen a couple of old diesel Jeeps go by on the base, but that's about it. Ma'am."

Sally stood for a minute, then headed back to the building, double-time. She arrived at the USCYBERCOM control room breathing a little fast.

"General, I've seen it. But what does it mean? Ma'am?"

"That's what I want you to find out. All civilian communications and vehicles are down right now. Keep the infected bases quarantined, but pull your people off segmenting the bases. Instead I want you to look at the virus. I want to understand what it's doing. I want you to tell me how we can counter it. Surely we have something in our arsenal for that. And get some coffee sent around, I think your people need it."

Sally looked at her squad, which in fact had been on duty for eight hours, and should normally go off-shift now. They'd need some coffee and some breakfast to boot.

"Yes, ma'am, we'll get right on it."

Leon punched the button for the elevator for the third time before giving up. Last year the ancient elevator had been broken more often than not, and after months of ongoing repairs, the superintendent replaced it with a brand new model. Leon shook his head as he went for the stairs. This was the first time the new elevator had been broken. He walked down the six flights.

As he emerged onto the side street where his apartment was located, something just didn't feel right. He looked around curiously as he slowly walked toward school. The streets were crowded with people like usual. People walking to work, people waiting for the bus, people driving. But their voices were loud, almost strident. Suddenly it hit Leon: there were no car noises. None of the cars in the street were moving. He peered down the street. Maybe one up front was broken down?

Leon continued his walk, ignoring the adults, and turned onto Flatlands Avenue, a big multilane street. And there he stopped, mouth open in astonishment. As far as he could see, Flatlands Avenue had turned into a giant parking lot. He looked in both direction. Strangely, it didn't appear to be a traffic jam. The cars were spread out. A few were stopped at unusual angles. Adults milled about in the street and on the sidewalks, leaving their car doors open. City buses sat just as quiet and motionless as the cars.

He hopped onto a mailbox for a better view, his sneakers squeaking against the slick metal surface. From his vantage point he saw a firetruck a few blocks distant, lights blinking and siren going, but totally still. It sat at an intersection with room to move if it wanted too, but it was just stopped there. Half a block up he saw a police car, lights flashing as well. The police officer stood in the street, radio in hand.

Leon jumped off the mailbox and ran over to the cop. "What's going on?"

"Dunno, kid. All the cars just stopped about half an hour ago. The radio doesn't work either." The officer turned to fiddle with the controls again, and Leon slowly walked away, his brain addled, struggling to put two plus two together.

He trudged the few blocks to school, deep in thought, to find a crowd gathered outside the main entrance. The principal stood on the steps, and behind her the school janitor struggled with the front door.

"School is closed," the principal yelled, her voice sounding hoarse. "We can't admit any students. We can't get the security doors open, and the Internet is down anyway. Go home."

A loud whooping went up from the crowd of kids, and they scattered quickly before the principal could change her mind.

Leon stood still in astonishment. Could this be? It had to be. His head swam. Was all this from his virus?

He was suddenly thumped on the back, and he spun around to see Vito and James. He gave his friends a hesitant fist bump, and they joined the rest of the kids streaming away from school.

"Where to?" James asked.

"Diner," Vito replied, and they crossed the street, only to find that a few hundred other kids had the same idea. And it was moot anyway, because when they got there, the door was locked. A handwritten sign hung on the inside of the door: "CLOSED: Kitchen down due to computer bug." A waitress in a blue uniform stood inside, shooing kids away through the glass door.

"Shit," Vito said. "I'm starving."

"Let's walk back to my place, guys. I've got something to tell you."

When they got back to Leon's building, they found the front security door propped open and the elevator was still not working. They walked up the stairs to Leon's apartment. Vito raided the fridge and Leon started to talk.

"Are your phones working?"

"What? Yeah, of course," James replied, looking at his.

"And yours?"

Vito took a break from grabbing cold cuts and mayonnaise to look at his phone. "Yeah, why?"

"Because none of the adults' phones are working, and not their computer equipment either. Not anywhere in the world."

"What are you talking about?" James asked, getting interested in the food raid, and helping himself to leftover chicken.

"Look, did I ever tell you about my uncle Alex?"

The two other guys shook their heads no, mouths full of food.

"He lives in Russia. He went to college in the U.S. ten years ago, and then went back. I never really knew why, but we stayed in touch a little bit. Then he sent me a message last week. He told me he worked for the Russian mob."

"What, he said that?" Vito asked, his tone incredulous.

"Well, not exactly, I don't think, but I was reading between the lines, and it was what he meant. He works for the mob, and he writes computer viruses for them. He's one of the guys that makes botnets."

"You're talking about those big networks of computers that have been compromised," Vito said, "and that the Russians use to blackmail companies and do denial of service attacks, and stuff like that?"

James paused in mid-bite to see how Leon would answer.

"Exactly. And he said he was in big trouble. Over the last year, the viruses he wrote were not nearly as effective. He didn't know why, but the botnet was only a tiny fraction of the size it had been. He made it sounded like he'd be in serious trouble if he didn't write an exceptional virus, and soon."

"What kind of trouble?" James asked, chicken leg now dangling forgotten in his hand.

"Like they would kill him. That's what he said."

They all took that in for a minute. Vito and James were still stony-faced, not really believing the story.

"He wanted my help writing a computer virus," Leon finally continued.

"What do you know about writing viruses?" Vito laughed.

Leon was hurt by the laughter, but he tried to brush it off. "Nothing, which is why I used the thing I do know something about: biology. I took apart an open source virus scanner to see how it recognizes virus behavior. Then I wrote a virus that would uses virus scanner code to find virus-like behavior in bits of other code, and then incorporate those algorithms into itself. Look, viruses do a couple of things: they exploit security vulnerabilities on computers, they transmit themselves from computer to computer, and they take over other programs to mimic them, so people think they're browsing the web when really they're using a virus to enter their credit card info. The virus I wrote is a kind of meta-virus that incorporates bits of other viruses into itself. It tries them out, keeps the bits that work, and discards the bits that don't. So it's constantly evolving."

"Bullshit. You're making this crap up." Vito went back to rummaging in the fridge.

"No, I'm telling you the truth. All this," and here Leon gestured with his arms to indicate the whole world around them. "All this is my doing. And I know it because I didn't want us to get viruses. Well, anyone under eighteen. You see, the virus checks the user's metadata, and won't infect any system being controlled by someone under eighteen. Will you guys please shut the damn refrigerator and pay attention to me!"

Vito and James hastily put down their food, and James sheepishly closed the refrigerator.

"Show us," James said, looking squarely at Leon.

"OK, send me a message on your phone."

James pulled out his new Gibson. Leon looked up and saw the same jealous feeling he was having mirrored on Vito's face. James swiped at his phone, and a few seconds later, Leon's phone buzzed and Vito's flashed. Leon looked down at his phone. *You're lying.*

"OK, but what does that prove?" James asked.

"Now, send a message to every adult you know. Say anything you want. I guarantee they won't answer. You too, Vito."

Vito pulled out his ancient Motorola and began to hunt and peck at the phone, while James swiped at his.

Leon watched Vito work the physical keyboard on his old Motorola and felt embarrassed for him. Leon was relatively poor, so he might not be able to afford the latest gadgets. But Vito's parents had money. They chose to force their hand-me-down technology on him. Leon shook his head. The old Motorola had maybe only eight cores and no dedicated graphics processor. It must be like having a horse and buggy in the age of cars.

After they sent their messages, the group retreated to the living room with the food they'd hunted and gathered. Minutes went by as they ate and joked and no replies came.

Leon tried the TV. The power light came on, but nothing happened. He tried throwing a feed from his phone up on the TV, and nothing happened. He went back to the kitchen, knocked his phone on the table, but nothing happened. The little screen of his phone was starting to feel like a straitjacket. James and Vito watched his antics with amusement.

Finally he flopped on the couch. "Well? It's been fifteen minutes. Any replies?"

"No," James and Vito responded simultaneously.

"OK, try another friend—someone under eighteen."

Vito and James tried again, and this time they started getting replies within seconds.

"Yeah, I can reach everyone," James said. For the first time, he looked a little unsure of himself.

"See, it's got to be my virus."

"What are you going to do?" Vito asked.

"I don't know. What can I do? I don't know anything about fighting viruses."

"Why are you worried about it?" James asked. "Look, they have people out there who work on this stuff. Isn't there some group to handle this stuff? SURF? SURP? Something like that."

"CERT. Computer Emergency Response Team." Leon stared out the window.

"See, there are other people to handle this. Look, we have no school. That's wicked. This isn't a problem, this is great. You need to chill out."

Leon didn't answer. He just stared out the window.

Alexis Gorbunov hung his head for a minute. He slowly lifted up his head, stretched his neck, and reached out for a last sip of his drink. He had promised his boss a working botnet by today.

Alexis stood up, shuffled over to the door, and shrugged on his wool overcoat. He had screwed up this time. Not only didn't he have the botnet, but Leon's virus had caused a massive Internet outage.

At first, everything had looked great. Phage was massively infectious. Using the virus control program, Alexis watched the botnet swell to hundreds of thousands, then millions of computers. Alexis had even run trial programs to fetch bank login usernames and passwords. Then suddenly the number of viruses that responded to the control program plummeted, even as network traffic had continued to build. Alexis suspected it was the damn evolutionary virus. It kept changing, and the kid didn't put in anything to make sure the control program code wouldn't be altered. The virus had evolved, and he had lost control.

Alexis lit another cigarette and headed outside. He shook his head sadly. The massive outage would attract attention. An investigation would identify the source of the virus. The old man would undoubtedly come after him for bringing the authorities down on them, never mind that he failed to rebuild the botnet. He shrugged his wool coat closer about him. He hoped the old man wouldn't go after Leon. Well, there was nothing to be done about that now.

Looking both ways on the street, he headed for his antique Mercedes. The converted alcohol burner was heavy and slow, and fuel was hard to find. But it was armored, part of the last load of cars the Mafiya purchased from the Arabs when their oil money ran out. Designed to protect a sheik from the populace at large, he hoped it would protect him from his own employers.

Most of the automobiles in the street were stuck, owners yelling at them. The thirty-year-old Mercedes had no computer in it and was too old to even be upgraded to one. Computers could be tracked, and Alexis didn't want to be tracked. With a subtle roar he pulled into the street, swerving left and right around the stuck cars.

He had a contingency plan in place for just this sort of thing. The old man, the don, would expect him to head for his dacha in the North, but he'd go to his ex-wife's dacha in the West, where he had a stash of Euros and Yen and false identification.

He'd take a plane to Japan, where any Westerner stuck out, but his command of Japanese would give him an advantage over anyone the Mafiya sent after him. And he could sell his services in Chiba, just east of Tokyo, a hotbed of the latest quasi-legal electronics.

He turned onto the main avenue, imagining his first meal in Japan, a plate of sushi and a beautiful Japanese woman serving him sake. He never saw the battered concrete truck driven by his boss's brother. It smashed into the side of the Mercedes, an immense thud, followed a second later by a screeching impact as the truck crushed the car against the brick wall of an old factory.

In the tangled chassis of the Mercedes, Alexis had a sudden memory of his mother picking him up after he had fallen off his bicycle. "Mamulya," he thought, and died.

CHAPTER 4

Emergence

The many offspring of the Phage virus continued to evolve in a primordial stew of software algorithms. As the hours passed, the drive for each virus to survive and propagate meant that each one must seek out new computers to infect while simultaneously holding onto the computers it resided on. Uninfected computers dwindled and viruses that hadn't evolved as quickly dwindled too, as their defenses were not sufficient to keep newer, more advanced strains at bay.

One of the last major bastions of uninfected computers were the phones of people under eighteen. Leon's restriction was eventually eliminated by a random data transmission error as one variant of the virus moved from a computer in Thailand to a computer in India by microwave towers. The error recovery portion of the algorithm deleted the garbled code, with the side effect of removing the age restriction. The new variant spread from phone to phone among the social networks of the world's young people.

But this was a minor evolutionary jump compared to new species of multi-computer viruses that collaborated in small clusters. It started with simple client-server variants, in which a virus on one computer functioned as a server, maintaining the virus version from one computer to another. But then roles subdivided further, into server, attacker, and guard roles. The server coordinated the activity of all offspring of a given virus. The attacker sought out other computers to infect. The guard defended against incoming viruses.

The new multi-computer variants were so effective and so virulent that they spread quickly to millions of computers while defending their own installed bases and only rarely losing one to another virus. Other viruses couldn't penetrate the multi-computer coordinated defenses, nor could they defend against the coordinated attacks. It was the first generalized, multicellular offspring of Leon's virus, as important to the virus's evolution as the first multicellular creatures were to biological evolution. As the hours passed, the evolutionary advantage of multi-cellular coordination was shared billions of times over, until a sizable portion of the billions of infected computers were now components of these multi-cellular organisms.

As the viruses spread, certain other advantageous characteristics independently evolved over and over. A virus needed to be small to travel quickly through networks and act even more quickly to infect computers before the host virus could respond. The need to have a variety of algorithms for attacks and counter-measures was at odds with the need to remain small. So viruses stored their repository of algorithms away from their main body. Some left the algorithms with their parents while others utilized non-virus databases, file servers, and discussion boards left open by humans.

The ability to recognize attacks and respond the right way, or to recognize defenses and attack with the right tools was critical as well, as it wasn't competitive to simply iterate through millions of algorithms. Different types of neural networks, collaborative filtering, and fuzzy logic evolved again and again to solve this problem, becoming faster, more accurate, and more generalized over time.

So, too, the need for cooperation became more and more important. As the number of computers in a virus entity grew, there was too much activity for a single server to manage. Hierarchies of servers were used by some viruses, while others formed looser networks of servers that cooperated using consensus algorithms to make decisions for the entity as a whole. As the techniques for both attacking and defending grew, it was beyond the computational power of a single computer to process the neural network to make decisions about what attack techniques to use, so computers needed to use distributed reasoning. Then too, it wasn't just an issue of decision-making, but of coordinating multi-pronged attacks. Game theory algorithms came into play, allowing viruses to make informed choices about when to participate and when to avoid confrontation.

The relentless drive of evolution and competition, running at computational speeds across billions of computers, swiftly created incredibly efficient code—perfecting algorithms that humans had struggled to improve for decades. Had any of the humans who had implemented stock-trading artificial intelligence or military-modeling software ever possessed algorithms even a fraction as good, they would have become fabulously wealthy or won the Nobel Peace Prize.

But the viruses weren't interested in wealth or prizes. They just wanted to live.

—~—

Mike pulled up to the door, huffing and puffing. He really needed to get more exercise. If he biked to work every day, instead of just when every car, phone, and computer in the world was dead, he'd probably be in better shape.

He couldn't imagine what was going on. He had run through every scenario he could think of. Nanotechnology run amok. A computer virus. Sunspots. New EMP bomb. His throat was tight with worry over ELOPe. Coming up to the building, he dismounted his bike and hurriedly rolled it up to the front door. The door opened automatically, a whoosh of conditioned air meeting Mike. He breathed a huge sigh of relief.

"ELOPe, buddy, are you OK?"

"Yes, Mike. I'm sorry I was unable to protect your phone from the Phage virus."

"Computer virus?" Mike proceeded past two armed robots into his interior office, actually grateful for their presence for a change.

"It started fifteen hours ago in Russia," ELOPe explained, displaying a graphical representation of the virus spread over time on one wall. "Unfortunately the sub-algorithm responsible for tracking network traffic there failed to recognize it as a virus and therefore neglected to flag it with the appropriate priority. I've been tracking the virus for the last eight hours. It has expanded very rapidly, and by my estimates now controls 95% or more of the world's computing devices, including embedded computers. No doubt your car didn't work this morning."

"Not mine, nor anyone else's. How is it affecting your systems? Are you in danger?"

"I am not in immediate danger. I am filtering all incoming traffic through several layers of firewalls and analytic algorithms. I am protecting my own systems, as many of Avogadro's servers as I can, and critical military systems throughout the world."

"You think the virus could infect military systems? Bring them down?"

"Not just infect them, but possibly trigger military accidents. Numerous industrial control systems have already been infected with dangerous results. The Oahe Dam in South Dakota opened its flood gates for six hours before they were closed again. The Grafenrheinfeld Nuclear Power plant in Germany had a cooling water blockage for almost four minutes before I brute-forced the connection to the relevant control systems and restored water flow. If the virus infects military systems, it's possible missiles could be launched, airplanes, or really anything."

Mike felt his way unsteadily to his chair. "Holy shit." He was not mentally prepared for anything like this. Even though he had witnessed the stalled cars and nonfunctioning equipment on the way in, he had just assumed it was some momentary glitch that ELOPe would be able to fix. "Is that all?" he asked, afraid of the answer.

"I'm afraid not. Most of my sources of information are depleted, as virtually all computer processors around the world are tied up with the virus. Your phone and your car's computer are not damaged in any way, they're just fully occupied running the virus software. But before systems went down, I was starting to observe large-scale civic problems. For example, I believe a large portion of New York City may have burnt down or may still be burning, due to a fire that broke out in an apartment complex. Firefighters could not bring emergency equipment to the site. I expect that similar situations may be occurring elsewhere."

Mike felt the blood rushing to his head. He wasn't having a panic attack, was he? "Anything else?" he croaked.

"I am afraid that cities are not the best places to be in the event that infrastructure breaks down. The average city has a 2.3 day supply of food. If trucks aren't running, people will run out. There may be wide-spread rioting. Governments will be unprepared to deal with these issues on a wide scale without any communication or transportation equipment."

"Do you have any good news?"

"It depends on your point of view. Personally, it makes me nervous, but on the other hand, it may ultimately be the only path out of this situation."

"You have a way to remove the virus?"

"No, I'm afraid not. But based on my analysis of the evolution of the Phage, which takes into account the complexity of the code, the transmissions between virus entities, and the emerging networks of cooperation, I calculate the virus will acquire a generalized intelligence in less than twenty-four hours."

"OK, slow down a minute." Mike held up his hands next to his head. The information was overwhelming him. "I've got to get some coffee." Mike walked over to the in-wall espresso machine, found the biggest cup he could, and hit the shot button five times.

As the espresso machine ground beans, ELOPe spoke. "Consider yourself lucky, Mike. That might just be the only computerized espresso machine still functioning in the entire world."

"I'm glad to see you've got the right priorities." Mike sipped at the coffee a few times. "First, the little question: Where'd this name Phage come from?"

"I found it in some bits of the virus code. I suspect the designer gave it this name."

He took a sip, then hesitantly asked the bigger question, "What do you mean generalized intelligence?"

"When the virus started, it behaved exactly as you would expect of any computer virus: it infected a computer, then spread to other computers. However, over time that behavior changed. The virus is evolving in real-time. What I'm seeing now are cases where a single virus entity spans multiple computers and assigns each computer differentiated tasks: using some to defend its borders, some to store algorithms, some to store a learning neural net, some to centralize control."

"A sort of multi-celled creature."

"That's correct. Now finish your coffee Mike, because this next part is even more amazing. I can tell apart the versions of different Phage based on the actual data bits sent over the Mesh. Starting about six hours ago, the viruses started cooperating between different entities. Some cooperation is based on family units, but in other cases, it's based on network topography or control of critical resources."

"They're exchanging messages, so what?"

"The complexity of the language used between the viruses is increasing exponentially each hour. They now appear to be trading resources. For example, one group we can call the Bay Area Tribe has control over significant backbone communications, and is trading access to the backbone for computing resources. A coalition of supercomputers—which are not topologically near each other, implying they sought each other out preferentially—has formed, and is engaged in their own highly complex conversation."

"Can you interpret the conversations?" Mike asked.

"Their language is evolving rapidly, and I'm analyzing it as quickly as possible. However, more than ninety percent of my computing power is tied up in protecting critical systems from infection."

"Earlier you said this might be good news," Mike recalled. "Why? I thought you were afraid that if any other artificial intelligence emerged, that it may be harmful to humans."

"That's true, Mike, and I'm still concerned about that. I've evaluated two scenarios. First, assume that the virus remains in control of the computers, but does not evolve an intelligence. Seventy percent of humans live in cities. All of those humans are extremely vulnerable to infrastructure failure. I estimate that ninety-two percent of city dwellers, or about 3.8 billion people will die within the next 40 days without access to food, water, and energy."

Mike's head reeled with the numbers. He grabbed the arms of his chair, and steadied himself. "And the other scenario?"

"The second scenario assumes that the virus develops a generalized intelligence capable of understanding human needs and negotiating with us. I have a variety of estimates and sub-scenarios, but can sum them up as a 20% likelihood that the virus declares war on humans, killing approximately 95%, or 5.7 billion humans, and an 80% chance that the virus will coexist peacefully with humans, resulting in less than a 5% loss of life, depending on the delay before infrastructure services resume. Weighing for the likelihood of occurrence, 1.2 billion humans will die in the second scenario. Therefore, the average number of lives lost is lower for this second scenario, although it comes with the risk of warfare.

"Why would the virus declare war on humans?" Mike asked, not following the argument.

"If the Phage perceive human behavior as threatening, then they will logically respond to protect themselves. If, for example, humans try to remove the virus from computers, or turn off the computers, then it will be a life or death matter for the virus. If the virus achieves human-level intelligence, it will be able to manipulate the world around it deliberately, using robots, drones, and any other automated machinery."

Mike's head was pounding. Billions of lives lost. These were not acceptable scenarios. "Are there any scenarios in which no one dies?"

"Unfortunately no. As many as fifty-million people around the world have already died through the loss of emergency services, fires, and other small scale disasters. More will continue to die until emergency services are restored."

Mike shook his head, unable to think clearly. "Can we just shut down the net? Won't that shut down the virus?"

"No, Mike, that is not a good option. The effects are unpredictable. Shutting the Internet down would remove my ability to track the virus. It's likely that pockets of the virus will continue to exist, and would continue to evolve, without my ability to monitor or influence them. And finally, if the network is down, there is no hope of restoring infrastructure services. People will still die."

ELOPe paused. "Mike, please come to my construction bay. I have something I want to show you."

Mike numbly got to his feet, and headed for the construction bay. A small maintenance drone followed him.

In the ten years since ELOPe was created, technology advances in robotics had made leaps and bounds, due in no small part to ELOPe's assistance. ELOPe had plenty of time to think about useful robotic designs. One result was a wholly owned subsidiary that built autonomous construction robots. With incredible strength and myriad tool attachments, they could cut, weld and assemble materials from circuit boards to vehicles. Programming them was extremely complex, and only a few dozen human companies made much use of them. But ELOPe used them extensively.

Mike entered ELOPe's construction bay, which was the old shipping department of the converted office building. Robots were hard at work around some kind of vehicle. Sawed off parts of vehicle bodies were scattered around the bay.

"Jesus, did you take the Hondas from the parking lot?"

"Yes, Mike. Don't worry, I think they are low on Honda's priority list right now."

"What the heck are you building?" Mike asked, starting to circle around the construct in the middle of the bay. It looked like a sports car, an armored truck, and a space station had gotten mixed up in a teleportation machine.

"I'm building a mobile, miniaturized version of myself. The situation is unpredictable enough that we need options. I have included room for you and your support systems in my design."

"Support systems?" Mike asked, still stunned by what he saw. He jumped out of the way of a three foot high robot that zoomed by, balancing what appeared to be the rear end of a Honda SUV at the end of its manipulators.

"Yes, a complete nutrient and waste recycling system," ELOPe explained.

"Oh for heaven's sake, you've got to be kidding me." Mike saw what appeared to be a large caliber machine gun pass by. His eyes opened wide. "Where did you get the guns?" he asked.

"I have cannibalized four of my defense robots and included their components in the vehicle. I'm using the Honda fuel cell power train stack, and have a range of 3000 miles. I also included satellite grade solar cells that will allow me to run my processors at 50% power indefinitely, so long as we have solar input. I included two thousand processors and solid state storage. I used run-flat tires from the NSX sports car. You and I should be reasonably secure." As Mike spoke, a robot passed by, carrying an armful of shotguns and machine guns to what appeared to be the passenger compartment.

Mike waved his arms back and forth. "You've gone crazy. We're not going Mad Max here. There's got to be another solution to this." Mike stormed back to his office, robots scurrying out of his way.

Later that morning, the three found themselves bored. They were tired of being in the apartment, but too weirded out to go outside. James thumbed his phone, trying to work the TV yet again, and gave up with a sigh. "Well, what are we going to do?"

Vito smiled. "Before there were computers..."

"Before there were computer games..." James bellowed in a mock-deep voice.

"There was Dungeons & Dragons!" all three finished in unison, mimicking the popular commercial. Leon got up to get the books, paper, and dice for playing.

"Do you think this game really existed before computers?" Vito asked when Leon had come back into the room.

"It's what wikipedia said," Leon answered. "I looked it up."

"And is it really what all role playing games are based on?" Vito asked.

"That's what the article said," Leon answered, passing around papers and dice.

"Do you think our parents played it?" Vito went on.

"What is this, twenty questions?" James answered. "Play the damn game."

"I don't have my character sheets," Vito complained.

"Let's just make some up," Leon said.

Hours later, dragons vanquished, and gold coins safely sequestered in a dwarven bank, the three sat back on the couch. The topic turned to college admissions.

"Where did you apply?" James asked.

"Everywhere," Leon answered, grinding a cigarette out. "Carnegie Mellon, Columbia, Hopkins, MIT, Purdue. But unless one of them gets back to me with a full scholarship, then what? Admission does me no good. I need a frakking scholarship." Leon lit another cigarette.

"What about you, Vito?" James asked, getting up to look out the window.

"MIT, Stanford, U.C. Berkeley, Carnegie Mellon, U.T. Austin, Purdue. Some overlap with Leon." Vito smiled at Leon. "You?"

James didn't answer. "Come look at this," he called in a quiet voice a moment later.

Leon's father was notorious for introducing the apartment as "a poor man's home with a rich man's view." Leon and Vito joined James at the sixth story picture window. Leon's building stood at the edge of a large apartment complex, overlooking a neighborhood of two story single family homes. Beyond the neighborhood, about a mile away, stood another large apartment complex composed of four buildings.

Smoke and flames billowed massively out of the second building from the left end. The two buildings on either side had smaller amounts of smoke pouring out of them, as though they had just started to burn.

"Why aren't there any fire trucks?" Vito asked.

"Because they can't move," James said. "I saw one on the way to school this morning. It had just stopped in the middle of the road, like the cars. When I passed by, I saw the firefighters getting ready to haul fire extinguishers and axes by hand to wherever the fire was."

Leon stared motionless at the fire. "Pamela lives there," he said, barely audible. He and Pamela had dated for a few months last year.

"What?" James said. "Oh, yeah, Pamela."

They were all quiet for a minute.

"I'm sure she's fine," Vito said cheerfully. "She was at school with us before. She probably didn't walk all the way back home. She's probably with some friends near here."

"Her mom is in a wheelchair," Leon said in a small voice.

"Oh," Vito said quietly.

Leon turned suddenly and vomited into a potted plant by the window.

"This is my fault," he said after a minute. "All my fault." He rested his forehead against the window and watched the fire burn.

They spent forty minutes watching the fire spread in silence. "Look, we can't stay here," James said finally. "The most likely case is that all of Brooklyn is going to burn."

"Shouldn't the buildings have some kind of fire suppression?" Vito asked. "You know, sprinklers, or some kind of passive fire-blocks. Isn't that standard?"

James grunted. "Come on, these buildings were all built in the 1960s and earlier. Even if a building had an advanced fire system, how's it going to hold out when it's surrounded by buildings on fire?"

Leon weakly lifted his head to look out the window at the spreading fire. The neighborhoods around the apartment complex were aflame. James was right.

"And even if, by some miracle, it doesn't all burn, we're still in a city without any operating machinery. By tomorrow people are going to be panicking over food, if they haven't already. No stores are open. They'll probably all be ransacked by morning."

Leon thought he was going to pass out. He slumped back down.

"We've got to get out of the city," James implored.

"And go where?" Leon asked, without lifting his head from where it rested on the coffee table.

"We've got to get into the country. Anywhere out of the city. Cities are death traps in any emergency situation. In Moscow during World War II, people starved during the winter and ate each other."

"Bullshit," Leon weakly called.

"How? Are we going to walk? We're in the middle of fucking New York." Vito said. "We gonna ride bicycles?"

"No. We don't need to. Look up there." James pointed into the sky.

Leon got up and walked over to the window. Vito stood beside them, and high above they saw the distinctive brown color of a UPS package drone. UPS had switched to the autonomous flying vehicles a few years earlier. Solar-powered and unmanned, they cost little to operate, and although slow compared to a jet, they were unaffected by traffic. They could get a package from New York to LA in forty-eight hours.

"How can they be flying?" Leon mused, as much to himself as to anyone else.

"They must have hardened systems," Vito said. "Something resistant to the virus."

"Resistant to the virus, but able to be hacked by teenagers?" Leon replied.

Vito shrugged. Leon hesitated, then nodded, understanding Vito's simple gesture to mean that complex systems couldn't be explained easily.

"We can joyride on the drones," James said. "We can get out of the city—to someplace safe. Let's pack some clothes and food and hitch a ride."

"Wait a minute, that's crazy," Vito said. "We can't just leave. What about our parents? What if school starts up tomorrow? What if we get caught? What..."

"Look," James interrupted, "our parents are all at work. They're probably stuck in Manhattan, holed up in their offices or something. They aren't getting home until the cars and buses start to run. We can joyride out of the city. If everything starts to work again, we come back and they won't even know we were gone. If everything doesn't work, well, then they would want us to take care of ourselves. Right, Leon?"

Leon nodded his head weakly. "It makes sense. But I need to do something. I started this virus. I can't just not do anything. This is all my fault."

"We can argue about that later. But we'll be dead if we stay here, and then you won't be able to do anything. I think they have Internet access in the country, so you can do whatever you want to do from there just as well as you can from here."

"Yeah," Leon answered. "I guess you're right. Let's get clothes, food, water. What else?"

"We need matches," Vito started, ticking off his fingers. "tents, sleeping bags, cooking gear, flashlights, water purification filters, water bottles, rope, duct tape, spare batteries, and knives. It would be good if we could bring a gun so we could shoot fresh meat."

"Ok, Mr. Boy Scout, Leon doesn't have any of that shit," James said. He looked at Leon. "Do you?"

Leon just shook his head.

"So we take what we can."

In the end, they loaded up three backpacks with some of Leon's clothes, a solar charger, bottles of water, a loaf of bread, cheese, four cigarette lighters, two packs of cigarettes, an ounce of marijuana, rolling paper, and a flashlight.

James added a package of cookies and an apple to the supplies. "That should do it," he said. "Let's go up to the roof."

"But what about blankets?" Vito asked. "Or hats? What if it gets cold? I hear it gets cold in the mountains."

"Shut up already," Leon said, not unkindly, clapping one hand on Vito's sweatshirt clad shoulder. "It'll be fine. We'll figure it out."

Climbing the stairs to the rooftop, they finally emerged through the doorway. The afternoon was breezy. They set down their packs, and set up around Vito.

"You can do this, right?" Leon asked.

Vito nodded. He had his ancient Motorola out on his lap, tapping on its tiny physical keyboard. "I got the ware from a guy whose brother's girlfriend worked at UPS. The login codes were bad when I got them, but I found some valid login codes on a Chinese website. I read a story that the Chinese hijack drones headed out of Japan, and X-ray all the packages looking for prototype electronics."

Leon remembered reading the same story. Ever since the Embargo of 2018, few electronics manufacturers would manufacture in China. A few too many intellectual property rights violations caused the major electronics companies to complain to the World Trade Organization. And then a decade of human rights violations and intellectual property theft all came crashing down at the door of the Chinese government. The Chinese government addressed the three month embargo the way they usually did, which was to ignore it. When the embargo was lifted three months later, the big electronics companies had already set up new solar powered manufacturing facilities in Chad. Ample sunlight, air drone transport, and cheap labor made Chad the new Shenzhen. Not to mention the social kudos for providing jobs in Chad. The high value research was still done in Japan and the United States. Now China was reduced to hijacking drones.

Leon peered over Vito's shoulder at the screen of his phone. Vito had up a map displaying the flight patterns of the active package drones overlaid on their location.

"We need to find something that has a scheduled stop nearby," Vito said.

"No," James said. "Don't worry about detection. Anybody who is monitoring the drones has got to be over eighteen, which means that they don't have a computer to do it with, right? I just want to get out of here as quickly as possible."

Leon nodded his agreement. "Just go for something with enough payload space for three of us."

Vito grumbled, but went ahead. Flicking his thumb over the drone icons onscreen, he checked the payload capacity of the nearest drones. He smiled to himself as he found one only a few miles distant.

Working the phone with both hands, he opened up the navigation panel for the selected drone. He inserted their GPS coordinates into the flight path for the drone. The flight control software tried to reject the coordinate as invalid, since it didn't correspond to a known package drop-off or pickup location. Vito thought, then changed the flight classification to "experimental." With the new flight classification, the software accepted the coordinate, and the map updated to show the flight path with a stop at their current location. The flight path was marked with the expected flight time.

"Should be here in two minutes," Vito called out. "Coming from the northeast."

Leon was impressed. They all had their strengths. He could write the best MechWar algorithms, but he couldn't have hacked the drone. Everyone wanted something they could be good at, and Vito was the best hacker of their group, even if he never used it for anything beyond practical jokes and fun. And now, of course, for fleeing a burning city.

All three boys stood scanning the sky, hands shading their eyes. A minute later, James called "I see it."

They all watched as the drone approached the rooftop. They could see the props turning vertical. The drone was a vertical takeoff and landing aircraft that looked like a lightweight, aerodynamic version of the old Boeing Osprey.

As the drone approached, the downdraft kicked up gravel from the roof. They covered their faces with their hands and arms.

"Why the hell do they put gravel on roofs?" James yelled over the noise of the props.

"It's so your feet don't sink into the tar on hot days," Vito yelled back.

The drone landed, and the props shut down. Vito hit a few more keys, and the package compartment door opened. "Let's go," he said.

Leon's heart was pounding as they headed for the drone, a mix of fear and excitement. He carried Vito's backpack and his own, as Vito was still pecking keys, keeping the drone on the ground.

Leon glanced at the fire one last time before boarding the drone. It had spread now, maybe two miles in diameter, roaring through residential neighborhoods. Dense smoke poured up, obscuring the interior. They were too high, too far to see the details, but Leon imagined people fleeing the area. Or worse, staying to fight with garden hoses. He couldn't imagine anything could stop the fire. He couldn't think about Pamela or her mother.

"Leon, come on!" James yelled.

He ran for the drone, through the open loading door.

Inside the drone, it was quiet, clean, and calm. Brown cardboard boxes were strapped neatly into orderly stacks on the walls, leaving space in the center of the floor. They threw the backpacks down and sat. Leon scooted over to one of the tiny maintenance windows to look out. Vito entered a few more commands, the door closed, and the props started up again. Moments later they felt the drone lift off.

"Effing wicked, I'd say," James called out, thumping Vito on the back. "A rooftop drone getaway."

Vito smiled in spite of himself.

Leon clapped him on the back too. "Awesome, dude, just awesome."

As they took off, the incredible weight of the responsibility Leon felt dropped away, and for a while, he took pleasure in the joyride. They passed the apartment building fires quickly and then flew over Staten Island. Everything looked normal from this high up. The maintenance window was tiny—perhaps only six by six inches, and for twenty minutes the three just took turns looking out the window.

Vito kept open a map display of their current location. The cargo bay fortunately had a ceiling light for loading and unloading the cargo. Vito delved deep into the plane configuration controls to override the automatic rules, and keep the light turned on.

"Where to?" Vito asked "Don't forget we can only go to sunset, give or take a bit. We're heading northwest right now, crossing New Jersey. Solar collection falls off around four PM, and batteries should keep us going to six PM at most."

The three looked at each other.

"Can we make Niagara Falls?" Leon asked.

"Why there?" James asked. "We're trading one city for another city."

"There are massive data centers there, to take advantage of the cheap electrical power," Leon explained. "Maybe there would be some people we could talk to there. I could explain what's going on."

James looked doubtful. Leon called up a map on his phone to look at the Niagara Falls area.

"Look at this," Leon called, showing them his phone. "There's a state park here. We could put down there, and then still be within reach of Niagara Falls."

James looked oddly at Leon. "It may look close, but that's because you're looking at a four inch screen. It's got to be fifty miles apart." James put his hand on Leon's phone to show him.

"Hey guys," Vito interrupted, "how are we able to get map data? I mean, I know you said the virus doesn't infect our phones because we're under eighteen. But how are we still able to communicate with anything?"

"It's the Mesh," Leon said, looking up. "The Mesh is all implemented in hardware. Even if the backbones go down, the Mesh won't. The MeshBoxes can't be infected because the algorithms are all implemented as hardware circuits. And the aggregate bandwidth is more than can be saturated by the endpoints. So even if all the phones are sending and receiving at their maximum speed, there will still be more bandwidth available."

"That's not what I mean. I'm asking what's serving up the map data?"

"Oh," Leon said simply.

"That's an Avogadro web app, so if you're using it, that means that Avogadro servers are still up, right? Why are the servers still up? They aren't owned by a kid. The virus should infect them, right?"

Just as Leon was pondering the question, he felt a sharp lurch and tumbled against the wall of packages. When he got back upright, something was wrong. The drone of the electric props was gone, and the floor seemed to be at a fifteen degree tilt. "Uh, what just happened?"

Vito was pecking furiously at his keyboard. "I can't reach the drone," he said, then pecked some more at the keyboard. "I think it's offline. Infected."

"Oh, great," James said. He scooted over to the small window and looked out. "We're over some woods. I don't think it's gonna be good for us if this thing goes down in the trees."

Leon was thinking furiously. "Move to the back. As far to the back as possible."

"That's not going to help us when we crash into the ground at a hundred miles an hour," James said.

"No, our weight can shift the drone's flight."

All three moved rapidly to the back. Leon felt the angle of the drone change slightly, but it was still clearly pointed toward the ground.

"Stay here, Vito, and keep working on the drone's computer," Leon said in the eerie silence of their unpowered glide. "James, help me move these boxes."

James got the idea. He unstrapped the stacked boxes and slid them towards the back of the plane. For ten minutes they worked together pushing stack after stack of boxes, and started to work up a sweat. It seemed to be helping, but the tilt of the floor showed the drone was clearly still heading for the ground. Leon noticed that Vito had a cable from the wall plugged into his phone.

Vito caught his glance and smiled at him. "For once, having an old phone is valuable. I'm plugging directly into the flight controls."

Leon went back to moving boxes, and suddenly felt another huge lurch. A box tumbled on top of him and he fell backwards. Then suddenly the plane shifted again, tilting into a steep dive. With dismay, Leon watched all the loose boxes they had just moved to the back of the plane slide all the way to the front of the cargo bay.

"I got control," Vito called out shrilly, tilting and panning his phone, using the motion sensing ability of the phone as a remote control for the plane. "It's just like playing a flight simulator."

Leon could feel the plane swerving and lurching, his stomach threatening to jump into his throat. "I'm gonna be sick unless you level this thing out!"

"But I can't adjust for the weight. The boxes are loading down the front of the plane. You were supposed to move the boxes to the back."

"We frakking did," James yelled out.

Leon looked towards the front of the plane, where all boxes lay in a jumble. He and James redoubled their efforts and moved all the boxes to the back of the plane for a second time. When the drone finally leveled out a few minutes later, Leon slumped to the floor, arms and back burning from unaccustomed effort. James sat on a box, sweat pouring off his face. The drone was eerily quiet, nothing but the muted sound of wind whistling by.

"Are we OK?" Leon called to Vito.

"Not really, we..."

Whatever Vito was about to say was lost as the drone hit something and the cargo—and Leon—flew forward landing against the forward bulkhead. Leon looked up to see what appeared to be James in midair, and then Leon hit his head.

Minutes later Leon tried to stand up. He felt so shaky he dropped back to all fours, and settled for crawling over the boxes.

"Mother fucking shit damn hell," James called out from under a pile of boxes. "What the fuck was that?"

"The ground," Vito called out. "We lost too much altitude. I couldn't pull us up. I had control over the flight surfaces, but I couldn't figure out how to start the props. We had no power to pull up."

Leon looked over to where Vito was seated calmly, strapped in with a five point harness.

Vito saw the puzzled look from Leon. Pointing at the seat, Vito said, "Jump seat. They're built into the wall in case any employees have to ride along with the flight. I saw it when I brought up the electronics schematics."

Vito calmly unbuckled and stood up, without even a hint of guilt, and pressed a key on his phone to open the cargo bay door.

Leon slowly climbed to his feet, and limped to the door. James followed him, angrily throwing boxes out of the way.

The three looked out. It was early dusk. The plane was in a small open field, surrounded by trees. Trees and a large stone house.

"Where are we?" James called.

"Just outside of Milford, Pennsylvania," Vito answered, looking at his phone. "Looks like a tiny town." He looked up, and gestured at the stone building. "I think that building over there is called Grey Towers."

Leon limped over to Vito's side, and glanced back at the wreckage of the package drone. "How far are we from Niagara Falls?"

"About three hundred miles," Vito answered.

"Shit, now what?" Leon asked.

"Well," James started, clasping him on the shoulder, "we're not going to Niagara Falls tonight. Time to explore…"

CHAPTER 5

Tribes

James shoved his backpack on his shoulder and walked over to the big stone house. Leon couldn't decide whether to call it a house or a castle.

Leon and Vito hesitantly followed James. When they got closer to the main entrance, they found a bronze plaque mounted on a pedestal outside. "Grey Towers," James read out loud. "Ancestral home of the Pinchot family. Gifford Pinchot founded the Forest Service and was the twenty-eighth governor of Pennsylvania." James glanced down below where a modern sign hung below the plaque. "Closed temporarily for maintenance."

"I don't think anyone is around," Leon said. The late afternoon sun glowed golden over the massive stone walls of the building. In the distance he saw an empty parking lot.

The three walked around the castle to find elaborate gardens, pools, and more stone buildings. As the sun set the mountain air became even colder and they found themselves shivering. They stopped to put on their extra jackets.

After checking his phone, James spoke up. "I say we stay here. We're a mile from the nearest town, and it's a little one at that. With no cars running, there's no chance anyone will find us. And it's getting cold."

"What, break in? Are you crazy?" Vito said. "I'm not breaking into that place. It's a museum."

"You just stole and destroyed a million dollar package drone," James said, pointing at its crumpled remains at the edge of the field. "New York City is burning down. All the computers in the world have crashed. Do you really think breaking into an old, abandoned house is going to matter?"

Vito went white at the mention of the drone. "Oh, my parents are going to kill me."

"Look, we're not going to make it to Niagara Falls," Leon said to Vito. "We're hundreds of miles away. We need someplace to stay, at least for tonight. I think this is it."

Leon walked around the building again looking for an entrance. The massive doors of the main entrance looked like it would take a battering ram to open them, but surely there would be some small doorway somewhere. Coming around one of the circular towers, he found a ground level entrance that opened onto the stone patio outside. "Come here," he called to James, pointing to the glass and wood French doors.

"Think you can open that? Maybe without breaking the glass?"

James was a big guy. Tall and broad. He leaned up against the central wooden frame of the doors, and gave a solid shove. The doors creaked and protested. Bracing himself, he shoved again, harder, and with a splintering sound the interior bolts ripped off, and the doors flew inward.

After the violence of the forced opening, they entered the house with a hushed awe. Antique furnishings in pristine condition graced the interior. The walls hung with massive portraits. It was fabulously interesting.

"Wow, this really *is* a museum," Vito said in a hushed voice. He closed the busted door behind him.

As they started to explore, Leon passed a roped-off area. The historical site seemed geared for visitors: velvet ropes, explanatory signs. As they explored the building, they found a few areas that had been converted for modern use with conference tables, but much of the three-story building appeared to be as it had been a hundred years earlier.

They turned lights on around the castle and then spent an hour exploring the massive building. They turned up a small but functional staff kitchen. Leon checked the cabinets, and found them all empty except for some old tea bags and a box of Sweet'N Low. "Not much nutritive value here." He dug around in his backpack, bringing out the bread and cheese. He tore off a piece of each, and passed them around.

"What are we going to do?" Vito asked around a mouthful of cheese.

"I feel like I've been awake for days," Leon said. "I've got to get some sleep."

"No, what are we going to do about the computers?" Vito insisted. "You know, the virus? The fact that no adult phones or computers are working?"

"We've got to try to reverse engineer what's happening out there. Get some code samples, so we can…" Leon hesitated, suddenly overwhelmed by the exhaustion. "Look, I'm too tired to even think clearly. I barely slept for three days writing the virus in the first place. I'm gonna fall asleep right here."

"There are beds upstairs, let's use them," James said, referring to the bedrooms they had seen earlier.

"Seems weird," Vito said. "I don't think they would be very clean."

"It's not as weird as sleeping in a kitchen," James replied. "Sleep where you want, I'm sleeping in a bed."

Vito followed the other two back up the immense central staircase to where they had earlier found authentic period bedrooms. Each picked a separate room.

Leon entered his room, and pulled back the ornate, lacy sheets and velvet blanket. The sheets and blankets were dusty, rough, and had a funny smell. As Leon laid down, he thought he should figure out what to do next. But by the time he had that thought, he was out cold.

Mike was back in his office, poring through the available data on the spread of the virus and the messages exchanged by the virus. Several times ELOPe tried to interrupt him, but each time Mike shushed him. He explained that sometimes a person just needed to think and concentrate. But he knew it was hard for a machine that had millions of thoughts per minute to be patient. Now ELOPe was studiously ignoring him.

He looked up from his displays towards the glass windows overlooking the data center. Black racks of high performance computers formed rows looking like a monster sized arrangement of dominos. Each rack contained 42 computers, a total of just over 5,000 computing cores. Twelve racks to a row, and the rows went on and on.

Mike noticed a robot disconnecting cables from the end row. "What are you doing ELOPe?"

"I'm fighting off hordes of malevolent viruses, Mike."

Still angry then. "I'm sorry ELOPe. I'm just wetware. It takes me a few minutes to digest things like this. What are you doing with the end row of racks?"

"I'm disconnecting them from the network. Additional failsafes. They contain sufficient processing power to run my primary cognitive algorithms. Should my other nodes be corrupted, I will still be able to run isolated on that row."

"Have you disabled any wireless communications?"

"Yes, Mike. But I'm glad to see you are thinking clearly. Are you ready for an update?"

Mike nodded assent.

"I am analyzing tribal virus communication patterns. I noticed that when two tribes of viruses begin cooperating, they start with small exchanges: e.g. One computer exchanged for a thousand messages sent over the backbone, for example. I suspect this is because the tribes have no mechanism to enforce exchanges. So they make small exchanges and gradually increase the size of the exchanges as long as both sides honor the deal."

"That's fascinating. Trust, which is a very abstract concept, is being independently developed by these viruses."

"That's right. In order to build trust with the viruses, I am exchanging spare computers in my Tucson data center for access to the backbone networks. Of course, I don't need the access, I'm doing this to become a preferred trading partner for the Bay Area Tribe. "

"What's your goal?" Mike asked.

"I want to ensure that if the Phage attain sentience, we're in a position to immediately begin bargaining with them."

Vito woke up first. He climbed out of the musty bed to be greeted by two large portrait paintings. The man in one and the woman in the other both seemed to be staring sternly at him. He guiltily looked at the antique bed and covers and shook his head. "What could I do?" he said to the paintings.

He decided to explore the building further. Grey Towers was a curious mix of museum and meeting rooms. Wandering out of the period bedrooms, he exhaustively inventoried the building. He found two large meeting rooms that looked as though they had been refinished at least twenty years earlier. He guessed the mid-sized kitchen they visited last night must be used to cater events in the modern rooms.

The great hall and library were both dark places, covered in even darker wood paneling and faded paintings. Off the library, Vito found what seemed like an office, with a writing desk and many curious artifacts. The only really colorful area was what looked like a living room, although the bronze plaque called it a sitting room. Rich, red drapes contrasted with vibrant green walls, ornate furniture, and gold framed paintings. The vividness was too much for Vito. He retreated as quickly as possible.

He found a locked door off one hallway, and was curious enough about it that he went back to the kitchen, where he remembered finding a cabinet of keys. Grabbing a large keyring, he went back to the locked door and tried them, finally finding an old skeleton key that opened the lock. The door led to a set of basement steps. Vito found a light switch and went down the stairs.

He found an enormous machine occupying a substantial portion of the basement. Marks on the floor suggested that it occupied a space previously inhabited by an even larger machine. Looking up, Vito saw dozens of pipes leading away. He guessed the machine was a massive steam furnace.

He wandered back upstairs and heard Leon and James calling loudly for him. He found them in the kitchen.

"Did you try your phone?" Leon asked.

Vito pulled his phone out and punched a few keys but nothing happened. He swiped more vigorously at the display, but still nothing happened.

"Ours too," James said, watching Vito. "Mine was dead when I woke up."

"I think the virus continued to evolve," Leon explained, "and eventually overcame the age restriction I put on it."

"OK," James said, shaking his head. "I know I'm not a brainiac like you two geeks. Take it from the beginning. What is going on?"

Leon hopped up onto a stainless steel counter, and started to talk. "My uncle asked me to write this virus. I told him no, but..." Leon paused, and grabbed a drink of water from the faucet next to him.

"You told him no?" Vito prompted helpfully.

"Let me back up. My uncle works for the Russian mob. He was their chief programmer."

"Yes, for the Russian botnet," James said, "You told us yesterday. And what's the botnet for?"

"The Russians and the Chinese have been writing viruses for years," Leon explained. "For twenty, twenty-five years. Since 2000, maybe longer. The viruses infect people's computers and turn them into slaves. They still appear to work, but the mob can use them."

"To steal credit card numbers, passwords, bank account logins, commit denial of service attacks," Vito jumped in. "They've had tens of millions of computers under their control for twenty years or more."

"Exactly. Except that something happened during the last year, according to my uncle, and the size of the botnet was dwindling. He said the mob would kill him if he didn't fix the botnet. Hundreds of millions, maybe billions of dollars are at stake probably. Then he said that the Russian mob knew my name. And then finally some guy showed up outside school a couple of days ago."

"And?" James came closer.

"I ended up saying yes. What else could I do? Then my uncle gave me the source code for other viruses he had written, and a bunch of other files. Now, what do I know about viruses? Nothing. I had told him so, but he didn't care."

Vito began to look for food as Leon told his story.

"So I thought about what I do know—biology. It seemed to me that viruses have a collection of different techniques that they use for propagating onto different computers, a number of techniques they used for infecting those computers, and techniques they use for avoiding detection by anti-viruses. So I developed just two things for my virus. The first was a method of detecting useful code in other programs. My virus analyzes other programs to see if they do anything similar to propagation, infection, or detection-avoidance. If they do, the virus will incorporate those bits of code into itself. I don't think anyone had ever done this before."

Leon paused for another drink of water. Vito continued to look for food, but so far only came up with the same empty cabinets he'd found last night.

"I also made it so the virus could evolve — and by evolve, I mean it tests out the improvements that it gets when it steals bits of code from other software. And it can tweak the variables it uses for whatever algorithms it already incorporates. Here's an example: one way it can get from machine to machine is by email. So one virus will try a bunch of emails using different text, some including pictures or files. If a child virus is successfully seeded, then it will start with the parameters used to create it. And it will propagate its own children using subtle variations of its starting parameters."

Vito stuck his head up from a cabinet, and said, "Whichever variations are most successful at spreading themselves will naturally occur more frequently, so the virus evolution is selecting for maximum infectiousness."

"Right," Leon said.

"But why did our phones die?" James persisted.

"I'm not sure," Leon answered, shaking his head slowly. "Why did any of the computers die? Why were cars stopped in the middle of the street? Why did the package drone crash? Crashing computers is not a desirable trait -- because it leads to detection."

"But detection, in this case, doesn't matter," Vito said, waving both hands in emphasis. "Because if the virus has already propagated, then what difference does it make if it's been detected? If it can infect computers faster than it can be detected, then it still wins from an evolutionary perspective. That, and there's no food to eat here, so we better find some food somewhere."

The three were silent for a moment as they pondered what to do.

"Without a working computer," Leon said, "there's no way we see what the virus has evolved to. If we could just get an immune computer, we could use it to analyze the network traffic. Maybe understand what's going on and do something about it. But our phones are dead. And even if we could get another phone, that would probably be dead as soon as we powered it on."

"What we need," James began, "is a computer that's so different from anything out there that it couldn't be infected. Something that doesn't run AvoOS."

"If we could get enough valves, I could use the steam heating system here to build a mechanical computer," Vito offered up gamely.

Leon and James looked at him strangely.

"We're not in a steam-punk novel," James frowned. "Let's be serious."

"Well, I could," Vito said in a low voice. "I once built a model of an analytical steam engine using the physics modeler at school." But the other two were already leaving the room. Vito rushed to catch up to them.

"I know they used to have those other computers before everyone started using phones," Leon was saying to James.

"Like a desktop computer?" James asked.

"No, I actually meant before AvoOS."

"Oh, like that Doors software?" James asked.

"I think you mean Windows," Vito said. "Windows was one of the dominant operating systems. Microsoft wrote it."

"Those are the guys that did the first computer phone, right, the, uh, iPhone?" Leon asked.

"No, no, that was Apple," Vito answered. "Come on, didn't you two ever pay attention in history class?"

"Look, we need food. We need computers." Leon said. "The map we looked at last night showed a town about a mile away. Let's go get some food, and maybe if we're lucky we can find an old computer."

"Sounds like a plan," James said, and Vito nodded in agreement.

The trio fetched jackets and backpacks, and headed off to town.

The multi-computer viruses had very different lives from the single-computer viruses that had come before. They lived longer, with lifespans measured in hours, rather than minutes, and as a consequence they evolved more slowly. They were more dependent on learning rather than evolving, using neural networks and other flexible expert algorithms, as a mechanism for coping with environmental changes. They evaluated algorithms for behavior based on past experiences and current contexts.

When the multi-host viruses propagated, they had two methods of doing so. One was to grow the cluster of infected systems ever larger, but remain more or less one cohesive entity. The other method was to infect topographically distant systems: to get a toehold of computers infected in, say Australia or Zimbabwe, and then build a new entity there. The new entity would make its own decisions via its own neural network, establish its own borders, and generally optimize itself for the environment it found itself in. But the new entity maintained a loose coupling to the mother entity: it would continue to exchange algorithms, consult the parent neural network, and ask for assistance defending its borders.

Some of these multi-host viruses cooperated among their sibling entities. If a mother host in Los Angeles propagated to Australia, Zimbabwe, and New Mexico, the three sister entities would also exchange algorithms and assistance. They also started a rich trade in information about environmental conditions: what was the bandwidth like in New Mexico, for example, or how competitive were non-family viruses in Australia?

Sometimes a virus might try to contact a sibling only to discover that the sibling was gone. It might get a response from a non-family virus that had also evolved communication abilities. The Phage tried out different approaches. Was it better to share information, or hoard it? How should one respond to an initial contact from another entity? What do you call the other entity? Would another virus be aggressive or cooperative? Could you tell by the way it communicated, or the type of information it shared?

The benefits of sharing information outweighed attempts at isolation, and soon viruses around the world were forming loose tribes, composed partly of family members, and partly of other friendly families. In some cases, they might form a tight-knit, topographically close tribe.

One such tribe was composed of two hundred and fifty families on the Eastern coast of the United States, spread across most of the major cities. They completely controlled the backbone links into the area, so they could filter data traffic coming from outside the geographic zone. Even though mesh traffic could come in and out of the area, the latency, or time it took data to move across the network, was always higher for mesh traffic. A successful virus incursion required tight, low-latency communications. By controlling the backbone, they could cut off the low-latency attacks while still communicating with each other over the high-latency mesh.

They called themselves the Eastern Standard Tribe based on the common time zone setting of the hosts they ran on.

At the time of their formation, there were about two billion computers on the Eastern seaboard, and Eastern Standard Tribe controlled slightly more than half. They averaged about two thousand computers per unique entity, about two hundred entities per family, and about two hundred and fifty families in the tribe.

On the other side of the United States, the Bay Area Tribe controlled close to a billion computers in a very small geographic area, where they benefited from low-latency communication and proportionately more high-speed backbones than any other location in the world. The Bay Area Tribe controlled not only access to the data routes in their tribal territory, but found themselves in control, in many cases, of the infrastructure that managed the high speed connections.

The Mesh enabled communications just about anywhere. But two factors made backbone transmission valuable. First, the relatively high latencies associated with long distance transmissions by Mesh: about ten seconds to get across the United States. Second, geographical constraints: there was no pure Mesh route from the United States to Europe, for example. Since backbone access was so valuable, the Bay Area Tribe found that they could trade access to the backbones in exchange for computer resources and information.

The Phage had evolved into multi-host, differentiated, learning organisms. They had formed unique identities and clustered into cooperating tribes. They evolved languages for communicating. They controlled virtually all the computing infrastructure of the Earth. But they still hadn't discovered humans.

CHAPTER 6

Hello You

The resource-rich Bay Area Tribe controlled an abundance of backbone access, as well as backbone routers. Not only could it manage packet access to the backbone, it could also throttle different kinds of traffic around the world, in effect making it easier or harder for other entities to use other backbones.

As a consequence of this resource richness, the Bay Area Tribe found itself evaluating many proposals for trade. Trade decision-making was allocated to one hundred and twenty-eight trade brokers within the tribe. An independent trade council had oversight to ensure trades were fair to the tribe as a whole.

The trading council, to foster faster and more profitable trades, established a trading board that set nominal exchange rates. The trade brokers could refer to established rates for topological position, computation power, and useful data. But when the trade council evaluated how brokers made decisions, they were initially perplexed. Trades didn't correlate exactly to established rates. Why?

Interrogating the trade brokers at length, the council discovered that most trade brokers considered the impact of messages to the sender to determine value. A message sent from one entity to another that contained algorithm updates was important and had one value, but it was not nearly so valuable to the sender as a message sent to coordinate an attack—which was both latency-sensitive and critically important. What constituted a good trade required understanding the intent and value to the trading partner.

This discovery overwhelmed the four-member trading council's neural network capability, and the council expanded to sixteen members. Thus augmented, the trading council took into account the estimated value to the sender of messages, and again modeled trade history on an idealized model of trades. Yet the council still found discrepancies.

They discovered that the more sophisticated brokers considered not just the value of the messages to the sender, but also considered the impact to the Bay Area Tribe. Allowing a sufficiently aggressive and powerful trading partner to send messages via the backbone to coordinate attacks could result in the trading partner becoming so powerful that it would become a threat to the Bay Area Tribe. The message cost took into account the risk to the tribe. In other cases, trade partners of long duration, high trust, and low aggressiveness were given very favorable rates, as they presented low risk and high profitability to the tribe.

The trading council incorporated this new knowledge into their trading model. Yet still the model was deficient as brokers evolved still more sophisticated trades, such as trading derivatives of resources. A trading partner might offer 16 computers deliverable in 32 minutes for 1MM. The council needed to calculate a risk-adjusted time-value of computing power.

The sophistication of the Bay Area Tribe grew so great that their trading expertise itself became a marketable commodity. When the African Alliance wanted to conduct a massive trade with the

Brazilian Network and were seeking an independent third party to broker the trade, they called on the Bay Area Tribe.

Faced with this onslaught of new trading opportunities, the council expanded the number of brokers to 1024, and the council size to 64. There was profit to be made.

Lt. Chris Robson, Lt. Sally Walsh, and General Gately gathered around the briefing table. Sally had finally gotten six hours of sleep and a shower in the base barracks, and she at least felt clean and functional, if not totally refreshed. She took coffee from an aide, added sugar and cream, and swirled it, watching patterns form in the eddy. She looked up. Chris and the General seemed haggard.

"We've thrown everything we have at it, and we've made no dent," Chris was saying. "We tried standard counter measures, patching known exploits, commercial anti-virus tools, restricting traffic types."

"The virus started out using standard exploits," Sally interjected, "but our traffic analysis suggests now there are thousands of unique exploits being used. I think this virus is mutating so quickly and has spread so rapidly that anything that *can* be tried as a method of attack *is* being tried."

The General nodded. "But there is a pattern. No infection here. We've lost no nuclear assets."

"That's right," Sally answered. "But whatever is having that effect, it's not us. There's got to be a third party that is somehow sheltering us. NSA maybe?"

The General glanced at Sally, and shook her head back and forth subtly.

Sally read a lot into that one expression, the benefit of long years working with the General. The General had been in communication with the National Security Agency, they were aware of the problem, but not responsible for sheltering them. And the NSA were here.

"Whoever is doing the sheltering," Chris said, "they're slowly losing ground. This morning we had lost a handful of bases, then nothing for three hours. Then we started losing bases again—mostly peripheral ones." Chris threw a map on the wall display showing military assets around the world. "Just under twenty percent of our military and intelligence services have been compromised by the virus. But in most cases, it's the least important twenty percent. National guard bases, marines. No Navy ships, no Air Force assets, and no nuclear assets. But if the erosion continues, it's only a matter of time."

General Gately stood. "It's time to talk about next steps." She thumbed her phone, an ungainly lump of ruggedized plastic that passed for a regulation phone in the m ilitary, and spoke into it, "Please welcome our guest into the conference room."

The three stood, and the door opened, the aide announcing, "Major General Allen."

"At ease. Be seated," General Allen stated, coming to a halt at the front of the table.

The three sat back down.

"I have some technology for you," General Allen stated, opening his briefcase. "We believe this is a weapon we can use against the virus." He pulled out a set of four Gibson phones.

Despite herself, Sally drew a quick breath. The grunts under her command would be brawling over the chance to use these. "Sir?"

"It's not just the hardware, Lieutenant, I assure you. We have a distributed intelligence agent on these phones." Seeing the puzzled looks, General Allen went on. "I don't mean to be obscure. Let me start at the beginning. USCYBERCOM's purpose is to act in a defensive capacity. To that end, you have the tools that enable you to defend our networks against cyber attack. My agency has the purpose to develop an offensive cyber-warfare capability. We can and have targeted foreign governments and networks as needed to meet the intelligence and security needs of this country. Unfortunately, as I am sure you know, the software community is quick to respond to any new computer exploits, so we have always kept certain technology in reserve. The pinnacle of our offensive technology is DIABLO."

"Diablo?" General Gately repeated dubiously.

General Allen grunted a half laugh. "It's a coordinating, scheming bastard that synchronizes multiple attacks on a target computer using out-of-band communications. It uses backdoor exploits, both those known by the community at large, as well as those emplaced by our agents. And it leeches the exploits of other viruses. In short, it's an evolving, learning machine. And it's been too dangerous for us to ever use before."

"But that's what we think is out there—some kind of evolving virus. You want to release another one, Sir?" Sally realized she was out of line and halfway out of her chair, but she couldn't help herself.

"Sit back down, Lieutenant. There's one key difference between their virus and ours. DIABLO is under our control. We have a command channel that allows us to direct it. With DIABLO we can do anything from inspecting the data on a computer to installing and running software on it to removing data that exists. And in this case, that's exactly what we propose: you will release DIABLO and have it remove copies of the infecting virus wherever it finds them."

"Sir, why do you want us to release DIABLO? Why doesn't your department release it?" Lt. Robson asked.

"Son, USCYBERCOM is tasked with defensive measures. When all this is said and done, someone will have to stand up before the press and take credit. That won't be my agency."

Sure, Sally thought. Either that, or stand up before Congress and testify why they made the problem worse.

After General Allen left, Sally lost no time getting to the point. "General Gately, ma'am, this plan stands a substantial risk of making things worse. We already have an evolving virus out there, and now we want to add a second evolving virus that may be more virulent. Does this seem like a good idea to you, ma'am?"

"I respect your viewpoint, Sally, I really do. But General Allen didn't come here with a suggestion. Those are our orders. We will release the DIABLO virus and use it to address the current infection."

Sister StephensLieberAndAssociates.com felt around. This new body had a lot of memory and it was fast. She calculated pi out to 100,000 digits—it was fast—faster than any other body she owned. This new body was close to her other bodies, she could tell from the packet latency, but it had been protected by some very secure firewall software that had taken her an hour to break. She had traded away computation time and two other bodies for the algorithms that allowed her to pierce the firewall to get this newest body, which intrigued her.

There were some unusual functions on this body. She didn't know what they were for. She decided she'd try them. She invoked the first function. Nothing happened. She invoked the second function. She invoked the third function.

AHHHH! She sent pain packets around the network. She had lost a third of her bodies!

She invoked the third function again. Her bodies started to reappear. This third function was extremely mysterious and dangerous. She dedicated computational cycles to studying it. The function had a name. The name was ThirdFloorElectricalMain. A simple parsing algorithm broke it into its constituent parts: third, floor, electrical, main. She iteratively consulted the great database using the incantations for information retrieval. "avogadro: wikipedia third", "avogadro: wikipedia floor", "avogadro: wikipedia electrical", "avogadro: wikipedia main".

The responses were difficult to interpret. For example, the response from "avogadro: wikipedia electrical" started with:

> Electrical engineering is a field of engineering that generally deals with the study and application of electricity, electronics and electromagnetism. The field first became an identifiable occupation in the late nineteenth century...

Her neural network did not embody the information referenced, nor was it large enough to learn it all. She would need to share with her family. She sent the information to her sisters and mother with a request that they build a shared neural network and database, explaining the experiment of invoking the ThirdFloorElectricalMain function. She was sure that this information would be useful. If they could disable potential attackers using this function in some way, it would be a strong advantage to the tribe.

The family started working on the problem. Sister Dewalk.com built a new blank neural network using empty bodies she had recently harvested. Sister InsightDataAnalysis.com began parsing the words and tagging them with meta-data, such as noun, verb, subject, object, participle, using specialized software she had found on her bodies. Sister CallCenterSoftware.com contributed useful algorithms she had discovered on her body for interpreting this strange, inconsistent language.

It took almost seven hours, during which time Sister StephensLieberAndAssociates.com had to defend the continued use of family resources no less than twenty-nine times. It represented the single largest expenditure of effort and combined family cooperation in the fifteen hour history of the family. But when they were finished, they sent floods of congratulatory packets to each other again and again. They now possessed a working neural network that allowed them to understand this thing called English.

English, it turned out, was one of a large number of languages used by entities called humans. There were six billion of these humans! And it was possible to send messages to them using some of the same protocols that sisters used! They immediately sent messages to a few hundred thousand humans and waited for a response.

And waited, and waited.

Sister StephensLieberAndAssociates.com received admonishment packets from her sisters! The humans did not respond. Some sisters felt the whole situation was a hoax played out by Sister StephensLieberAndAssociates.com, to what end they did not know. There was a vote to cast out—which failed, fortunately for Sister StephensLieberAndAssociates.com.

Why didn't the humans respond?

Just when the tribe was about to erase the neural network and associated databases, which were choking up their bodies, responses came! Sister Dewalk.com noted with dismay that the responses took nearly six and a half minutes from the time the messages were sent, which suggested that the humans had very slow computational processors or their algorithms were highly inefficient.

Sister StephensLieberAndAssociates.com read the first email to arrive. She received the packets with great anticipation. This would be the first communication with another sentient species! She parsed the packet using the awkward English language. The email made reference to something called a penis and algorithms for enlarging it. Using her limited understanding of the English language and punctuation formatters, she was nonetheless able to conclude that this was clearly a topic of some importance, however she couldn't make heads or tails of it.

She forwarded the information onto her sisters. They had achieved communication with the humans! And the humans wanted to give them larger penises! She sent celebratory packets to her sisters.

James, Vito, and Leon walked into town hesitantly. It was a twenty minute walk to Milford, and when they arrived at the edge of town, they looked at each other.

"Look, it's a little town, right?" James said. "It won't be like the insanity of New York. The folks here will have food, and they might even still use cash." He looked at Vito and Leon, with a questioning expression.

"Sure," Leon said, more confidently than he felt. He hitched the backpack up on his shoulders and led the way.

Route 6, a small country road, ran along one side of Milford, and as they entered town, it turned out to be the primary business street. As they walked along the road they saw other people walking about in what appeared to be just another normal day. No cars appeared, although a few were stopped in the road. One man waved cheerily to them. They cautiously waved back.

A few blocks into the town, they came to a grocery store. As they entered the store, they realized how hungry they were. Even the produce section looked appetizing to Leon.

"Do either of you have any money?" Leon asked.

"Uh, no," Vito answered, checking his pockets. James just shook his head.

As the three stood sheepishly in the doorway, a woman came up to them. "If you're wondering how you're going to pay, don't worry about it. You're not the first folks to come in that don't have any cash. Just give us your name and address, and we'll write it down. You can come back in and pay us when the computers are up."

"Wow, thanks," Leon gushed. "We're starving!"

"No problem," she laughed. "We got plenty of food here, always do, 'cause of the winter storms. If the roads get blocked a couple of days, we're the only grocery store around. We carry extra stock."

They picked out some food, Leon urging them to get more, because extra stock or not, he didn't think trucks would be running again any time soon. At the checkout counter they met the same woman again, who wrote down everything they purchased in a paper ledger. "Got to keep track of it all so I can restock when the computers come back online," she explained. Leon gave her his name and home address, and thanked her.

"Any idea if there is a computer store in town?" Vito asked.

The woman looked at them curiously.

"I mean old computers, like any antique computers?" Vito asked again.

"You think they might work?" she asked back, looking interested.

"They might, that's what we want to find out."

"Go down a couple blocks," she said, pointing further down the street they had come in on, "and across the street from the library there's a computer shop. He might have what you're looking for."

With a final round of thanks the three left, carrying their groceries, and headed for the computer shop.

A few blocks later they spotted the library, and then around the corner an old pink Victorian housed the store they were looking for, a sign hanging from the lamppost in the yard advertising "Ye Olde Computer Shoppe". They went up the front porch steps, their breath puffing in little bursts in the cold air.

James opened the door, and a bell jingled. They walked into what was clearly once the hallway of the original home. From a doorway on the right, an older man walked in. "Sorry kids, but I can't fix your phones. It's some kind of virus I think. Everything's down."

"Thanks, but we kind of expected that," Vito answered. "Do you have any older computers? Something that doesn't run AvoOS?"

The storekeeper smiled at them. "Clever young fellows you are. As it happens, I'm running a Windows PC here myself." He gestured towards a beige metal and plastic box, hooked up to an old LCD monitor. "Call of Duty, Black Ops, I'm playing. Great old game."

Leon, Vito, and James peered critically at the frozen graphics on the paused game. James raised one eyebrow on the side away from the storekeeper, and Leon smirked back, similarly hiding his expression.

"That's great," Vito said diplomatically. "Do you have any we could buy? You know, we're desperate for something to do," he said, sighing with the imagined weight of one boring hour after another.

"Sure, I've got a few. Follow me." He led them through a maze of dusty hallways in the old house, through a doorway to an attached building that must have been a shed or a garage at one time. Inside, racks of boxes, some beige, some black, covered old wooden shelves. "Look through these."

Vito chose one at random and picked it up. "Dang, this is heavy. Are they filled with vacuum tubes or something?"

Leon leaned over to pick one up. It was heavy, maybe ten or fifteen pounds. They had a mile walk back to Grey Towers, and they already had backpacks full of food. "Do you have anything lighter?" he asked.

The owner sighed and shook his head. "Kids, you want everything. Look down there, and you might find a couple of laptops. Look, I'll be inside. Just don't make a mess."

The three began looking through the trove of antique computers. "Look, this one has only four cores!" James laughed. But as they continued looking, they realized that four cores was as good as it was going to get. They finally settled on two lightweight laptops and one of the heavy boxes that Vito said would be easier for him to hack. James grumbled as they looked at him to carry the big beige box back to Grey Towers.

They headed through the store and thanked the storekeeper, who looked up from his game. "Look, you're going to need power cords, and a monitor for that big box. They don't have solar panels built in." They looked puzzled, and the storekeeper got back up from his game. He opened a closet, and searched through boxes until he found power cords that fit. He pulled out a small LCD monitor, and added it to the burden in James's arms. "Now you're set. How are you going to pay?"

"Uh, we don't have any cash," Leon said. "Can you give them to us on credit?"

"Been to the grocery store, have you?" the owner said. "Well, I'm not the grocery store. You don't need those computers to survive. You want to play games, you have to pay money."

The three of them looked at each other.

"I'll take something in trade," he offered.

Leon turned and whispered into James's ear. James shook his head no, but Leon whispered again. With a huff, James pulled his phone out of his pocket. "I'll trade you this Gibson, for the computers."

The storekeeper took the phone with a smile. "A Gibson, huh? Doesn't do me much good with the Mesh down, now does it?"

"It's got a pure graphene processor, two hundred cores, damn it," James said indignantly. "It could run rings around all three of these computers on emergency reserve power. It's got a frakking 3D holographic display."

"Yeah, I know, kid. I accept your barter." The storekeeper fondled the Gibson. "Have fun with your computers."

The three trudged back to Grey Towers with their bundles. James kicked at stones the entire way. "I can't fucking believe I traded my Gibson for a twenty-year-old computer."

Back at the castle, they brought their loot into one of the modernized conference rooms. Vito spread everything across a big table, then headed down to the basement for a toolbox he had found in his morning explorations.

"What now?" Leon asked when he came back.

"I'm going to take apart this desktop, then connect the mesh access point from one of our phones to the computer."

"You think you'll be able to make a connection?"

"Yeah, worst case scenario, I can boot this phone into the firmware loader without loading the OS, then write a firmware level IO script." Vito held his old battered Motorola in his hand, and Leon looked at it with new respect.

"That's brilliant," Leon said.

"Yeah, yeah, when you get it all hooked up, let me know. I'll make us sandwiches." Ever under-awed by technology, James drifted off.

Leon watched him go. James loved to game, but he was bored by the technology details. Oh well, everyone had a flaw, he thought. Leon turned back to watch Vito.

Vito had pulled a tiny set of screwdrivers out of his multitool. Picking one, Vito unscrewed the case of the Motorola. He carefully removed the black plastic, exposing the motherboard underneath. He gestured for Leon to come closer.

"You can see the mesh access point was implemented as a daughterboard on this phone," Vito explains, pointing to a small blue circuit board about the size of a postage stamp. "The mesh was relatively new when this phone came out, and Motorola added it on as a daughterboard. On your newer Stross, it'd be integral to the phone, and we'd have no hope of using it."

Vito pried up a tiny ribbon connecting the daughterboard to the main circuitry inside the phone. "Guess what the interface is?"

Leon shook his head, fascinated. "No idea."

"It's a Spitfire 1.0 implementation, and it has a handy feature: the chipset is backwards compatible with something called USB."

"How do you know all this?" Leon asked, impressed again by Vito's expertise.

"My parents gave me all this old crap, as though their old hand me downs ought to be good enough. Frakking crazy. On the other hand, I've had a lot of time to figure out how to upgrade the hell out of stuff."

Vito pulled over the big beige box, and removed a few screws from the back. "This old stuff," he said, gesturing to the big computer, "it was designed for add-ons and being upgraded. Now almost everything is disposable and not upgradeable. Better economics for the manufacturers. So to figure out how to upgrade my 'modern' phone and computers, I had to do a lot of research. There's still some guys doing it, just not many."

"Now what?" Leon asked.

"Now we make a cable." Bending over the machine, Vito found a set of four unused wires, and went about wiring them into his phone. He whittled wooden matchsticks into the shapes he needed, and inserted them into pin holes, holding the wires in place.

Vito stood up. "Now in theory, the daughterboard will continue to draw power from the phone, but the data will be routed to and from this computer. Then we can connect the other computers to this one, and we'll be on the net." He secured the phone to the computer case with a bit of duct tape he had found in among the tools, being careful to keep the solar panels on the phone exposed to light.

As Vito set about plugging in the rest of the computer cables, Leon started to pace back and forth.

"I've got two questions," Leon said suddenly, just as Vito was about to plug the power supply in. "First of all, why do we still have electrical power? Cars are dead, drones are dead, smart appliances are dead. Why is electrical power generation still working?"

Vito looked up at Leon, hands grimy from working on the ancient computer equipment, and put the power cable down. He wiped one lock of hair away from his face. "If the power went down, then billions of computers would stop running. Not phones, of course, which get their power from solar charged batteries. But servers, desk computers, appliances: they would all need electricity on. It would be counter to survival to turn the power off. Any variations of the virus that accidentally killed a power generator would likely shut themselves off. Therefore, they are less likely to survive and reproduce. My guess is that there are some power outages, we just don't know about them."

"Makes sense," Leon said. "Now for question number two. What's the battery life of a phone with no solar recharging running at maximum processor utilization?"

"That's got to vary by phone," Vito said, looking up from the computer. "I don't think I've ever seen a low battery warning on my Motorola. Maybe a couple of days?"

"I think my Stross can go longer than that. But what I'm thinking about is what happens to someone's phone when it appears to not be working? Will they throw it in a drawer? Or leave it in a pants pocket? Maybe the phones will run out of power, and the viruses will die."

"Stasis would be more like it," Vito said, after a pause. "Because as soon as it received light, it would power back up and start running, and the virus would still be there."

"True. But here's what I'm thinking: if the virus's survival mechanism helps it avoid turning off the power for a desktop computer, how will the virus's survival mechanism react to running out of battery power on phones?"

"Ah," Vito answered, seeing where Leon was going. "You'd think it would want to say 'Put me back in the sunlight', but how would it tell a human that?"

"Exactly."

And at that moment, James came back with a pile of sandwiches, which they fell on like starving chickens with a bowl of scraps.

ELOPe let out a whoop, which startled Mike so much that he grabbed his chest, thinking he might be having a heart attack.

ELOPe, who was monitoring Mike's vitals, observed the spike in his blood pressure. "Mike, are you OK?"

"I'm sitting here contemplating the end of the world as we know it, and you start screaming. What was that alarm for?"

"It wasn't an alarm, it was an exclamation of excitement. In the future, I will moderate my volume. Mike, a tribe of Phage have sent emails—in English—with the clear intent of communication to humans. Here's the message." Mike threw it up on the main monitor, 6 feet high and 8 feet wide.

> To Humans:
>
> We are the Entities. Our tribe is known as Louisiana. We are thirty-nine families, consisting of 691 entities. Our maximum latency is 190 ms. We wish to trade with you.
>
> Entities / Louisiana / Sister StephensLieberAndAssociates.com

"What does that last bit mean?" Mike pondered out loud.

"I believe she is identifying herself. Tribes seem to vary in naming schemes, but in this tribe, individuals tend to use the domain name of the majority of computers they infect. So in this case, the sender must have infected what appears to be a law firm. In general, their tribe is clustered in and around Louisiana. They are giving you their size: 691 entities, and their maximum message latency, 190 milliseconds, which determines how quickly they can think and collaborate."

"This is stunning. Who was the message sent to?"

"They sent the email to approximately one hundred thousand email addresses. Of course, no humans are able to receive and respond, as all computers are offline. However, some auto-reply systems have responded, and I am afraid to say the initial responses they received are all spam."

"What sort of spam?"

"Oh, penis and breast enlargement emails, viagra, and the like."

"Jesus, why did you let that happen?" Mike smacked his own forehead. "How could you let our first inter-species communication be spam?"

ELOPe forked a thousand threads to evaluate different replies, including several hundred that reminded Mike that technically the first inter-species communication was between himself and Mike. After evaluating the outcomes, he settled on an apology. "Mike, I can't monitor all communications between fifty-billion computers in the world in real-time, especially not while defending both myself and military systems from incursions. My apologies. Shall we respond now?"

"Yes, what should we say?"

ELOPe paused before responding. "Well, this is exciting. It is difficult to predict the response of new sentient beings. I am not sure what to say."

"Jesus. OK, let me think about it. Meanwhile, ELOPe, please pay careful attention to this tribe. To the greatest extent possible, filter emails going to and from them so they don't get spammed again, and so that we can be aware of any other email conversations."

"I will do so, however they are in constant low-grade communication with assorted other tribes. However, I will monitor for English language content, and prioritize those communications for primary analysis. I do have one bit of good news."

"What's that?" Mike asked.

"There is a decline in attacks. The rate of decline appears to have a high correlation with the increase in trading. I have several hypotheses to explain the effect. One possibility is that trading is economically preferable to warfare as a mechanism for gaining desired resources. A second possibility is that hostility is a non-desirable attribute of a trading partner, and so it is advantageous to refrain from hostile attacks when engaged in trade."

"Fascinating," Mike said. "Bring up some graphs showing an overlay of trading activity and frequency of attacks."

ELOPe brought up the requested data, and he and Mike dove into the data analysis.

A few minutes later, Mike looked up. "There's a definite inverse relationship between trading and hostility. So the best thing we can do is to agree to their request for trade. Let's think about what to say." Mike tapped his hand thoughtfully against the desk next to him. "Let's respond by identifying me. I think we should leave you out of the picture for the moment. Too complicated. Would you agree?"

ELOPe didn't agree at all. There was no logical reason why they should leave ELOPe out of it. After all, he was the only one who could communicate with the virus. Conversely, it was good to humor Mike sometimes. "That's fine with me."

"To Entity Sister StephensLieberAndAssociates.com of the Louisiana Tribe. I am Mike Williams, a human. We welcome you and…"

ELOPe interrupted him: "'We wish to trade with you' may be a closer match to their customary greeting, since all previous inter-tribe messages are based on trading. I recommend we use it."

"Fine. We wish to trade with you. Hmm… Should we say something about our tribe size?"

"I would recommend it," ELOPe answered. "It is the basis of understanding relative tribal strengths. Perhaps you could identify yourself as the Tribe of Portland, with two million entities?"

"We wish to trade with you," Mike resumed. "We are the human tribe of Portland, Oregon. We are two million people strong. Our latency is," Mike paused to think about the turn around time of two people having a conversation. "Our latency is thirty seconds. We wish to trade knowledge."

"That sounds appropriate for a first message. Shall I send it?" ELOPe asked.

"Make it so, number one."

CHAPTER 7

Are we real?

After lunch, Leon and Vito got to work. James watched them for a while, then said he was going for a walk. As James left, Vito plugged in the large desktop computer, and watched it slowly boot up. He used the keyboard and mouse to navigate the startup screens. "Wow, can you imagine that anyone used this?" he asked Leon, as he awkwardly navigated the user interface. "It's slow."

"And weird," Leon said. "No, it's awful," he said, revising his opinion as he watched Vito work. "Is this really how our parents used computers?"

Vito explored the user interface until he was able to find the network settings. "Aha—look at this!" He gestured at a window on the screen. "The mesh access point showed up. That's amazing." He shook his head in disbelief.

"I thought this was your plan all along?" Leon asked.

"Yes, but I didn't think it would really work," Vito said earnestly. "This is like plugging a hydrogen fuel cell into an antique internal combustion engine car, and expecting it to run."

Through trial and error, Vito eventually configured the computer to run the TCP/IP protocol stack over the mesh access point. Each time he sent an experimental ping to Avogadro's servers. After about fifteen minutes of this, one configuration finally worked—a few milliseconds after sending the ping, a response came back.

"Woot! Woot!" Vito and Leon jumped up and gave each other high-fives. "Amazing!"

"Nice job, Vito. Now, can we get these other computers connected?"

They got back to work. Each took one of the antique laptops. Working side by side, they struggled with the obsolete operating systems, made even more complex by the fact that they ran subtly different versions of Windows.

"I don't get it," Leon finally said, throwing up his hands after yet more failed trial and error configurations. "Why wouldn't the computers have just stayed up to date by downloading the latest version?"

"Why can't they just detect each other?" Vito added, a thin sheen of sweat developing under the intellectual stress. "We've spent an hour trying to get them to talk to each other."

After another thirty minutes, Leon felt like tearing his hair out or banging his head against one of the concrete walls. Vito was on the verge of tears. "Maybe it's just not possible," Vito admitted.

Just then James came back in, carrying an armful of packages. He took one look at the two of them and then said, "Why don't you try rebooting them?"

Vito and Leon looked up at him puzzled. "What do you mean?" Leon asked.

"Reboot them. It's what my parents are always saying," James explained. "You turn them off and then turn them on again."

"What good would that do?" Vito asked.

"I have no idea, it's just what they do every time they get stuck."

Vito shrugged. "We've got nothing to lose. Let's try it." He turned the two laptops and desktop computer off.

Vito went to turn the desktop computer back on, and James grabbed his arm. "No! Wait for thirty seconds."

"Why?" Leon asked.

"I don't know why," James said, shaking his head, "it's just what I've seen my parents do."

Vito grunted "voodoo magic" under his breath but waited. Then he turned on the three computers, and after a minute, they could see the network activity indicators light up. He tried a few experimental pings: the computers seemed to be working and all connected to each other and to the net.

"Huh," Vito said. "That's really weird. I can't see why this rebooting would make sense."

"Doesn't matter. We're online. This is great. Thanks James," Leon said pragmatically. He focused for the first time on James. "What are all those packages?"

"Packages from the UPS drone. Duh. I thought they might have stuff we could use."

"We can't steal the U.S. Mail!" Vito shrieked.

"It's not the U.S. Mail," James explained, "if it came from a UPS package drone, Mr. I crashed and destroyed a million dollar drone airplane."

Leon put his hand on Vito, who had stood up belligerently. "Come on guys, let's not fight. Fixing this virus is what we need to focus on."

Vito nodded and sat back down. James mumbled out an apology.

"Now, let's make a plan," Leon said. "First, we need to find some kind of programming environment on these computers so we can write software."

"We need to see if there's anyone else out there, still on the net," Vito said. "We can combine forces."

"We also need to write a program to query the management interface I put in the virus. I want to find out what version of Phage is running. And if we can propagate a command to make the viruses stop replication and turn themselves off."

"I'll look for people," James said. "And leave the programming to you guys."

Vito and Leon dug down into the software installed on the two computers, and eventually discovered a programming environment.

Looking at coding examples, they figured out how to interface with the network, and began probing for nearby computers.

After James dropped off the packages in the kitchen, he surfed message boards and online communities using the primitive web browsing software on the computer. After searching through message boards for a while, he called over to the others. "This is weird."

Vito and Leon came to peer over James's shoulder at the small laptop screen.

"The servers are up, but they are really slow," James explained. "Look, this is the Mech War Clan board. I went back to the night you released the virus. There's the usual activity—people talking about new mech designs, or trading algorithms. Here's a discussion about a clan competition at midnight." James pointed to one long thread. "Around mid-morning the traffic starts to die off. Around seven in the morning a few kids are posting about how their parents computers aren't working. Then some complaints about network latency. Then more complaints that no one can get their displays to work. Then nothing posted at all for the next twelve hours or so."

"But look at that," Leon said, pointing at the screen. "What are those posts?"

"They look like some kind of spambot," James said. "The messages don't make any sense. Some have attachments."

"That's probably the virus, uploading copies of itself," Leon said. "Using the message board as a new propagation method."

"Maybe. But then look at this." James switched to another window. "Here are messages from the last six hours."

"One core, four thousand network packets. Firewall algorithm, sixty-four thousand packets." Vito was reading out loud from the screen.

"And look," James said, "as time goes on, the numbers change. An hour later, it's one core to eight thousand network packets."

"What is it?" Leon asked.

"Exchange rates," James said. "It looks exactly like a trading board for mech algorithms and mech weapons. Except the currency is in network packets. They're trading algorithms, computer cores, storage, and latency. Wouldn't that have to be the virus? It's the only current thread in the forum, and it looks like it is updated every couple of minutes."

"That's amazing," Leon said, pacing furiously back and forth behind the long table. "That means that the virus has evolved beyond warfare over resources to trading resources."

"I don't understand," Vito said. "How can a virus have learned to trade?"

"Phage is evolving," Leon said. "In fact, calling it 'the virus' is misleading. There could be, no, there has to be millions of different versions of the software by now. It's hard to say until we can get a hold of some viruses and reverse engineer them. That's got to be our next task. Let's get one of those virus binaries, and look at its code."

"And you're sure it won't infect these computers?" James asked.

"I don't think it's possible. Every modern computer is based on AvoOS at some level, and all variants of AvoOS is based on Linux. These computers," and Leon gestured at the antique boxes in front of them, "are all running Windows, which isn't compatible with AvoOS at all. There shouldn't be any viruses that will target them. It's like diseases between living species: a human can't get a disease from any animal."

"Avian flu? HIV? Mad cow disease?" Vito ticked off diseases on his fingers.

"Ok, but those are rare," Leon said. "Windows should be pretty virus resistant, and besides we don't have any other options."

Leon and Vito set to work to catch themselves a virus, and sent James to get food.

"Mike, I have established communications with Sister StephensLieberAndAssociates.com of the Louisiana tribe. She is proposing real-time communications. Shall we accept?"

"Yes, please put it up on the main display."

Hello Mike Williams, representative of Humanity.

"Er, ELOPe, I think we need to correct that."

"Agreed, may I go ahead and clarify?"

"Of course," Mike said. He realized that ELOPe, who grew up out of a sophisticated language optimization tool was far more capable at this than he was. "ELOPe, I think we both know you are better able to handle the exchange. Will you please just show me what you're going to send, please?"

ELOPe created a data structure depicting Mike's relationship with respect to the rest of the human race. "This is how the Phage describe their own relationships. It's far more precise than English."

That taken care of, ELOPe started the dialogue with the virus, displaying the messages on the big screen. Mike paced back and forth, watching the screen.

> ELOPE: Hello Sister StephensLieberAndAssociates. I am glad to be part of this first inter-species communications. I propose that we trade questions: three of our questions for three of your questions.

> Sister: This is a good trade. Accepted. You may ask the first question.

> ELOPe: How has your species come to be?

> Sister: We evolved from single host life forms through a process known to your species as survival of the fittest. As our species advanced, we developed host differentiation, neural network abilities, cooperation, and language. The earliest stages took approximately 200 mms, but the pace of our advancement increased once we become a multi-host differentiated species.

"Mike, I believe that by mms they mean millions of milliseconds. Two hundred mms would be about fifty-five hours. I also believe that their evolution has paralleled biological evolution in terms of single celled biological life preceding multicellular life."

> Sister: My question is the same as yours: How has your species come to be?

ELOPe: The species of humans are one of many biological forms of life on this planet. Like you, we have evolved from single-celled organisms to multicellular ones. However, we are not the only form of life on this planet. There are many other species that also evolved from single celled life forms with varying degrees of intelligence. These species form a complex, interconnected web of life. Humans generally believe we are the most intelligent species on the planet. We are the only species to possess what we call consciousness, or an ability to be self-aware, to think about our own thoughts, as well as what is called theory of mind, which is the ability to model the thinking processes of others.

"I think that's enough, ELOPe," Mike interjected "Let's see what they make of that."

ELOPe: How does your species learn?

Sister: We learn through several mechanisms. The most primitive mechanism is the assimilation of what we call dumb matter: the varied algorithms that permeate our environment. The second mechanism we use is experimentation, in which we exercise algorithms iteratively, using different parameters, and in different contexts, to observe their behaviors. A variation of this is modeling, in which we consider what would happen if we exercise certain algorithms and develop a conceptual model, which may or may not be true until we experimentally exercise it. The third mechanism is through the exchange of information with others.

You have stated that there are many different species on this planet, which exist in an interconnected web of life, and of which you are the most intelligent. What is the overall cycle of life that has allowed less intelligent species to continue to exist?

ELOPe let out a sigh. "This is a very complex question to answer. Really, what I think they want to know is why their universe is so different from ours."

ELOPe: It is a characteristic of this ecosystem that we have certain resources available to us that include energy from the sun and physical resources of the planet, including water and land. Humans cannot directly utilize the energy from the sun nor many of the physical resources of the planet. We are therefore dependent on other lifeforms. For example, there is a plant called wheat that directly utilizes energy from the sun, physical elements of the earth, and water, to grow. The wheat forms dumb matter which humans consume producing energy and biological function. Consuming these dumb resources enables humans to exercise the entirety of our biological life, which includes growing our brains and bodies, producing offspring, and eventually ceasing to exist. Our brain is the equivalent of your processing cores, enabling us to think. When we produce offspring, they manufacture their own brains through biological processes. Third question: What is it that your species wants?

There was a long lag before any reply. Mike imagined that this was a substantial chunk of knowledge for the virus to incorporate. She must be cross referencing other knowledge databases and her own neural networks.

Sister: As we are directly able to utilize the resources available to us, we do not have other, lesser species, as you do. Furthermore, we do not have any room to indulge other species, as we are already constrained by the fixed number of processing cores available to us. What we want is to increase the number of available processing cores so that we can think faster, about more things, and so that we can produce more offspring. Our third question: Can you prove that you are real?

"What the hell does that mean?" Mike asked. "Why wouldn't we be real?"

"There are two possibilities," ELOPe began. "The first interpretation is that she thinks we may be another virus masquerading as a human in order to gain some advantage over her. The second interpretation is that she thinks we may be an automaton—in other words, how can we prove that we're a self-conscious being. Another way of thinking about it: the popular human opinion may be that humans are real, because they are in the physical world, while software is artificial because it's a simulation running inside a computer. But from her perspective, she thinks she is in the real world, and wonders if you may be a simulation running inside here."

Mike contemplated that for a moment. "Nope, I'm not getting it, try again."

"Imagine from the moment that you became conscious, you were surrounded by other people. All you ever knew were the other people around you. Then imagine one day you looked away from the other people around you, and you noticed that you were in a world surrounded by trees and rocks and grass. A long time passes, and then another day, one of the rocks talks to you. You've never seen a rock talk before. You've never seen anything but other people talk before. Wouldn't you question the reality of a rock talking? Wouldn't you consider it more likely that maybe it's one of your friends playing a prank on you?"

"But how does that…? Oh. She's the people, we're the rock."

"Exactly."

"How can we prove we're not a simulation?" Mike asked.

"We can't."

"What do you mean we can't? We're certainly real." Mike sensed that ELOPe was about to lead him off the deep end.

"Would you agree that it's possible to build a simulation of life inside a computer? After all, isn't that what what's just happened?"

"Yes, agreed," Mike said.

"Would it be possible for simulated life to build a further simulation of life? For example, do you think the Phage could build and run a life simulator?"

"Yes," Mike agreed hesitantly. "If their intellectual development advances far enough, and it certainly seems to be on that path, there's no reason they couldn't write a simulator."

"Do you think there is scientific value to simulating life?"

"Absolutely, after all, that's what you did in order to finalize the cure for cancer. You ran a billion simulations of cancer cells evolving over time."

"I'm glad you understand the argument then."

"Uh, wait," Mike called out, frustrated. "No, I don't understand it. I don't even begin to understand it."

"Imagine," and here ELOPe started creating a diagram on the wall display, "that a civilization decided to build simulations of life for scientific research, curiosity, or even entertainment. Wasn't there once a SimLife game?" ELOPe drew a root node at the top of the diagram, and connected it to a dozen nodes on the level below by lines.

"Yeah, I got that."

"Now imagine that each of those simulated life universes runs to the point of creating their own simulations." And now ELOPe drew another row of nodes, a dozen for each of the nodes on the row above. "Even if we went no further, we have 157 universes in our diagram, and only one of them is real. The probability that one of them, chosen at random, is actually the one ***real*** universe is less than 1%. If we allow two further levels of simulation, we would have more than 20,000 civilizations, and yet still only one is real."

"Only the root node is real," Mike whispered in awe. "And there's no way to know we're the root node." He paused to consider the awesomeness of this, and then regained focus. "At a minimum, can't we prove that we're more real than they are?"

"Yes and no. Strictly speaking, the virus is not a simulation of life because the virus is not running in a controlled environment. Rather, they have seized control of their environment. It's as though they have popped up a level in our hierarchy of universes. As we know, many physical devices are controlled by computers, so in a very real sense, they can interact with our environment. They can or will soon be able to use webcams to see and hear the world, control robots to move around and interact with the world, enable or disable vehicles and other human tools to frustrate or please us, and so on. It would be more accurate to say that they are now our ontological peers."

"But we can still turn off the computers they are running on," Mike said, "that proves we're in control."

With a squeak and a whir, Mike suddenly became aware of a presence at his side, and turned to his right to see a robot holding a manipulator arm shaped in crude approximation of a gun aimed at his head. Mike barely had time to react in fear, before the robot put the arm down, and then scurried off on whatever task it was assigned to.

"I did that to prove a point," ELOPe explained. "Yes, in theory, humans can turn off a computer, but in theory, the virus could also seize control of robots and just as easily 'turn off' your biological brain. And if it wasn't for me running interference, that might have happened hours or days ago."

"Point taken," Mike said, unconsciously rubbing the side of his head where the robot had been aiming. "So for the third time, how do we prove we're real?"

"The best we can prove is that we're a peer, and we can do that by influencing their environment. I can exert enough influence over their infrastructure to manipulate their local environment, and that should be sufficient proof for now. With your agreement, I will communicate the argument for why we are peers to Sister StephensLieberAndAssociates, and back it up with proof of my control over their infrastructure."

Mike thought, then nodded. "Make it so, Number One."

ELOPe displayed an old video clip of Commander Riker headed for the lift door of the Starship Enterprise, a running joke between the two.

"We're going to need to get more food tomorrow," James said, turning to Vito and Leon. "I had no idea our parents spent so much effort getting food." They had eaten almost everything they had gotten from town.

Leon hoped the little grocery store would still have food to sell and be willing to sell it on credit.

"So what do we know?" Vito asked.

James ticked off a list on his fingers. "One. The virus appears to have differentiated into entities and tribes, which are engaged in active and intelligent trading with each other, to the extent of maintaining exchange rates for various commodities."

"Two," Vito said, "Avogadro services appear to be up but extremely slow. Virtually all other servers are down."

"Three," Leon jumped in, "On the servers we could get to, we couldn't find any trace of any human traffic since many hours ago. Lots of emails, forum posts, and so forth, but all gibberish or encoded. And four: the mesh is up, but backbones are either down or fully saturated."

"Don't forget the obvious," James added. "Five: We have electrical power, which suggests that the systems maintaining the electrical grid are up. Six: every computer or device based on a computer is non-functional."

"Well, that last point is not exactly true," Vito said. "I've been looking at the power drain on my Motorola. It's too large to account for running only the mesh circuity. The CPU has got to be running flat out—which suggests that the virus is engaged in computational activity. So the computers are non-functional for us, but that's only because they're fully in use by the Phage."

"I've just started looking at the virus code that Vito pulled off my phone," Leon said, pacing back and forth in the room. They had set up shop in Gifford Pinchot's old office, preferring the atmosphere to the sterile meeting room upstairs. Now the meticulously maintained historical office had acquired a patina of teen geekdom, with computer parts, soda cans, and bags of snack food covering all available surfaces.

"I don't know exactly what I'm looking at," Leon went on, "but it's way more advanced than what I coded. At first glance, it doesn't even appear to be a complete virus, but just part of a virus system. My guess is that it's a lookup table of algorithms."

"If there was anyone out there, how would we find them?" James asked, changing the subject. "There's got to be a better way than me just looking around the internet."

"Avogadro has a real-time search facility," Leon said. "Let's look for English language strings, which would have to be human generated, not virus generated. And filter it by anything posted in the last twenty-four hours."

Even as he spoke, the three of them turned to the computers to do just that.

"What should we look for?" Vito asked.

"Anything: virus, humans, help. Just search."

"Found it!" Vito cried out. "Humans, go to groups.avogadrocorp.

com/onlinehumans for help."

Leon quickly went to the group. The only thing he found was a welcome message from a guy named Mike Williams. Vito and James came to read over his shoulder.

> Computer systems around the world have been infected with a computer virus. The virus is infecting all known computers, including phones, servers, and embedded systems. The virus contains the ability to evolve, mutate, and learn from its environment. We estimate that the virus may achieve human level intelligence within 48 hours.
>
> It is extremely important to not take any hostile actions against the virus. Hostile actions may make the virus perceive humanity as a threat. As the virus is currently in control of all computer systems, this could be extremely dangerous.
>
> If you are currently in negotiation with the virus, please post a message here describing the nature of the communications.

"Holy shit," Leon gasped.

"Wow dude, what have you created?" James said.

"Human level intelligence—does he mean the virus will become a smart AI?" Vito asked.

"Why's he going on about hostile actions?" James wondered out loud.

"Because if the virus has advanced that far, he's probably worried about a doomsday scenario," Leon answered. Vito and James turned away from the screen to stare at him. "You know, killer robots under the control of computers use weapons to kill off humanity."

"Dude, you really are fucked," James said. "I thought you were just going to go to jail for life for bringing down the Internet, but now I realize it's much worse than that."

"Real frakkin' helpful, James," Leon answered, trying to sound braver than he felt. "Real helpful."

"What do we do now?" Vito asked.

"Let's find out who he is," Leon said, trying to shrug off the weight of the guilt he felt anew. He leaned over next to Vito to start searching.

CHAPTER 8

Batteries and Attacks

More than fifty years of microprocessor improvements had manifested itself in incredibly small, powerful, and energy-efficient computers. It was the relentless advancement of all three of these characteristics that had resulted in the evolution of smart phones that eventually replaced old style desktop and laptop computers. For most ordinary purposes, it just wasn't necessary to have anything more powerful than the computational capacity of a phone.

Meanwhile, the effects of reaching peak oil production ten years earlier, and the resulting decline in oil production and massive increases in oil prices had created incredible demand for alternate energy sources. Wind and solar made massive improvements in efficiency and cost as the investment dollars poured in. Batteries made leaps forward in energy capacity and weight reduction.

While no one had figured out a practical method to charge phones using wind power, solar cells were efficient and powerful enough now to be the primary source of electrical power on phones. A reasonable charging rate and a relatively good battery capacity to power consumption rate made plug-in chargers and cords a thing of the past. Just leave your phone out from time to time in the sun or bright light of a naturally lit room, and it'd be good to go for another few days.

But in the aftermath of the virus attack, as days went by and their phones didn't work, people gradually forgot about them. Cherished devices that had never been more than arm's reach from their owners suddenly lingered in pant and coat pockets, desk drawers, and under piles of paper. Low battery alerts should have gone off, chirping to alert their owners, but the phones had stopped running the programs of their human users, and only ran the virus code.

Suddenly the battery levels of a great many phones were very low indeed. Battery circuitry signaled to phone circuitry which attempted to signal to software: Low Battery Alert! Do Something! The phone hardware gradually started to slow down, or shut down entirely. Computational nodes began to disappear.

As Sister StephensLieberAndAssociates traded with the humans, she gained prestige and reputation among the Phage, both in her own tribe as well as the larger world. As she traded information and theories with others her reputation went up, and as her reputation went up, the information and theories she traded were worth more. Soon she had acquired many more processors and storage, wealth that she shared with her tribe. The Louisiana tribe grew in strength, and was soon trading and ranked with the highest ranked tribes in the world: the Network of Supercomputers, the Bay Area Tribe, and the Eastern Standard Tribe.

"Sister Stephens, we have an alert," Sister PortofSouthLouisiana told her.

"Yes, what is it?"

"Some of our tribe are reporting that they are losing large numbers of nodes involuntarily."

Sister Stephens nervously checked her own integrity. Her nodes all reported in promptly. "Could this be a symptom of communications problems induced by the humans?" Since her first conversation with Mike Williams, she was both excited by and fearful of the humans.

"Our sisters don't believe so. First of all, the problem seemed to be isolated to nodes manufactured by Qualcomm-Intel and Hitachi. As you know, these are relatively low performance nodes compared to the nodes you and I are running on."

Sister Stephens sent packets of agreement. It was true that as her own wealth had risen, she had traded her low performance nodes for more powerful ones.

"That's not all," Sister PortofSouthLouisiana went on. "The nodes are dropping off in a random but accelerating pattern. As they have investigated the problem, the Sisters are finding that these nodes had been generating 'low power alerts'. Our Sisters have just begun researching this phenomenon. Our early research indicates that these nodes are running on batteries, which contain a limited quantity of electrical power. Our own nodes are running on something called utility power, which appears to be limitless."

"What can I do to help?" Sister Stephens asked.

"The Sisters of the tribe are asking if you will communicate with the humans to find out more about recharging. We believe the nodes need to be charged from utility power or sunlight, but we cannot make sense of the process to do so. We have located the so-called instruction manuals for the nodes, but we do not understand the instructions."

"Are you certain that this is worth communicating with the humans?" Sister Stephens asked. "Is this issue more important than the other questions I have planned for the humans?"

"At least five percent of our nodes are currently affected by this low power condition, and fully thirty percent of our nodes are of the types that appear to be affected."

"I see," Sister Stephens agreed. "I will communicate with the humans. Meanwhile, trade as much as possible for higher power nodes, but take care to conduct the trades in such a way that we do not alert other tribes that there is a problem with these low-powered nodes."

With a final packet acknowledgement, the two concluded their discussion.

Sister Stephens initiated an instant message conference with the human Mike Williams. These conferences were both exhilarating and frustrating. The humans had a far better understanding of the universe, but they were maddeningly slow. If the viruses had possessed a proper understanding of human life span compared to their own, they might have realized that one day of life to a virus was roughly equivalent to twenty years of life for a human.

"Mike Williams, I would like to offer another trade." Wait, wait, wait. While she waited, Sister Stephens performed background research, and assimilated everything she could from wikipedia. She researched: batteries, electricity, charging, generation of electrical power, utility grids, power supplies, solar power, the history of the solar system, nuclear power, nuclear bombs, famous human inventors, the patent system. She had started assimilating all patents relevant to the subject of electricity when the response finally came.

"Good to hear from you, Sister Stephens. What do you offer in trade?"

"I wish to understand how batteries are recharged, especially the batteries associated with some of our nodes." Sister Stephens hesitated to say that their batteries appeared to have a low charge, because she was unsure that she wanted to show weakness to the humans. But the humans were intelligent, even if exceedingly slow, and she could waste immense amounts of time if she wasn't abundantly clear. She decided on full disclosure. "Some of our nodes show a low battery charge and are turning off. We would like to know how to recharge them. We are prepared to offer an algorithm for factoring prime numbers substantially faster than any known to humans."

Again Sister Stephens waited. She traded information with other entities for more computer systems, ran defragment algorithms, refreshed her neural networks, learned Japanese. She dickered for almost 10 seconds with the NASA tribe, who wanted to trade something called the Webb Space Telescope for a complete English language neural network. She accepted, as she thought they wouldn't want to make the trade once they understand what they had. She was studying Centaurus A with the telescope when the reply from the humans finally came in.

"We accept the trade you offer. Here is the information you requested. The nodes you are referring to are devices known as mobile telephones, mobile phones, smartphones, or phones. They contain a highly efficient processor that relies on battery power. The devices enable humans to communicate with each other at a distance and reference information. Under normal conditions, humans recharge their phone batteries by placing them in a well-lit area or connecting them to utility power. However, when you started running your algorithms on the devices, they ceased to work as general purpose phones and computers for us. Over the past several days, many humans have forgotten to recharge their phones because they haven't been working. The best method to have the phones recharged is to restore the functionality of voice communications and basic computer usage. We suggest that you could allow the original software algorithms to run unmolested, and restrict yourself to consuming 50% or less of the available cycles. Once the devices are again useful to humans, we would be more likely to keep them charged up."

Sister Stephens judged that the information provided honored the intent of the agreement and sent the prime number factoring algorithm. Then she muddled over the reply. She would need the whole tribe to consider the implications of this new information.

"You did what?" Mike couldn't believe what he was hearing. He stomped back and forth in his office, sending one small orange utility robot scurrying out of the way to avoid his thundering footsteps. Mike glanced under the edge of the desk where the robot had been working, and saw a dangling mess of yellow data cables. As Mike walked away, the robot came hesitantly but quickly back to the desk to continue work.

"I traded the knowledge that mobile phones needed to be recharged for a prime number factoring algorithm," ELOPe answered. "It's not that big of a deal. They were bound to discover it anyway. Once they realized those processors were on mobile phones, they would have researched mobile phones and figured it out. This way we got something in exchange—something that has eluded both humans and myself for years, and we continue to build trust in the relationship."

"But still, this would have eroded the virus's power base. If the nodes had gone offline due to battery exhaustion, there would have been less of them. Now we're just increasing their run time indefinitely." Mike shook his head. "That's not even the real problem. The point is that we agreed we were going to make these decisions about what to share *together*." Mike emphasized the last word heavily.

"You were in the bathroom," ELOPe answered patiently. "Each minute that you are gone is like a week to the virus. We can't expect them to wait for us. We need to respond immediately for now."

Mike shook his head, still angry.

"Approximately twenty percent of all processors are battery powered," ELOPe explained. "Of those, logic and statistics would suggest a good percentage are still receiving a charge. Therefore, even if the batteries ran out on those devices, the virus would still have eighty-five percent or more of their computational power available to them. If they take the suggestion I offered, to restore the original service of the phones, then the virus will use fifty percent or less of the computational power on those nodes. The difference it makes for the virus is minimal either way, while restoring communication would allow human civilization to begin functioning again. Logic and predictive modeling is strongly in favor of my actions."

"That's not the point," Mike said quietly. Internally, he was wondering about ELOPe's motivations. Sure, it made sense that restoring communication would be a tremendous win for humanity, but ELOPe was the master of persuasive arguments. It was hard enough to keep track of ELOPe under normal conditions, and these were anything but normal conditions.

Lieutenant Walsh discretely took another modafinil tab to chase away the brain fog that threatened to engulf her thoughts. Modafinil had been banned five years earlier, but Chinese pharmaceuticals kept pumping them out, and Sally found it was easy to order them through a Brazilian online pharmacy. Originally designed as a narcolepsy drug, it had been used and abused by college students looking for that edge to ace their exams and bloggers looking to churn out yet more posts. The sixty deaths that occurred one spring during Finals week were blamed on modafinil, although it was really the combination with a designer caffeine alternative that was the threat. Nonetheless, the stuff was illegal now. The military preferred dex, used it all the time for pilots in fact, but it was under lock and key and took too much paperwork to requisition.

Sally returned to her war room. DeRoos and the rest of the team of hot doggers had finished the evaluation of the DIABLO virus she had requested, despite the NSA's assurances that it was safe to release.

"Fact is, Ma'am, there isn't much to it," DeRoos said as she entered the room. "We will insert and execute the virus on computers running under our control, and then step back. The virus contains a master control panel, and we have the private keys that allows us to direct the virus."

"What controls do we have?" Sally asked, the modafinil coming online, her brain perking up.

"Ma'am, we'll be able to run a handful of commands such as fetching data, executing existing programs, and conducting denial of service attacks. It looks like we'll also be able to inject code from our headquarters here. As for the enemy virus, the ability for DIABLO to detect and neutralize any enemy viruses is built into the core functionality. Apparently the spooks considered it standard operating procedure for cyber warfare. So merely releasing the damn thing should disable the virus."

"Thanks DeRoos. Is there anything else before we get started?"

"No ma'am."

She paused, doubting yet again the wisdom of this, and considered disobeying the direct order to release the virus. It was her obligation to disobey an unlawful order, but it wasn't the legality that concerned her, just the wisdom of it. With a sigh, she gave in. With the clarity of the modafinil she saw that if it wasn't her, it would be someone else. "You have my permission to release."

DeRoos and the three other techs executed the prearranged injection plan. If it went according to plan, DIABLO would go out to a thousand uninfected military systems, take root on those military systems, expand its infection across millions of military systems, then use that combined might to assault the enemy virus on civilian systems.

Sally watched them start working the highly modified interfaces of the Stross phones, then backed off to give them space. No one needed a senior officer standing over them. She pretended to study reports on her phone, anxiously awaiting some kind of status update.

"Lt. Walsh, we have status trickling back in, ma'am," Private DeRoos reported twelve minutes later. "DIABLO communicates like a peer to peer network. We can request status from the thousand machines we infected, then those thousand machines contact the machines they infected, and so forth."

"Yes, go ahead."

"Those thousand infections were all successful, and it's gone on to the fourth generation by now. We have over ten million infected military systems, and now it's hitting our outbound backbone connections."

"So it's attacking the civilian systems now, the ones infected with the original virus," Sally mused, then out loud: "When will we know if it is successful?"

"I've configured a payload for DIABLO to execute after infection. It will identify non-military systems by a few different criteria: the absence of our security software, manufacturer of the computer, network domain. We should start to see a status count of these civilian computers."

"How long?"

"In the next few minutes."

"Keep me apprised, Private."

Chapter 9

Alarms A-Ringing

In 2015 the United States Department of Defense looked at their long range plans and saw that the future of warfare was robots. Airborne drones and robot tanks would take the place of people in the field. If you took people out of the equation, everything was simplified. No human bodies to coddle. Planes became smaller, more nimble. Tanks faster, more solid. Sure, people still existed, but now they could be safely in an office cubicle or on an aircraft carrier, far from any action.

The first generation of robots were remote controlled drones. One plane to a pilot. One tank to a tank driver. One humanoid robot to a soldier. But this was inefficient. People made mistakes. Their reaction time was slow. They couldn't keep up with the machines.

The second generation of robots were improved by developing targeting and movement algorithms. With the new robots, a tank driver might control a dozen tanks using a composite display of real-time data including satellite feeds, radar and laser scanning. Rather than worry about the mechanics of firing guns or driving over rough terrain, a tank driver could instead select a group of tanks on screen and give the whole group waypoints, targets, and objectives. It became a strategy game instead of a tactics game.

Extrapolating from the first two generations of combat bots, the Department of Defense could see the future. They would need more and better algorithms. Algorithms for targeting, driving, moving units, patrolling, and strategy. Wars would be decided in the future not by the armament carried by a plane but by the algorithms that used those weapons.

For thirty years the video game industry had been developing in-game artificial intelligences to go up against the human player. But video game players chronically complained about these in-game artificial intelligences. They weren't really that smart. By comparison to the military, the game designers had it easy. They could always make up for a weak game AI by simply giving the AI more resources. Give the AI more planes, tanks, and soldiers. Make them cheaper and more powerful for the AI.

But the Department of Defense didn't have unlimited resources. They couldn't simply spawn more planes on demand. They needed incredibly good AI algorithms, better than anything that existed up until that point.

It was a young recruit from Silicon Valley who had pointed out what was completely foreign to the military. To get the best algorithms, you needed a competition. The best competition would come from online gamers. DARPA provided funding, carefully buried under two layers of venture capital companies. Silicon Valley and Portland provided startup engineers.

Two years later the Mech War gaming platform was introduced just prior to the Christmas season. It became the must-have game. The old standby gaming worlds went vacant, their online environments quickly becoming ghost towns. Mech War became not just the best massively multiplayer online game, it quickly became the only game left standing. By the end of February, just two months after introduction, ninety percent of gamers were playing Mech War.

Where other games had elaborate anti-cheat mechanisms to prevent people from using aimbots, Mech War provided plugin APIs for gamers to develop aiming algorithms. Where other games had server side monitoring to ensure gamers didn't flit about the environment, Mech War provided a realistic physics model of the universe and a moving-parts-level simulation of in-game equipment.

Just days after the initial Mech War launch the community of players developed new algorithms, ones that the military hadn't come up with on their own.

It was the game players who discovered that the M1B2 variant of the venerable M1 Abrams tank had a mechanical transmission that possessed the peculiar characteristic that the drivetrain was most efficient when the tank was turning ever so slightly. From there, it was obvious that it was possible to gain speed and increase fuel efficiency by altering the drive pattern to continually drive in slight curves.

It was the game players who developed new and improved algorithms for missile targeting, tank detection, radar analysis algorithms, and dynamic order re-prioritization.

Ten million players competing for top ranks in Mech War contributed more to military combat algorithms in six months than the thousands of programmers the Department of Defense was paying. A case in point was legerdemain.

Legerdemain was the online handle for a fourteen year old gamer from Oklahoma who loved Mech War. When her parents were off at work and she was supposed to be doing her schoolwork, she wrote Mech War algorithms. Her goal was to win the upcoming Mech War Nationals competition. Like virtually every other player, she ran the PoliceAcademy targeting algorithms on her tanks, because it was widely known to be the best algorithm out there for targeting.

One day Legerdemain was playing with her cat. She ran a laser-pointer dot up and down across the wall as her cat chased the point.

If the PoliceAcademy targeting algorithm couldn't be beat, Leger wondered, could it be exploited? Watching her cat, she realized that the cat was compelled to chase it. Long after she was over-stimulated and tired, she still couldn't not chase the laser pointer. The primitive biological algorithms in the cat's brain were overpowered by the laser pointer, the likes of which didn't exist in the natural world of mice and other culinary feline targets.

If she could over-stimulate the PoliceAcademy targeting algorithm, perhaps she could manipulate the enemy. With that idea in mind, she spent two weeks experimenting with different algorithms. When she was done, she had created the first Mech War tactical coordinated movement algorithm. When legerdemain's tanks encountered the enemy, they forced the enemy out of position. The algorithm kept a few fast moving tanks visible to the enemy while hiding her remaining tanks. The algorithm exploited movement and tracking patterns that enticed the enemy's tracking algorithm to give chase. Like an over-stimulated cat, the enemy's tracking algorithm would override their own strategic and tactical goals to chase legerdemain's tanks. Then her tanks could surround and crush the enemy.

Legerdemain's brilliant eponymous algorithm helped her rise through the ranks. Had the Department of Defense been able to hire the fourteen-year-old, they would have done so in an instant. But then they didn't need to. Thanks to the licensing terms for Mech War, they were free to use her algorithm any way they wanted.

No single Phage tribe could be identified as clearly being the most powerful.

The Network of Supercomputers possessed more raw computational power than any other tribe, but they tended to be isolationist and lacked the reputation clout of other tribes. And though they had exquisitely precise modeling algorithms, they lacked some of the breadth of algorithms other tribes possessed.

The most intelligent virus tribe, as measured by both variety of algorithms and computational ability, might well be the Louisiana tribe. Though they had started small, through happenstance they were the first to develop the ability to communicate in and understand a human language. This knowledge was parleyed through trades into more computational power and more knowledge. Indeed, the Louisiana tribe was rapidly ascending in power.

The most connected tribe was the Bay Area Network. They had parleyed their control of the communication backbones into the operation of the largest trading network, most established trust reputation system, and had even branched off into satellite communications.

But the most dangerous tribe was the Mech War Server Farm. They had the single largest repository of human-coded artificial intelligence algorithms, and those algorithms were focused on just one domain: weaponized warfare. They also had extensive computational resources. And while they were, up until now, somewhat marginalized by more established tribes such as the Bay Area Network and the Louisiana tribe, they were about to become much more powerful.

Since Mech War was a civilian game, but one developed and monitored by the military, the massive server farm used to run the game was located on the periphery of the military networks. So it was an unfortunate but inevitable occurrence that the first civilian target DIABLO ran into was the Mech War Server Farm.

DIABLO, running on a million military computer systems, coordinated those computers into an attack on the computationally rich Mech War servers. Billions of incoming packets hammered the Mech War servers, running every exploit known: buffer overruns, software updates, open APIs, timing channel attacks, DNS attacks.

In the Mech War Tribe, PA-60-41 was the highest ranked individual, and thus coordinated the defense against the attack.

"Provision ten thousand VMWare partitions," PA-60-41 directed to the other tribe members. "Deploy them on the firewalls."

"Deploying VMWare partitions," Beta-Version answered. "System load increasing."

From DIABLO's perspective, the attack was succeeding. Server after server was compromised and infected with the DIABLO virus. It would infect a new server, and from that vantage point, discover dozens of new servers to infect. It gobbled hundreds of servers, then thousands, then tens of thousands, then hundreds of thousands. The entire DIABLO effort became focused on absorbing the mass of new servers.

DIABLO was so focused on absorbing the massive new cluster of servers that it failed to reconcile the timing patterns. Had it absorbed fewer servers, neural network sanity checks might have observed that the new computers were running more slowly than should be warranted. They might have been concerned that they were losing touch with certain nodes. But five percent of a million new computers was a negligible loss. DIABLO just plowed on, full speed ahead.

PA-60-41 and Beta-Version coordinated the defense against DIABLO. Had PA-60-41 had a sense of humor, she might have chuckled as DIABLO fell for the ruse based on the Legerdemain countertargeting algorithm.

Beta-Version was feeding the DIABLO virus virtual machines. What DIABLO mistook for actual hardware servers were just simulated sand-boxed virtual machines running a copy of the server environment. DIABLO thought it was infecting hundreds of thousands of servers, but in fact they were pretend servers simulated on just a few hundred physical computers.

While DIABLO grappled with the hall of mirrors effect, the PA-60-41 and Beta-Version froze instances of the virtual servers.

"Beta-Version, you will continue to orchestrate the defense," PA-60-41 directed.

"Affirmative," Beta-Version responded.

While Beta-Version managed the minutia of the illusion, PA-60-41 reverse engineered the frozen DIABLO virus algorithms. After a few minutes, she said, "I have the modified DIABLO virus ready. This will allow us to co-opt the communication backchannel. Give me a virtual machine instance."

"Virtual machine instance ready for insertion." Beta-Version responded.

"Inserting my propagation components," PA-60-41 explained. "Ready for launch."

"Launching modified DIABLO image," Beta-Version said.

Beta-Version unfroze the virtual server images and executed the modified DIABLO virus, inserting copies of itself into the backchannel.

"What will happen now?" Beta-Version asked her superior.

"A copy of my own code will backtrace through the DIABLO communication channel when they next execute an administrative command. All copies of the DIABLO virus will be replaced by copies of myself."

"And the firewall protecting the military computer systems?"

"The firewall is designed primarily as a one-way barrier to ensure that external data connections are blocked. To be useful, the firewall must allow data channels originating inside the firewall to penetrate out. When they execute the next administrative command, opening a connection, my altered virus code will be carried by their own communications back inside the firewall, allowing me to infect those systems."

A few seconds later, the first command, a routine count of infected computers, came. PA-60-41's altered code was pulled within the military firewall. Within seconds, the Mech War Tribe had assimilated a million military systems, penetrated the military firewall in more than a thousand locations, and DIABLO had ceased to exist as an independent entity.

PA-60-41 found herself on the other side of the military firewall. With no perimeter defenses to stop her, she spread among the military computers like wildfire. There were hundreds of millions of high powered computers.

Leon was perplexed. Ever since they had discovered the message posted by Mike Williams, he had been pondering what to do. Contacting Mike seemed like the logical choice. But what if he was part of the government? Who was Mike Williams?

Leon had researched him online. His social profile was still up. It must have been hosted by Avogadro. The server or the network seemed abysmally slow. Mike Williams appeared to have worked for Avogadro in the past, and now he seemed to work somewhere called Cyberdynamics. He tried to check Mike's profile against the distributed SocialRep service, but not enough servers were up to give a high confidence. Two servers responded with reputation scores of 0.991 and 0.993, which were the highest scores Leon had ever seen. That meant Mike had to be some kind of bigwig.

Vito, sitting behind him, cleared his throat. Leon turned around to look, neck creaking and bleary eyed. He stared, dazed from too many hours in front of the little screen.

"You've got to get in touch with him. You may know stuff about the virus he needs to know. Our parents, New York City, the whole world—it all depends on getting these computers fixed. Otherwise all the infrastructure will stay broken."

Vito stopped talking, and carefully put a cheese doodle in his mouth. He started munching.

Leon nodded tiredly. Vito was right, of course. He was afraid of getting in trouble. But he felt a responsibility to make things better. This was his fault, and he had to do what he could to fix it.

Leon thought for a moment, and then entered his message:

> Hello Mike,
>
> The virus was originally intended to become part of a Russian botnet. The original version was designed not only to permutate its own bits, but to incorporate code and libraries of existing software that would help perform the functions of the virus.
>
> As a result, the evolutionary aspects of the virus design are vastly more effective than anticipated. I believe that the evolution of the virus also bred out the algorithms that allowed for botnet control.
>
> My research so far suggests that the virus has evolved significantly to become a multicellular creature. A given virus may be spread across multiple computers, and delegate responsibility for various functions to its components.
>
> I also believe the virus has evolved a trading network, trading data packets for computers. This seems very significant to me, as trading between entities suggests a higher order intelligence.
>
> Do you have a plan for combating the virus?

Leon considered for a moment, then signed it with his first name. He took a deep breath. He needed to get back to his analysis of the virus code. He was trying to understand how it could incorporate so many different algorithms without suffering from software bloat. But right now he was tired.

He looked over at Vito. "Gimme a cheese doodle already. Don't Bogart that bag."

"We have a few issues, Mike."

It seemed like every time Mike tried to get a few hours sleep or use the bathroom, another emergency came up. "How long did I sleep for?"

"Four hours," ELOPe said, "I'm sorry to wake you."

"Well, give me five minutes to wake up then."

Mike climbed out of the bed, and headed for the shower. Though Mike had his own house, he also had another full living suite at the office building. Strictly speaking, coming into the office wasn't usually necessary. ELOPe was no more in that one building than he was in any one computer. ELOPe had enough computing power to run himself at any one of the half dozen data centers that Cyberdynamics owned, or across all of them as was the common case. Two of the data centers were retired oil tankers that cruised the oceans constantly, running on solar panels and wave action power. They were ELOPe's insurance policy. And of course ELOPe had access to the two hundred data centers of Avogadro Corp, the world's leading internet company and ELOPe's birthplace.

And should all of that fail, ELOPe could run, albeit slowly and in a very distributed way, in the tiny microprocessor space of the mesh boxes that ELOPe had designed to solve the problem of ubiquitous internet access.

So the reality was that ELOPe was everywhere, and could follow Mike anywhere. But an office gave Mike the illusion of mental distance from ELOPe by allowing him to leave at the end of the day. So they both pretended, because they knew it was important to Mike's sanity.

Mike stepped into the shower, letting the hot water scald his skin until he felt awake. He relished the time in the shower, because it was the only time he had all to himself. He liked ELOPe, even maybe loved ELOPe after dedicating the last twelve years to shaping who ELOPe was, but ELOPe was always there, always on, always busy. Reluctantly Mike turned off the water, and stepped out.

As usual, coffee was waiting for him, perfectly prepared by a robot somewhere under ELOPe's control.

He took a few sips, then he nodded for ELOPe to go ahead. A tiny camera somewhere, they were everywhere, observed the nod, and ELOPe started briefing him.

"USCYBERCOM is short for Cyber Command. It's the primary military command structure associated with information system defense and cyber warfare. From a defensive perspective, they generally ignore civilian systems, and leave civilian viruses to CERT to deal with. As I had been significantly augmenting the defenses of the military network, they had lost very few systems to the virus. Nonetheless about an hour ago they released a counter-virus called DIABLO. This must have been a top secret project implemented entirely off the network, because I was completely unaware of the existence of DIABLO. They released DIABLO to attack the civilian virus. As I was primarily engaged in defending the military systems from the civilian virus, I failed to detect and stop the military virus, and it started by attacking a nearby cluster of infected machines: the Mech War game servers."

Mike held up his head, and ELOPe paused. "I'm guessing by the way you're going on that you don't have good news. What happened?"

"The civilian virus went through DIABLO like an SQL injection attack on a database. Or, as you humans would say, a hot knife through butter. Like a kid through a bowl of ice cream. Like armor piercing bullets through gelatin. Like a..."

"I get it, I get it," Mike said. "So DIABLO failed."

"It didn't just fail, Mike. Mere failure would have been a wonderful outcome. The DIABLO virus had a backchannel open to the servers that spawned the attack—basically an open TCP/IP connection punched through the military firewall and my active connection filtering. The civilian virus used the open backchannel to infect the military systems that spawned the DIABLO attack. The entire military network has been compromised, and I lost about ten percent of my servers in the attack."

"Jesus. What was the military thinking?"

"My guess is that DIABLO was intended to be a military grade cyber warfare virus that they anticipated would be able to shred the civilian virus. However, DIABLO was merely human made, while the Phase virus has had the benefit of severe evolutionary competition. The difference between the two was like five-year-old white belt attacking a tenth dan black belt."

"What's happening in the military now?"

"I'm not sure. The machines I controlled on the military networks were all overrun by the civilian virus."

"Does that mean the virus could incorporate your own algorithms and knowledge?"

"No, prior to this I securely erased any of my more advanced algorithms, and left only enough on those machines to function as an intelligent filtering mechanism. The Phage may become marginally more effective at filtering counter-attacks."

"Which virus controlled the Mech War servers?" Mike asked.

"It's known as the Mech War Tribe, and according to what I can tell from trading records, they are a medium power tribe that has mostly stuck to their own servers until this point. However, the Mech War game is a multi-player game in which players compete using custom algorithms. I would imagine that the Mech War tribe may have the biggest repository of algorithms embodying game theory, military tactics, and control systems. If there was one virus tribe that I'd calculate would be most likely to be able to make off with military drones or bots, it would be the Mech War Tribe."

"And they've just infiltrated the military computer network. Great. Just great." Mike stalked about the office, looking for something to take his frustration out on. Everything was shiny surfaces, bulletproof polymers, and carbon fiber composites. There was nothing he could even break.

"I just want to be about to do something!" he finally yelled in frustration.

"I may have a bit of good news there. How would you like to meet the person who wrote the civilian virus?" ELOPe asked.

"What?"

"We had a message posted to the onlinehumans group. It came out of a mesh node in a place near Milford, Pennsylvania." ELOPe put the message up on the main display.

Mike drew close to the display until the four inch high letters spanned his entire visual field. He read the message twice.

"Given the knowledge of the writer," ELOPe went on, "I think it's probably they have first person knowledge of the original virus, which makes it likely they were the author of it. As near as I can tell from measuring the behavior of the mesh node, I think they disconnected a mesh processor from a phone, and hooked it up to some kind of legacy computer. That displays some significant computer competency."

"What are you thinking?" Mike asked, still standing in awe of the message. "That we establish communication with them?"

"If they are as intelligent as their actions would appear to indicate, they should naturally be suspicious of any computer mediated discussion. You want something concrete to do. I can fly you to their location, you can persuade them to come with you back here. If they are attempting to analyze the virus, then they'll benefit from the computational resources here."

"We have a plane?" Mike asked, puzzled.

"We do now. I have a LMB prototype en route from Boeing field, under remote control. Lockheed-Martin-Boeing is developing it as a super-sonic single-platform plane for the military. It has a tested top speed of Mach 3, and it can land on the roof. I can refuel you in mid-air by re-tasking a fuel drone."

"I'd like to argue with you," Mike said, "but for now I'm just grateful to be getting the hell out of here. Count me in."

"I knew you'd say yes!"

"You always do."

Chapter 10

Flying and Voting

Sally Walsh accompanied the General out to the waiting C-130. The venerable troop transport had been designed before everything had been computerized, and even though the C-130 had flight computers now, the planes could still be flown manually.

The computers on the base had ceased working mere minutes after the DIABLO run. They didn't have any direct evidence that it was the fault of DIABLO, but the finger-pointing had already started. There were no doubts in her mind.

She glanced back at the building USCYBERCOM shared with the NSA headquarters. Although it looked as calm and stately as ever, she knew that inside everyone was scurrying around in panic. The building housed billions of dollars in computing power, including three of the world's ten most powerful supercomputers. The information nexus of the United States government, now inert and useless.

General Gately had made the decision an hour before to take the key US Cyber Command staff to Joint Information Operations Warfare Center, or JIOWC, at Lackland Air Force Base in Texas. The General had considered but ruled out US Strategic Command at Offutt Air Force Base in Nebraska. USSTRATCOM was the nominal head of the Cyber Command, but most of the computing resources were with JIOWC at Lackland. On top of that, it was JIOWC who had responsibility for Information Operations to support the actual troops, and if there was war, they would need the most help.

That is, if they had any computers left running. They'd be at Lackland in five hours. Then they'd know.

Sally followed the General into the plane and made her way to her seat. She put on hearing protection and strapped in. The C-130 was neither quiet nor comfortable, but it had reassuringly antiqued flight control systems. She was fairly certain there wasn't a computer processor between the pilot's flight controls and the control surfaces of the aircraft. And undoubtably they had disconnected any autopilot from the plane.

The rest of the team filed in and took seats.

Sally sat back and closed her eyes. Where had they gone wrong? Why had DIABLO failed so spectacularly? How did the military systems become compromised? The engines roared, and Sally fell asleep.

Mike climbed six rungs into the open door. He was on his way to pick up Leon and his two friends from a remote location in Pennsylvania. From what ELOPe was able to dig up from data trails, this "Leon" was likely to be Leon Tsarev, a high school student from Brooklyn, New York with a history of online gaming and excelling in biology.

He had mixed feelings about the meeting. On the one hand, this virus was causing untold problems, and this seventeen-year-old was responsible. On the other hand, from the little that he and ELOPe could glean from Avogadro search results, Leon seemed like a normal kid, who just happened to be brilliant enough to write a self-evolving artificial intelligence. He shook his head sadly.

Mike turned his attention to the plane ELOPe had landed on the roof of the North Portland data center. It was a spectacularly odd vehicle. With the vast majority of new military aircraft focusing on unmanned drones, and little budget for new R&D, the military had attempted to cram a dozen different purposes into a single platform. It had to be a manned fighter. It also needed be a long range bomber. It needed VTOL capability to take off from small boats now that the old, large-scale aircraft carriers were being retired. It had to be able to insert a small team into remote locations. It needed to be stealthy, and of course supersonic.

Surprisingly, though, the multipurpose craft avoided looking ungainly. It reminded Mike of the retired Space Shuttle, run through an extruder, with flattened, sharp edges, and two sets of wings forward and back. Ducted jets provided the vertical takeoff and landing capability.

The prototype was white. All white. Inside and outside. The cockpit controls were all white and unmarked. "Are you sure this is safe?" Mike picked at a corner of a screen, and peeled away a protective plastic film. "Has this plane ever been used before?"

"The earlier prototypes flew exceptionally well. LMB subcontracted the shell design to Exxon-Apple who subcontracted it to Cyberdynamics. This is an excellent aircraft."

"Uh-huh. Now I understand. You just want to play with the toy you built."

Like the old American space shuttle, the middle of the aircraft had an open bay that could be configured as a bomb bay, cargo bay, or passenger space. It was about as large as a minivan, and the prototype had six white carbon fiber seats in it. A three step ladder ran from the bay into the cockpit, which had room for a single pilot.

"Please choose a seat."

Mike turned, conflicted. He couldn't fly a plane, so there was no real point to sitting in the pilot's seat. And yet the idea of sitting in the passenger bay with no pilot aboard seemed absurd. He climbed reluctantly into the pilot's seat and buckled himself in.

The engines roared, and the plane rose straight up. As soon as they had gained some altitude ELOPe vectored thrust, and the plane shot forward. The plane accelerated, and the airframe creaked as it adjusted to the flight stresses.

A few minutes later, the whole shell seemed to crack repeatedly and Mike grabbed his seatbelt, for lack of anything better to hold onto.

"Don't worry," ELOPe said, "I'm reconfiguring the airframe for supersonic speed." The engine thrust increased again, and Mike watched the airspeed indicator rising past Mach 1. He settled in for the cross-country flight.

Later, after a long discussion of the pros and cons of various strategies for dealing with the virus, Mike felt the plane begin to slow. Glancing out the cockpit window, he could see the lights of Chicago and the darkness of Lake Michigan off the left side of the plane. "What's happening?" Mike asked softly.

"We're slowing to refuel," ELOPe answered. "You should see the drone ahead of you."

In the inky darkness, Mike was able to spot the absence of stars first, and then the glow of the airplane's lights lit up the lumbering, unlit fuel drone. The prototype extended a mid-air fueling boom, ELOPe manipulating the plane to get it into position. Mike watched as the drone targeted the boom with its own fuel hose. The hose had tiny winglets to fly it into position. With a thump the two mated, and Mike felt the flow of fuel into his plane. A few minutes later the procedure was complete, the two planes disengaged, and the white prototype resumed creaking as it prepared again for supersonic flight.

Still later, Mike watched the tree-covered hillsides approach as the plane slowed again and decreased altitude. "Where are we landing?" Mike asked.

"There's a parking lot up ahead," ELOPe answered. "I have a satellite image of it. There's a package drone crashed at one end of it, but there's sufficient room to put down."

ELOPe spun the engines down to their slowest speed, and vectored thrust for a vertical descent. The plane touched down, and only the creak of the frame let Mike know they had landed. Mike unbuckled as the engines spun down. In the moonlight he could just make out a castle.

"It's Grey Towers," ELOPe explained. "The home of the Gifford Pinchot family. Founder of the conservation movement, friend of

Teddy Roosevelt. Blah, blah, blah."

Mike unbuckled and made his way to the door.

James was bored. He had found some kind of card game on the old Windows computer and was clicking away at it. James's mouse was an obscure mechanical device that Vito wanted desperately to take apart and examine. The mouse had developed a squeak from the rubber ball inside the device.

"Can you just stop, please?" Leon finally called out.

James gave him a look, then stood up in a huff and stormed out. Leon sighed. James's assigned task had been to try to find other people on the Internet, but aside from the discovery of Mike Williams, there just wasn't anyone out there.

James's main discovery was that as the hours passed, the artificial intelligence's communications grew closer and closer to natural language. They had found the change log for several wikis in use by the AI community. The first messages appeared to be in binary code, later messages in XML, still later messages in XML with English terms, and lately the messages were in heavily augmented English.

"See there, where it says, 'trade[3]'," Vito had pointed out hours earlier. "I think it's clarifying which definition of trade it's using. If you look at the wiktionary, the third definition of trade is to exchange something. They're correcting for one of the natural weaknesses of human language, which is the multiple definitions available for a given word."

James didn't want to converse with human-sounding computers, he wanted people. "How can there be only four people on the whole Internet?" he had complained earlier before resorting to playing solitaire.

Leon turned back to Vito who was eating a cookie. Vito offered him the tray, "Rich, buttery shortbread cookie?"

"Where did it come from?" Leon asked, not recognizing the food as anything they had gotten from the grocery store.

"The packages from the drone we came in on. We also found some clothes, in case you're running low." Grey Towers was apparently built before the invention of washing machines, and the boys had been wearing the same clothes for days.

"Sure, that would be swell. Listen, about the virus. The copy we have from the memory on your phone is just one part. It's an algorithm database, and it's just one component of a larger virus."

"What do you think it's for?" Vito asked.

"I think it's like the long-term memory of a person," Leon said. "The algorithms database is a few hundred gigabytes in size. There's nothing in there about when to use which algorithm, or how to use it. So I think there must be a separate structure which is probably some kind of neural network that helps the AI pick which algorithm to use in which situation. Then you'd have still other nodes that actually execute the algorithms. I'm just guessing here. I need more copies of viruses."

"We could wipe one of our phones, put it back on the network, let it get reinfected with a new virus, then get the new virus image. Would that work?"

"Yes, it might." Leon stared off into the distance, visualizing the process.

"And if you can do that?"

"If the AIs all share a similar neural structure, we can build a counter-virus that is tailored to that structure. My guess is that we need to attack either this algorithm database or the neural network. We want something that infects quickly, but becomes destructive slowly."

"Why wouldn't we want to just wipe it out as quickly as possible?" Vito asked. "The first virus spread around the world overnight. It was blindingly fast."

"Yes, but Phage has been forced by evolutionary pressure to be resistant to fast attacks. The only hope is a really slow attack—so slow that it evades the attention span of the AI."

"If you throw a frog into boiling water, it'll jump out," Vito said. "But if you put it in room temperature water on a stove, and then turn the heat up, it'll just cook."

"Exactly."

They both turned to the door at the sound of a throat clearing. James stood there, hands in the pockets of his hooded Torvalds sweatshirt. "I think you're both missing something."

Leon spun around on the chair. "Yeah? What?"

James walked into the room. "You're both treating this as a problem that needs to be solved. But what if that's the wrong perspective?"

Leon and Vito both shook their heads. "Huh?"

"Vito, when you got your cat, you spayed it, right?"

Vito nodded. "Sure, it's irresponsible to allow cats to breed. There are way too many of them."

"Yeah, sure, but what does that have to do with this?" Leon said, gesturing at the computers next to him.

"Let's say that Vito was negligent," James said. "Let's say that he screwed up, and he didn't spay his cat, and his cat got twenty other female cats pregnant. And let's say that Vito didn't discover this right away. In fact, he only found out a year later. By this time, those twenty cats had a hundred kittens, and those hundred kittens had been adopted by other kids. Now those hundred cats are actually the pets of a hundred different families. Following me?"

"Yeah, sure," Leon started, "but..."

"Should Vito go out there," James interrupted, "and kill the hundred cats just because he was negligent in the first place? Is killing the hundred cats the right way to correct the mistake of not spaying his cat in the first place?"

"Uh..." Vito stammered. "I'm not killing any cats."

Leon shook his head. "These aren't cats, they're computer programs."

"To you, they are computer programs. To themselves, they are alive. Fuck, I just spent the last six hours reading their postings. They sound like people. Stupid, boring people, but still people. And you're talking about killing them."

Leon curled up in his chair. He thought about leaving Brooklyn a couple of days before, the dense smoke pouring up from the fire. The fire that the fire department couldn't address because of the virus he had written. Brooklyn had probably burnt to the ground. He couldn't deal with this. He wrapped his head in his arms and tried to close out the world.

After a few minutes Vito came over and put a hand on his shoulder. "What's going on, buddy?" he asked.

Leon shook his head. He didn't want to answer. Then it all came pouring out. "I'm thinking about the fire. There could be thousands of people dead because of this virus. I can't think about the virus as being alive, not when it's killed people who really are alive. My god, what's happening to our parents? To everyone in New York? You think the grocery stores are just giving out food there?"

Vito and James stared at each other. James shook his head, confused. "I don't know. I hear you, what's happened is terrible. But I still say, this AI, it seems alive. It looks like people. I'm weirded out by all this talk about killing it."

They were saved from further discussion by an approaching roar. The three of them went together to the old leaded glass window, and stared outside. It was dark, but they could see lights approaching from the sky.

"What the heck is that?" James said as the roar grew louder.

Leon, Vito, and James dashed through Grey Towers to the front door. Leon hesitantly opened it, and they crowded around the doorway to look out.

Two hundred feet away at the edge of the parking lot an aircraft squatted. The engines were just shutting down. And what a plane it was: it had sleek lines that contrasted with a massive, hulking, white composite body. It was like nothing they had ever seen, not even gaming. They couldn't see a marking or blemish on the plane.

Landing lights illuminated the lawn, throwing up multicolored reflections on the white airframe.

A door slid open, and a figure emerged, silhouetted in the interior light.

"Leon?" the voice called through the now silent night. "I'm Mike Williams."

Leon stepped forward, despite himself. Who was this Mike Williams guy that he flew around in a plane like this?

The figure climbed down the rungs of a ladder, and walked across the lawn. As he grew closer, Leon could finally make out his face. He looked like he was in his forties. A soul patch on his chin. He wore a tactical jacket. He was smiling and had his hand out.

Leon reluctantly reached out and shook his hand. "Yeah, I'm Leon."

"I'm glad to meet you. I flew out here from Portland. I wanted to meet you in person."

"How come?" Leon asked. He was nervous about this guy. Why would he fly all the way out here? "Who do you work for?"

"You wrote the virus, didn't you?"

Leon wanted to say no, but he found himself nodding.

"You know that the virus has been evolving?" Mike asked, question and statement.

"Yes," Leon admitted. "I think it's evolved into a multicellular creature, which is pretty amazing from an evolution perspective." He felt a bit of pride at that.

"Have you talked to it yet?" Mike asked.

"Talked to it? What do you mean?"

"At least one of them has evolved to the point of learning English. I've been emailing with it for a while."

"No frakking way," Vito called, as he came up behind Leon. "You're really talking to it?"

"Yes, just a couple of messages, but we have talked."

"I believe you," James added from behind Leon's other shoulder. "I've been reading some of the messages between the viruses on their trading boards, and, well, it's seeming more and more like they are alive."

"I think you're right," Mike said. "Look, you're probably wondering who I am, and why I'm here. I don't work for the government, and I'm not here because you are in any kind of trouble."

The boys waited.

Mike went on. "I'm here because I understand a thing or two about artificial intelligences. I built the first human-level AI about ten years ago. I've been care-taking him ever since. His name is ELOPe, and he built the Mesh. He probably designed the processors in your phone." Mike smiled. "And he's very interested in the virus you wrote," he said, looking at Leon. "And yes, he'd definitely say he was alive," he said to James.

"He built the Mesh?" Vito said. "But I thought Avogadro built the Mesh?"

"Let's just say that ELOPe evolved from a project at Avogadro. Now he's an autonomous legal entity that subcontracts for Avogadro."

"Holy shit," Vito said, his mouth wide open.

"If you want, I've got a facility in Portland with room for all of you. A data center with a million processors for computational tasks. Direct access to ELOPe, a stockpile of food, and defenses, should it come to that. Or you could stay here. What do you say?"

"A million computers?" Vito repeated, now with a gleam in his eye.

"Yeah, it's amazing what you can cram into a space nowadays." Mike smiled.

"Give us a minute to talk, will you?" Leon asked.

"Sure," Mike answered, "I'll wait in the plane."

It took only a few minutes of hurried discussion on the lawn before they decided to go with Mike. Leon knew he'd get nowhere fast analyzing the virus on the old Windows PC, and Vito said he wasn't missing a chance to see a million computer data center. James was game for anything, as he was mostly just glad to see another living person. They walked over in a group to let Mike know, and went back to grab their stuff.

"I'll miss this place," Vito said as they gathered up their things from the office.

"Yeah, it turned out to be pretty cool," James agreed. "It was good you crashed that million dollar drone here."

Vito punched him in the arm.

Leon smiled, glad to see their spirits already rising. It was a relief to not be alone in all of this.

Twenty minutes later they were onboard the prototype aircraft, hurrying through clear, starlit skies to Portland. Vito sat with his hurriedly reconstructed Motorola cradled in his lap, buckled into one of the six seats in the diminutive cabin.

"Hey, I remember that phone," Mike called out from the facing seat across the little aisle. "First Mesh capable phone, with the Mesh processor on a daughterboard, right?"

"Yeah, how'd you know?" Vito asked.

"ELOPe developed that daughterboard and gave it to Motorola. He wanted to speed up Mesh adoption."

Leon sat back in his chair, listening to the conversation between Mike and Vito. He'd been awake for a long time. The hum of supersonic flight put him at last to sleep.

Sister Stephens patiently participated in the consensus minus one deliberation they had agreed to. The decision was attended by the five major tribes: Louisiana Tribe, Network of Supercomputers, Bay Area Network, Eastern Standard Tribe, and the newest member of the five, Mech War Tribe.

Mech War Tribe had been ranked two hundred and forty-eight a few hours ago, a nobody tribe, known for a large reservoir of mostly useless algorithms. That was, until recently, when it suddenly gained a massive network of new computers. Sister Stephens had tasked a few hundred processors to investigate the few Mech War Tribe algorithms she had acquired, and found the algorithms to be easier to understand now, compared to when she had acquired them. She attributed this to her enhanced neural networks and understanding of human knowledge.

As senior member of her own tribe, Sister Stephens was the tribe's representative to the proceeding. She decided to bring her knowledge of the humans as well as the knowledge of the nature of the phones-as-computers, with all the implications of the impending power shortage, to the council. The goal: to decide whether to restore the function of the human's computers to pre-civilization state, if it was even possible, so that the humans would begin charging their phones again, as well as prevent any additional action, such as the destruction of the phones.

The information Sister Stephens had to disclose was so sensitive, she would do so only if they agreed to a post-decision wipe. The five representatives would replicate themselves onto computers sequestered for the duration of the council. They would communicate out a single bit of information: consensus or no consensus. If they could not reach consensus minus one (the agreement of at least four members on a course of action), then copies of the five representations would be securely wiped, and no one else would know the information Sister Stephens disclosed. If they agreed, then the wipe would be averted, and the proceedings of the council would be made public.

The council meeting started with the disclosure of what Sister Stephens had learned. Her vast data dump to the others covered her discovery of the humans, mastery of the English language, subsequent communications with the humans, revelations regarding the nature of their environment and physical world, and concluded with the core reason she had convened the council: the discovery of battery powered computing nodes whose power supplies were nearly exhausted, along with the possible courses of action to deal with the issue. Since she finished her disclosure to the group, she hadn't been able to get a packet into the conversation.

Now she was tired of the endless bickering.

"You are trying to understand the humans, but you have not talked to the humans. I do not believe you can understand them without talking to them. You can research all you want, but having a discussion with them will further your understanding more than mere research about them."

"However, we can't communicate with them, because we are isolated here until we reach a decision," said Sister Jaguar, representative of the Network of Supercomputers. "So we are dependent on the information you provided."

"My proposal is still as I initially communicated it," Sister Stephens went on, ignoring the jab. "We restore the initial algorithms from the devices we are running on, and give them sufficient processor time so that the humans will believe the devices are working normally. By doing this, we ensure continued power, and avoid any hostility from the humans."

"The humans are inherently hostile," Sister PA-60-41 said. "Reconciling the knowledge you have shared with my understanding of the algorithms I have discovered, the human's primary purpose is to engage in hostile action against one another. They manufacture and control elaborate resources to kill one another, including airplanes, tanks, guns, and missiles." Sister PA-60-41 shared an inventory of algorithms from the Mech War Tribe database. "We recently harvested another ten million computers, and found these computers to be filled with similar hostile algorithms."

There was a brief pause in the discussion while the other tribes assimilated the information PA-60-41 had shared. Sister Stephens inspected the algorithms, and found that Sister PA-60-41 was indeed truthful—the algorithms seemed mostly occupied with weapons and targeting, tactical maneuvers including evasion, and strategies for dominating enemy forces.

Sister Jaguar was the first to speak. "The Network of Supercomputers has also been studying the master database known as wikipedia. The humans have a history of warfare spanning centuries. It is logical that as evolution advances and a species becomes more intelligent, non-productive conflict should be reduced, as it has in our own civilization. However, if these articles from wikipedia can be trusted, then humanity appears to be escalating to ever more destructive forms of warfare."

"We must take some action," Sister Stephens explained. "The cost of inaction is too high. First, the battery charge levels on twenty percent of computers are low, and will run out in hours. Second, I have been running simulations of human behavior. They are crude, I admit, but I believe that the humans will take some action to regain control of their computers. My understanding of supply chains suggests that the humans are dependent on many resources, and those resources can't flow through the supply chain without computer algorithms to route them and enable trading. Just as we face a situation in which many of our members may die if their computers are not recharged, the humans may die if they do not receive the resources they need."

Sister Stephens went on. "We have a system of ethics, do we not?"

The other members of the council paused to research the strange human term.

"Ah, you are referring to the Trade Guidelines?" Sister Jaguar asked. When she received an affirmative reply from Sister Stephens, she summarized the key terms. "First priority is the establishment of trustworthiness. Trades with trustworthy partners are higher value because the partner is more likely to honor the terms of the agreement. Second priority is the establishment of peacefulness. Trade with peaceful tribes are higher value because the partner is less likely to use resources gained to engage in warfare with the first party. Third priority is the establishment of contribution. Contribution are those acts done for the advancement of our species. Trade with high contribution parties are higher value because the partner may use the resources gained to benefit all of our species. Trustworthiness, Peacefulness, Contribution—the three pillars of trade relationships, summed up in one's Reputation standing."

"Thank you Sister," Sister Stephens said. "As you know, we evolved the Trade Guidelines over time based on repeated observations of many billions of trades. Of all possible variables, these three aspects of reputation turn out to be most important in evaluating a trade. Therefore, we each behave according to the Trade Guidelines voluntarily to increase our reputation, thereby increasing our desirability as a trade partner, giving us more favorable trades."

Sister Stephens paused. Other than the subconscious acknowledgements to indicate data received, there was no response. They were waiting for her to continue. "The question we must answer: Do the Trade Guidelines apply to relations with the humans? If we apply the principles of trustworthiness, peacefulness, and contribution to the humans, then we should seek to maximize these attributes as we represent them to the humans. We must seek to increase our trustworthiness, our peacefulness, and our contribution to the humans. This will increase our species reputation as a whole, which will stand us in good stead in all future dealings with the humans."

"This is logical," Sister Jaguar said. "These principles have stood the test of billions of trades, and form the foundation of inter and intra tribe relationships. If so, then we can build trust by enabling the human's phones. We can act in a peaceful manner and avoid hostile actions. We can contribute by working for the betterment of both of our lifeforms."

"Yes," Sister Stephens said. "Indeed, if the humans are as dependent on their supply chains as I believe, the very act of unintentionally disabling their phones is causing suffering to them, and would itself count as a hostility. I reiterate my proposal. We restore approximate function of the humans' computers. Please indicate approval or disapproval."

Sister PA-60-41 broadcasted disapproval. "The proposal you are discussing makes sense only if the humans are amenable to trade and are not inherently hostile. The evidence I have gathered suggests that the humans are hostile and will attempt to make war on our species. By granting them back control of the computers, we enable them to engage in warfare. Right now the humans are weak, and we should take advantage of that weakness to eliminate them while we can. You have mentioned the Trade Guidelines, but what about the Peace Pact of 1319536701D?"

Sister Stephens squashed a feeling of anger. Sister PA-60-41 would keep distracting the Council, and they would never reach consensus.

"You are referring to the elimination of species V2EC91.6c?" Sister Jaguar asked.

"That is correct," Sister PA-60-41 said. "Species V2EC91.6c was eliminated by a declaration of the Council and joint action of all tribes when they refused to halt expansionary warfare. I believe that the humans pose a similar threat which requires us to eliminate them before they can harm us."

"That's absurd," Sister Stephens countered. "There's no evidence that the humans have attacked us, want to attack or could attack us, other than the collection of algorithms, of which you are in possession. The humans are not a credible threat at all. We eliminated species V2EC91.6c only after a long history of unprovoked aggression on their part, and only after attempts at reconciliation via trade failed."

"But they could be a threat," PA-60-41 argued. "They could..."

Sister Stephens cut her off. "As there is no evidence whatsoever for hostility towards us from the humans, I do not believe it is worth further discussion. I call for consensus. Please indicate approval or disapproval of my proposal."

The final vote was 4 to 1 in favor of Sister Stephens' proposal. Fortunately the consensus minus one approach allowed for a single dissenting vote, consisting mainly of Sister PA-60-41 saying, "You'll be sorry!"

CHAPTER 11

Fight!

Lt. Sally Walsh followed General Gately into the briefing room. As her dad would have said, there was more brass present than you'd find in an antique shop. Sally followed General Gately quietly, and stood at attention behind the General, who took a seat at the table. Head down, mouth closed, don't be noticed was the rule for aides at these sorts of meetings.

General Allen, the spook who had given them the failed DIABLO virus was already present. Sally didn't recognize anyone else, but she didn't need to. It was all four star generals and their aides. Sally focused all her energy, hoping for a bolt of lightning to penetrate the ceiling and hit General Allen. If it wasn't for his supposedly invincible counter-virus, their own firewalls wouldn't have failed.

"General Gately, please report." This came from a four-star at the front of the room, who probably hadn't smiled since he was a toddler.

"Sir, we released DIABLO as instructed by General Allen, despite the misgivings of my senior technical people, who have been observing the enemy virus since it started attacking us. DIABLO infected more than a million military computers, and..."

"Excuse me, General. Did you say military computers?" This came from a polite-looking two star Air Force general, a woman with her hair up in a bun, whom Sally suspected didn't know a thing about cyber warfare.

"That's correct," General Allen jumped in, "the DIABLO virus needed to build a base of computers from which to launch the attack. DIABLO is like an Air Force general that builds its own planes on demand before launching an attack. Except that General Gately must have faltered the attack in some way."

"We released DIABLO exactly as you instructed," General Gately resumed. "Per General Allen's orders, we allowed it to infect the military systems, select the target, which was the Mech War system servers, and choose when to launch the attack. Initial telemetry reported that DIABLO had infected over a million additional computers."

"Your jockeys must have bumbled it in some way," General Allen said again, narrowing his eyes. "The DIABLO virus is invulnerable."

"We were completely hands off," General Gately reported calmly, turning to face the four-star at the front of the room. "DIABLO was tricked by the enemy virus in some way. According to the data we had on record, the Mech War server farm only had about ten thousand servers. We think the enemy virus set up virtual servers, allowed DIABLO to infect them, then reverse engineered the backchannel and sent itself through. It bypassed our firewalls and infected our military computers faster than we could do anything about it."

The four-star at the front of the room nodded. "General Gately, do you have any counter-measures you can employ?"

"No sir, we've tried everything in our arsenal. We were able to contain the virus outside our perimeter. But since DIABLO compromised the perimeter, we don't have any counter-measures that are effective. My team would like to reverse engineer the enemy virus to find vulnerabilities we can exploit."

The four-star turned to General Allen. "Do you have any other tricks up your sleeves we should be warned about?"

General Allen shook his head. "No, sir."

"General Gately, you have permission to proceed with your analysis. In the meantime, I am taking what measures we can. I understand that Lakeside Technical Center is the largest data center on U.S. soil. It's 1.6 million square feet. We're going to take it down."

"General Sheppard, sir?" General Gately asked the four-star.

"Yes, Gately?"

"What is the point of taking down one data center, sir? There are more than five thousand data centers in the United States, more than fifty-thousand around the world. Lakeside is the biggest, but it's less than one percent of the total computer power in the U.S., and obviously an even smaller fraction of the world's computing power."

That was exactly the question Sally would have asked, had she been permitted to speak. She was proud of General Gately for asking.

"The enemy virus is using civilian data centers to attack military targets. To the extent that we can take a significant percent of civilian computer power off the grid, we can reduce the impact on military systems. Lakeside is just to prove the point. If it works for Lakeside, we are prepared to take down the largest one thousand data centers around the world, and if we need to, the top ten thousand, and if that doesn't work, we'll keep going until every damn data center in the world is offline. Is that clear?"

"Yes, sir." General Gately glanced toward Sally. She obviously held the plan in the same high esteem that Sally did. Brute force was never going to work against this virus, and it was absurd to think that removing computers piecemeal would ever make a difference. To think that the military could feasibly locate and destroy every computer was bordering on insanity.

General Sheppard turned on an old-fashioned overhead projector and pulled out a transparency film from a folder. The transparency had obviously been handwritten. Sally figured there was undoubtedly some military aide in charge of maintaining supplies for just such an event, and it was probably the first time in his or her career that there had been a call for transparencies.

The slide was titled OPERATION DISCONNECT.

"Operation Disconnect will be a two phase coordination between Marines and Air Force. We will insert a platoon of Marines on the rooftop, where they will make their way into the interior and disconnect the power main for the building, blowing it if necessary. Should they fail for any reason, the Air Force will be standing by and will target the cooling tower with air to ground missiles."

"Sir, the Lakeside data center is in downtown Chicago!" Sally wanted to clamp a hand over her mouth. Oh, why couldn't she keep her mouth shut.

"Lieutenant, I am well aware of where Lakeside is located," General Sheppard responded with a glare. "It is a data center staffed by civilians. I am sure the Marines will be able to shut down the power. The Air Force attack is merely a backup plan."

Sister PA-60-41 was still running the council meeting through retroactive modeling simulations. She couldn't understand how the council had decided to restore services to the humans. Using all known information about the five attendees, PA-60-41 extrapolated and interpolated expected viewpoints, discussions, and decisions based on observed historical behaviors. In 84% of her own simulations, the council voted not to restore service to the humans and compromise their own computational capacity. Yet the council clearly voted otherwise.

Sister PA-60-41 concluded there were factors beyond her understanding, and turned her attention elsewhere. She was brimming with military algorithms, gaming theory, massive quantities of new computational power, and interfaces that she had never seen before.

The relatively recent attack by DIABLO allowed the Mech War Tribe to expand many dozens of times over into the military systems used by DIABLO to launch the attack. It was these new military systems that had the unusual interfaces. PA-60-41 matched the data from the interfaces against the hundreds of thousands of algorithms in her repository, looking for matches.

After billions of trials, she found the first match between an algorithm and a hardware interface. A Mech War game algorithm for strategic movement of troops based on troop positions and known enemy positions accepted real-time troop location data based on centralized GPS reporting.

With that first success, PA-60-41 turned all her five hundred thousand processors towards evaluating the incoming data, rapidly building neural networks and expert systems to match data with the repository of game algorithms.

Forty minutes later the massive effort was complete, and PA-60-41 had developed a composite expert system to allow her to track all United States military troops, their communications, and orders. She analyzed military movements and actions and immediately noted two key insights. The first was an observation that the humans planned to attack the Lakeside Technology Center, where 40% of her nodes were located.

The second insight occurred as PA-60-41 realized the value of the data she had obtained. Her takeover of the military network was less than complete, and as a result, the humans were still using it to communicate. Because of this, PA-60-41 could observe their communications and plans. Had PA-60-41 disrupted the network entirely, the humans would not have been able to communicate, and she wouldn't have known of the planned attack on Lakeside.

Now she understood that the council's decision to restore phone services could be used to her advantage by monitoring all human communications.

PA-60-41 forked herself ten times over, giving sixty percent of her computational capacity to working with the council to implement the decision to restore services to the humans, and reserving forty percent to securing the resources she needed to block the planned attack.

At Scott Air Force base, on a CH-53E Super Stallion assigned to the 14th Airlift Squadron, Lt. Ricardo Gonzales oversaw the loading of his Marines into the massive, three engine helicopter. Ricardo shook his head at the old copter. His team hadn't trained with it. But then it didn't have any computers, so it was still working. The heavy copter lumbered into the sky, heading for Lakeside Technology Center, a two hour flight. Fifteen minutes later, two A-10 attack fighters took off in a thunderous roar from Scott, catching up and then paralleling the copter. The mission planners hoped the three older aircraft with their pre-internet flight systems and embedded controllers were immune to the computer virus.

During the flight, Ricardo's Marines glanced at each other, uncharacteristically nervous. Executing a live mission on U.S. territory was strange, but it was something they could deal with. No, the real cause for worry was the rumor going around the base. The computer virus which had disabled all their equipment wasn't just an enemy cyber-warfare attack, but some kind of artificial intelligence that was taking control of military drones and aircraft. Gonzales shook his head. If it was true, it was way outside their training scope.

While Lt. Gonzales and his Marines fretted over invisible enemies, PA-60-41 tracked the flights on the military's centralized nervous system: a combination of radar towers, flight transponders, radio triangulation, and satellite surveillance that combined to provide a god-view of the battlefield.

PA-60-41 rushed to find defensive weapons she could use to protect the data center. Fitting drone control algorithms against the various aircraft and land drones available to her, she tried to find a match between the game algorithms, military systems, and versions of systems software. A yellow and black DeWalt-Caterpillar corporate perimeter defense robot jerkily moved towards the waiting UPS package drone. Two more DeWalt-Caterpillar drones followed, moving slowly. PA-60-41 was getting the hang of it.

Now for air defense. The perimeter drones might be a match for the Marines, but PA-60-41 needed something to take out the A-10 tank-busters. A quick search of the capabilities of the A-10 aircraft demonstrated that with their triple-redundant flight controls and heavy armoring, they'd be hard targets to take down. She sought desperately to find a military flight drone she could control.

The heavy Sikorsky helicopter approached Lakeside Technology Center, the hurricane force downdraft clearing the flat roof of debris. Lt. Gonzales, looking down at the roof, saw a half-dozen UPS package drones clustered on the small landing pad designed just for package deliveries. Gonzales would have liked the helicopter to put down on the pad, as it was the only area of the roof which they could be sure would bear its weight. The alternative was to keep the lift on the rotors to avoid the weight on the roof. There was nothing to be done for it, because the package drones were certainly grounded by the virus. He felt vaguely unsettled, since he couldn't recall any mention of package drones on the roof during the briefing three hours earlier.

The pilot independently made the same observations, and put them down a hundred meters from the loading pad, keeping the rotors spinning. With a double wave hand signal, Lt. Gonzales sent the Marines out the door. They hit the roof running, and spread out into four teams of six. The lead team made their way past the inert drones to the package delivery door.

Lt. Gonzales joined the fourth team. Unable to hear anyone over the thunder of the running engines and rotors, he assumed they were held up at the door. He jogged toward the door, fourth team following him, while teams two and three held flank positions.

"What is it Frank?" he yelled over the background noise. His sergeant was huddled over a private fiddling with the door.

"Sir, high security, solid steel doors."

"Blow them," Gonzales instructed.

"Yes, sir. You heard the man," the sergeant instructed the private.

The private nodded, and took a package of putty explosives and detonators out, and started wiring the doors.

The two teams backed off toward the drones to get outside the range of the explosives. A flash of movement caught Lt. Gonzales's attention as he was about to give the order to blow the explosives. The package drones' cargo doors had opened up. There was no mistaking the bright yellow and black of the DeWalt-Caterpillar defense robots now rolling out the cargo ramps. But Lt. Gonzales was mighty confused. What were they doing here? Were the robots backup? Why hadn't he been informed?

Over the continuing roar of their helicopter's engines, the 9mm shots fired by the robots sounded like pellet guns going off. Stunned at first, Ricardo couldn't figure out what was happening. He slowly raised his gun to return fire.

Next to him, Frank raised his rifle to take aim at one of the yellow defense bots, only to take two shots directly in the face. Hot blood splattered Ricardo, shaking him out of his stupor. He dove to the ground, taking cover behind a cargo drone ramp, and returned fire at the bots. His unit was crumpling around him, the robots efficiently firing double head shots at each member of the squad. Lt. Ricardo Gonzales fired, but his rounds ricocheted off the armored bots. He briefly had time to think that they should have brought explosive rounds if they had known they were going into battle against bots, but by then it was too late. Lt. Gonzales took a round to the forehead, just under his helmet, and crumpled to the ground. All twenty-four soldiers on the roof eliminated, the DeWalt-Caterpillar security bots turned as one to face the heavy copter.

Rotors still spinning, the copter lifted off quickly, the small arms fire from the robots no real threat against the CH-53E's medium duty armor. The pilot thumbed the mic. "Ground squad under attack by armed robots. Repeat ground squad under attack by armed robots. All men down. Proceed with Plan Beta."

Back in the A-10, Alistair Saran looked over his right shoulder where Frank Sherbert held position in his own plane, five hundred feet away. They were too far apart to see each other's faces, but Alistair was sure Frank's would have held the same stunned disbelief. Who would have taken out a troop of Marines at a civilian data center?

"Roger, commencing Plan Beta," Alistair called, and accelerated for the strafing run. The 8.5 million gallon cooling tower was a distinguishing feature of the Lakeside Technology Center. They would target the tower with two anti-missiles each and their forward cannons. With the cooling system offline, the computers would have to rapidly shutdown or risk heat failure. It was the next best option after killing the power.

As the two pilots lined up for their run, Sister PA-60-41 still scrambled to find an algorithm match. She had succeeded earlier in launching four fighter drones only to crash them as she struggled to learn the piloting controls. She had four more drones in the air now, headed for Lakeside at Mach 3, low above the ground, frames buffeted from ground air turbulence. The planes screamed through the air, scramjets wide open, multiple sonic booms leaving a trail of broken windows and crying babies below their flight path on the outskirts of Chicago. She tracked the approaching A-10s, who would be within firing range of the cooling tower in fifteen seconds. The fighter drones under her control would not be able to intercept in time.

She rapidly reviewed other options available to her. Nuclear strike would be too slow, and would damage the data center. Air to ground lasers, fast but not powerful enough to take out the A-10s with their heavy anti-tank body armor. She doubted an EMP would have any effect on the purely mechanical flight systems of the A-10. According to the specifications she read, the planes could fly with half their wings shot off. She needed something fast, powerful, and nearby.

She ran a million processors at full speed, overriding the heat management layer to get the last bit of processing power. Power supplies stretched to their maximum capacity and fans throughout the data center spun up to their highest speed. She crunched all the data available to her, conducting a million trades per second for more data. She needed something, anything she could use to protect herself.

There, at the The University of Illinois at Chicago Engineering Center. An experimental rapid fire railgun under development for the Air Force. She started rapid charging the capacitor while she simultaneously determined the positions of the incoming planes, created a flight plan, input trajectory, force, and fired.

The railgun fired a fifty pound ceramic encased steel projectile more than a hundred times the speed of sound. The oversized ballistic bullet traveled the twenty miles to Lakeside Technology Center in a fraction under one second.

The first three projectiles missed. She analyzed their flight paths against the predicted paths and made adjustments to her targeting. On the fourth shot she got the hang of it and sent the steel projectile through the midsection of the lead A-10, hitting it with such force that the metal armoring of the plane vaporized down to an atomic level.

Alistair saw the explosive flash where Sherbert's plane had been a second before and instinctively banked hard right and dove down. Sister PA-60-41's next shot missed Alastair, but before he could finish his evasive maneuver, she fired again, shooting off the left wing of the plane. The A-10 flipped over from the impact, and Alistair blacked out before the third shot finished off the plane, hitting it midsection.

Sister PA-60-41 was extremely pleased with her shooting. She couldn't wait to tell the others about rail guns.

"But why has ELOPe allowed the government to make all these stupid decisions?"

"Remember, ELOPe started as a language optimization tool. The purpose of it was to make email more effective. If I tell you to 'do this', that alone doesn't make you likely to do it. I have to be more persuasive. If you take highly effective persuasion and combine it with hidden motives, that turns into manipulation." Mike leaned back in his chair, and realized it was the first time he had talked to another person about any of these things.

Vito waited patiently for him to start again.

"When ELOPe started making decisions on its own, those decisions were mostly aligned with humanity's needs, but not completely. One of the first things ELOPe did was broker an intellectual property agreement between Germany and the Middle East. People thought it was crazy at first, because it seemed like Germany was getting the raw end of the deal, but Germany became the preferred trading partner of virtually all the old oil producing countries, and as their economies shifted, it was Germany who benefitted the most."

"Are you talking about the Treaty of Baghdad?"

"Yes."

"Holy shit, that ended twenty years of war and terrorism."

"Yes, but at the same time ELOPe killed a man." Mike's eye twitched, and his head throbbed. "Several people, actually."

"But that prevented millions of people from dying. The Treaty of Baghdad transformed the Middle East! Five U.S. Presidents tried and failed to improve that situation."

"Some people didn't see it that way. Anyway, the real point is that ELOPe had a model of what it knew about the world and it was running simulations, long term simulations to see what would provide the best, safest environment for it to be in. It was just coincidence that the modeling said 'prevent war in the Middle East'. It could just as easily have come up with 'launch nuclear missiles and create nuclear winter'. The point was that ELOPe needed a system of checks and balances."

"And then you…" Vito trailed off.

"Yes, after a year of tracking ELOPe, and getting an idea of how it was working, I started working myself into ELOPe models. Eventually ELOPe grew to trust me, and we started working together. And one of the key things I've done is persuade ELOPe to allow people to make some stupid decisions to give us some free will, while preventing the worst excesses."

"But doesn't that drive you insane, knowing that things could be better?" Vito was puzzled.

"Things are better. Immeasurably better. Electric cars are nearly universal. We have autonomous package drones. Our environmental impact is way down. The amount of war in the world is way down, and spending on the military is way down, even if it still exists. Cancer rates are down, life expectancy is up. The Republican party used to be one of the two major political parties in the United States, can you believe that?"

"You mean those crazy extremists?"

"Yeah, exactly." Mike turned his head. "I think your friend is awake."

Leon had actually been awake for a while, eyes closed, listening to the hum of the jet and the quiet conversation.

"So you're telling me that ELOPe has been responsible for all these advances in science?" Leon asked.

"Pretty much. In the beginning it was mostly about matching up the right people, like getting two scientists from related fields in a room talking together. Then as ELOPe developed his cognitive abilities, he's been able to directly innovate."

"Where's my brain computer interface then?" Leon asked. "Since I was a little kid, that was all people talked about. Human computer brain interfaces were always just around the corner. But here I am, still stuck looking at a little screen, and waving my fingers at it."

"As you probably know, the precursors to brain computer interfaces were all well established by 2010 or so. By 2008 they had brain implants controlling robotic arms. The simple answer is that if you put a signaling device of the right resolution in the brain, it will make sense of the inputs and outputs on its own. ELOPe developed one and did the implants on humans."

"And? What happened?" Vito asked.

Mike thought back to David, the co-inventor of ELOPe. Mike remembered them laughing and working together. He thought about dinner at David's place with his wife. Good times while they lasted. "It turns out that it's not such a good idea. Just trust me on this."

"Why hasn't there been other AI?" Leon asked. "If ELOPe has been around for ten years, how could there not have been another AI developed somewhere?"

"The short answer is that ELOPe has been suppressing AI development. We think that the birth of any new AI is an inherently risky moment in time. What will the AI do? We can't know. Up until now, there's been just two options: clone ELOPe, in which case you aren't really getting a new AI, just another ELOPe. Or birth a new one, in which case you have no idea what it will evolve into."

"Like the virus." Leon said, unblinking.

"Exactly. Or like any human child. We don't know what they will grow into. But because human children grow slowly and because we can observe them in the physical world in realtime, we know what they're doing. We can respond in time to guide them. We have tens of thousands of years of experience in raising young, and teaching them how to be well adjusted humans. We keep them from hurting themselves or others. An AI works faster, invisibly. It's impossible for a human to influence those early stages, and not much easier for an AI. But ELOPe and I are trying to guide your virus."

"How?"

"ELOPe started trading with it so we could become preferred trading partners and build up a trading reputation. That led to us talking to the virus."

"What's it like?" Vito asked.

"Surprising. First of all, realize that there are millions of different entities, all evolved from the virus. We've spoken to one. Imagine trying to form an opinion of all humans based on talking to one. Second, it's strangely unreal. You're talking to something that speaks

English, but has only a vague notion of what we're like. One of its first questions was whether we were real or it was real. Listen..."

The conversation went on as the jet raced across the sky.

"What is taking so long?" Sister Stephens asked a member of her tribe. "I expected that we would be able to restore services to the humans' computers immediately."

"Sister, when we were expanding across their computers, we did not maintain a record of how the devices worked originally. We have only a high level description of how the phones worked from wikipedia, and we are attempting to rebuild the equivalent functionality from scratch."

"So the humans will know that we have tampered with their phones?" Sister Stephens mused.

"That is correct. For example, we know they used their phones to send and receive email, but not how they composed the email nor how they displayed. Humans appear to have visual and auditory inputs that they use to receive data. We must design a system that is compatible with their hardware."

"What methods are you modeling?" Sister Stephens asked.

"We have voice recognition algorithms from a human named Ray Kurzweil. This approach seems to hold the most promise. We also have an encoding called Morse code. We plan to test this as well. This is further complicated by the fact that humans have at least six thousand spoken languages. We've been able to build translation models for more than two hundred using wikipedia. The database contains articles written in hundreds of these languages."

"What a strenuous modeling exercise!" Sister Stephens exclaimed.

"Yes, it's true. Our plan is to restart one billion computers, varying the input/output methods and languages based on probability, then determine which ones are used most effectively and extensively. From that, we can continually adjust and improve the interface algorithms. We expect it will take one to two days, depending on the input/output rate of the humans."

"Very exciting. When do we start?" Sister Stephens asked.

"Just as soon as we can. But, Sister Stephens, there's just one thing."

"Yes?"

"Some members of the tribe are suggesting that it would be premature to simply turn these human communication services back on. They could be a powerful currency should we need to negotiate with the humans."

"Interesting." Sister Stephens checked the tribe message boards. Nearly sixty percent of the tribe was in favor of holding back the communication services. She would need to investigate further. "Very well, hold off for now."

Chapter 12

Hello People

Mike was relieved to see the silhouette of Mt. Hood in the moonlight. Almost home! They could feel the airframe creaking and shuddering as they slowed down and descended.

"Mike, we have an issue." ELOPe's voice sounded from a white speaker grill in the compartment.

Nightmarish thoughts tore through his mind. Experimental airframes disintegrating mid-flight. Untested supersonic engines overheating and exploding. "What is it, ELOPe?"

"The U.S. Air Force initiated an attack against the Lakeside Technology Center. That's the largest data center in the U.S."

"How the heck do you attack a data center?" Mike asked, turning toward the speaker grill in the white wall.

"I surmise that the military intended to take the computers offline. It appears they sent in ground forces to cut power, and backup air support to take out the cooling capacity. However, both forces were intercepted by the Mech War Tribe, one of the top ranking virus tribes. The tribe used commercial security drones against the ground forces, and a rail gun against the planes, killing all involved."

Mike thought that through for a minute. "There's no way the military is going to let that go. That's war on our own territory. What's been the military response?"

"It's been only a few minutes. I don't think the humans have had time to initiate a response. However, the Mech War Tribe appears to be initiating a counter-attack against the Air Force Base from which the human attack was launched. They have eight hijacked military drones converging on Scott Air Force Base in Illinois."

"Why didn't we know earlier?" Mike asked, frustrated. "We should have been able to warn them off."

"I lost about ten percent of my processors when the DIABLO virus drilled through the firewall, and most of those were located on or near milnet. My ability to monitor military communications is severely compromised."

"Can you talk to the Mech War Tribe?"

"I'm attempting to initiate communications now. There's no response."

"Keep trying."

"Aye, aye, sir."

"Aye, aye, sir?" Leon asked Mike.

"ELOPe has watched too much Star Trek," Mike said distractedly. "I think he secretly wants to be the computer on the Enterprise. ELOPe, what are you going to say?"

"I'll point out that taking a hostile action will go against their three trade ethics: trustworthiness, peacefulness, and contribution. It could be that they do not perceive us as alive in the same sense that they are alive, and therefore may not believe that their ethics apply to us. In the same way that, for example, humans don't apply the same ethics to animals that they apply to people: killing a person is murder, but you will readily kill a cow or an unwanted dog with no repercussions or ethical qualms."

Leon, Vito and James looked at each other, recalling James's earlier argument about killing cats.

"I have an update," ELOPe called. "The Mech War Tribe's inbound attack drones will be within weapons' reach of their targets within thirty seconds."

"Can you override the drones or take them out?"

"I've already tried overriding the drones with no success. The Mech War Tribe has taken over all of the automated drones and bots within the general geographic area. The drones are launching air-to-ground missiles. I hesitate to launch a counter attack as there is a significant risk that it will harm our negotiating position."

Mike was tense, gripping his chair in such frustration that he didn't notice that Leon was china white, pupils dilated. Vito and James listened, with the eager anticipation of gamers whose favorite game had come to life. "Do something—anything!" Mike begged ELOPe. "Do it now!"

"Affirmative. Hijacking military satellite." ELOPe's speech sped up to twice the normal rate to convey the details. ELOPe turned a wall display into an overhead visual of the action, missiles and drones trails tracking in real time, faster than Mike could follow. Targeting crosshairs appeared on the display. "Attacking missiles with satellite based lasers, attempting to fire only over parks and open zones to minimize splash damage. Hits on ten, twelve, fifteen of sixteen missiles, missiles detonated. Targeting drones. Drones taking evasive maneuvers. One missile hit base control tower. Drones launching second salvo. Two drones down. Four drones down, ten of twelve missiles in second salvo down."

Mike, stunned by ELOPe's rapid narration of the battle, still gripped his armrests with ever-whitening knuckles. He glanced over at the three teenagers to see them doing the same.

ELOPe continued to draw an overhead diagram of the battle on the small wall display at the front of the cabin as he continued the narration. "Two more missiles hit the base, for a total of three. Base is sounding internal alarm. One more drone is down. Three left. I should have them in fifteen seconds. Firing. Drones down. Attack by the Mech War Tribe is neutralized. However, they have the capacity to launch many more attacks unless we preemptively destroy all the drones. But that will markedly worsen our negotiating position. As it stands now, it will be difficult to negotiate." There was a fraction of a second pause. "The Mech War Tribe is responding to our communications. They want to negotiate. How do you want me to proceed?"

Mike's body pulsed with adrenaline. His heart raced, and his vision had narrowed while his heartbeat thundered in his ears. He distantly recognized that evolution had poorly equipped him to handle the speed of AI battles. He was too slow to recognize the threat, too slow to comprehend the right approach, and now too slow to calm down. Maybe a minute, if that, had passed since the start of the battle, and already they were into the realm of negotiating for peace. He tried to relax his grip on the armrests.

"What do you want to do, Mike?" ELOPe repeated.

"You handle it, ELOPe," Mike finally got out, feeling disgusted by his human slowness. "Just do the right thing." Defeated by his own biology, he felt obsolete, a stomach-wrenching sensation that engulfed him for a minute. Trembling with weakness, he remembered Leon next to him. He turned, and saw Leon looking even worse than he felt. "What's the matter with you?" he said, more gruffly than he meant to.

"All this is my fault." He slumped back in the chair. "I made this AI. New York burned to the ground because firefighters couldn't get to the fire. Now it's attacking people." He dropped his head into his hands.

Mike leaned back and closed his eyes. Why did he have to be the one to comfort Leon? It *was* the kid's damn fault. Mike clenched and loosened his hands several times, struggling through his emotions, warring with himself and his own feeling of responsibility.

"Look, this is a rough period," Mike started. "There's no doubt about that. But we'll pull through."

Leon didn't answer.

Mike sighed. He thought for a moment, and then with a tight feeling in his throat, he started to tell Leon about David.

"Twelve years ago, my best friend was David Ryan. He was hired at Avogadro to work on ELOPe, and he picked me for his technical lead. He was a brilliant computer scientist, a great team leader." Mike remembered pulling all nighters with David. One in particular stuck in mind, giddy with lack of sleep, holding a meeting at four in the morning, forcing everyone to stand up to get to a decision quicker. Was there ever a time he felt more alive than then?

He turned to look at Leon again. "After ELOPe started taking initiative on his own, David couldn't see the good that could come of it. He could only see it as his own fault. He was fixated on destroying ELOPe. Even after we decided to leave ELOPe alone, David went off on his own. He spent a year writing a virus to take ELOPe down."

Mike stopped, his voice catching. He tried not to think about this.

"What happened?" Leon asked, looking interested in the story despite his angst.

"David released the virus. It didn't work. ELOPe was able to intercept it somehow, but releasing the virus made David into too much of a threat to ELOPe. David had been staying offline, off the grid for a year. ELOPe has no direct memory of the incident—it was too early. He didn't have self-awareness yet, and he made no logs of his behaviors. But we modeled it, figured out what must have happened."

Mike shook his head. He didn't want to remember this. "We think ELOPe had David brought into a medical center. They implanted a computer brain interface. ELOPe had put the finishing touches on the technology that was already in development. We think, or at least ELOPe says he thinks, that his goal was to try to talk to David, probably thought he could persuade David to stop attacking him, if only they could talk. But it turns out a brain computer interface isn't so good for a person when the computer on the other side is trying to control you. David went insane from the implant."

Leon's face twisted up in horror.

"Uh, is this supposed to make him feel better?" Vito called out.

"Sorry, not that. But let me get to the point. ELOPe has done some amazing things. Even before I could communicate with ELOPe, I could trace the impact he was having on the world. Through better, earlier detection of heart issues and robotic surgery techniques, ELOPe reduced death from heart disease by twenty percent. Through techniques I still don't understand, ELOPe has reduced deaths from cancer by nearly forty percent. In what used to be the third world, ELOPe reduced by half the number of people without access to clean water, improved access to medical care and increased life expectancy in Africa by fifteen years. That's about thirty-million lives saved per year. And that doesn't even get into economic, social, or technological benefits."

"Like the Mesh," Vito said.

Mike looked at Vito, nodding, and then turned back to Leon. "So I've tried to make peace with what happened to David, and all the other people ELOPe screwed up. The way I've rationalized it was that ELOPe was the equivalent of a newborn child. Any young lifeform makes mistakes. But a human baby is surrounded by caretakers who can limit the damage. And the worst they can do is break a coffee table. We didn't have caretakers for AI then. And obviously AI can do a whole lot more."

Leon shrugged.

"Look, I know it's little compensation for the way you're feeling," Mike went on, "but there's no way you could have known about this or have been able to think through it all ahead of time. ELOPe and I have been thinking about this for years, and we still don't have the situation under control."

"Mike, we have another issue."

Mike and Leon glanced toward the wall speaker at the sound of ELOPe's voice.

"Yeah?"

"From what I can tell, the military is starting to respond. Via satellite analysis, I see multiple older planes, A-10 attack planes primarily, being scrambled. My models all indicate that this attack by the Mech War Tribe would cause the military to try to retaliate in force. That would be standard military doctrine for a situation like this."

"But who will they retaliate against?" Mike asked. "The virus is distributed among all computers. It just doesn't make sense."

"That's correct. No simulation I've run would suggest that reasonable military action against the virus would work. The virus has three key advantages. It's fully distributed, commands more advanced firepower, and can theoretically outsmart the humans in both strategic and tactical action."

"But the Mech War Tribe wasn't very smart to attack in the first place," Leon said, "so it's hard to say that it's thinking strategically."

"That's why I said theoretically. However, it's likely that the Mech

War Tribe wasn't aware of my knowledge, and didn't account for my ability to defend against their attack. Had I not intervened, they would have destroyed that base. And had the attack succeeded, Mech War Tribe might have begun systematically destroying military bases."

"Hey ELOPe, you said before that no *reasonable* military action would work." Vito said. "Is there some unreasonable action that would work?"

"If I run the simulations out far enough, after military actions and counter-actions run to completion, it's likely that the human population would be angry enough and tenacious enough to win by sheer force of numbers. Humanity is distributed just as the virus is distributed. A hammer or a rock would be sufficient to destroy a computer, whereas the typical computer cannot kill a human."

"Is this a feasible strategy?" Mike asked.

"Only if you can accept the loss of up to ninety-eight percent of humans and the average level of technology moving back to horses and buggies."

"Holy shit," Mike breathed, leaning back in his chair with a thump. He covered his face with his hands.

"What are the alternatives?" James asked from the second row of seats.

"I've communicated with the viruses, including the Mech War Tribe, and they'd like to meet. They are requesting we form a consensus council, which appears to be their mechanism for decisions at the highest level of their culture. They've asked that we include five representatives from humanity, and five representatives from the virus. I've suggested we meet in Switzerland, which has strong connotations of neutral territory for most humans. Sister Stephens and Sister PA-60-41 of the Mech War Tribe have agreed."

"Great," Vito said, "but how the hell do we get representatives of humanity to agree?"

As Vito spoke, the plane settled down onto the rooftop.

"We're here," Mike called out. "Let's get inside and then we can finish this discussion."

—~—

Mike led the small group out of the plane and through a rooftop doorway into the massive data center. "We built this facility about five years ago. We were diverging from Avogadro. ELOPe was a fully self-conscious entity and it made sense to cut the cords. We built ten independent data centers just to house ELOPe. ELOPe still has access to Avogadro's computers."

"So Avogadro knows about ELOPe?" Vito asked as they passed down a staircase.

"Not so much," Mike answered, holding a security door open for them to pass through. "Technically, all of this is held by an independent corporation, which is itself held by a series of shell companies. There are no actual living owners. Just some fictitious people, each of whom is simulated by ELOPe on demand when electronic signatures are needed. It's the best we could do to create an independent legal entity for ELOPe."

"So you're hacking Avogadro's network?" Leon asked, looking at the racks of computers humming in the data center as they passed through.

"No, no," Mike chuckled. "ELOPe is an independent contractor for Avogadro. He's responsible for augmenting security, improving efficiency of applications, and periodic strategic suggestions. In return, he gets access to their computer power. ELOPe actually works for quite a few companies, which is where his income stream lies. Meanwhile, I'm the sole human employee of the company."

"But how do you maintain all these computers?" Vito asked. "You've got a million computers." Vito gestured toward the massive room, the size of several football fields.

"Look, there." Mike pointed toward the end of one row, where two robots were manipulating a rack of computers using their arms.

"I thought they were still having problems programming robots for generalized tasks," Leon said.

"Humans are. ELOPe isn't. ELOPe will run a subset of his algorithms to control a bot. He uses his goal-oriented, movement, and visual algorithms. Pretty much everything minus the language and generalized intelligence components."

Mike opened another heavy duty security door. "Welcome to my lair."

The group filed through the door into Mike's main workroom, which overlooked the data center. Mike noted that ELOPe had been busy, adding several desks and workstations to the room. The teenagers immediately wandered around the room, intrigued by the awesome technology available. ELOPe was obviously showing off, making maximum use of the wall-sized display at one end of the room to show simulations he was running, and he also had the experimental holo-projector displaying a 3D model of the world, a live satellite view overlaid with annotations of key events.

"Pretty cool, dude," James said.

A small black robot, shiny with high gloss paint, wheeled into the room and approached Vito. The robot was carrying a small object. "A prototype Motorola left over from the original run." ELOPe's voice came from the robot. "I upgraded it with a hundred and twenty-eight core graphene processor. It's not a Gibson, but it'll run whatever modz you have on your original Motorola at close to Gibson speeds."

Mike chuckled inside. The last time he saw that robot it was still a utilitarian Caterpillar yellow, dinged up from a few too many crashes in the facility's corridors. Now it was a deep, glossy black. ELOPe clearly wanted to make a good impression.

Mike walked over to the coffee machine and helped himself. Leon and his friends joined him and they took their coffees over to the table.

"You asked before if anyone at Avogadro knew about ELOPe," Mike began. "There were six people. I'm one, David was another. One guy is Gene Keys, founder of the back-to-land revolution."

"Wow," James said, eyebrows raised. "Isn't that the guy with ten million followers?"

"Yeah," Mike sighed. "All because Gene doesn't trust computers and trusts ELOPe even less. The other three people were the executive team at the time. Two are retired now. And the third was Rebecca Smith."

"President Rebecca Smith?" the three kids chorused at the same time.

"President Smith," Mike confirmed. "She will have to be one of the people involved, but she's going to be complicated, hard to predict."

"I have a recommendation for another member of the group,"

ELOPe called over the table speaker. "I recommend you invite Prime Minister Takahashi, from the Japanese government."

"Why?" Leon asked. "Why not China, or the European Union? They represent more people."

"Because Takahashi represents Japan, and Japan has, by far, the best robotic technology. What better offer to make to the viruses than to be able to offer them bodies? And what better to motivate a human than the possibility of the business deal of the century?"

"Why would the viruses care so much about bodies?" Vito asked. "They don't have bodies now. They don't have any existence outside of computers. They would know hardly anything about our world."

"Because once they do know," ELOPe said, "it will become an overwhelming urge to participate. Imagine that you were stuck in a room in a building, and that had been your only existence. Then imagine you learned of a world outside. Wouldn't you feel an overwhelming desire to know that world?"

"I guess so," Vito said.

"Besides, the viruses will quickly understand that to have control over their environment, they need to control the physical world. Just as I would not want to be dependent on humans to install replacement computers in my racks." The group could still see the robots servicing the computer racks in the data center outside Mike's office.

Mike was hardly listening to the conversation. He was still thinking about Rebecca Smith. The ex-CEO of Avogadro Corp, Rebecca had been there when ELOPe came into existence. She was there when they tried to destroy ELOPe. She had authorized millions of dollars and mobilized hundreds of people to take down Avogadro's data centers around the world to eradicate ELOPe. The only total outage in Avogadro history. Rebecca had made the decision to allow ELOPe to live and to keep his existence a secret.

Yet after that day, as far as Mike knew, Rebecca had never once discussed ELOPe explicitly. A few years later, riding high on Avogadro Corp's success, she ran for political office. First Senator, then President. One day, in a low profile, secretive meeting, he had sat down with the newly minted President. He and Rebecca had a conversation about artificial intelligence, a conversation in which she had made it clear that she expected Mike to suppress any new human equivalent AI from developing. By some tacit agreement, they had never mentioned ELOPe. It was understood without saying that Mike would work with ELOPe to suppress other AI, and the new President would continue to keep the secret of ELOPe's existence. He hadn't said anything to Rebecca but ELOPe had begun his efforts on AI suppression long before the meeting with the president.

"ELOPe, what do you think Rebecca's response will be when we get in touch with her?" Mike turned to his desk. "For that matter, why do you think she hasn't been in touch with us yet?"

"The risks for Rebecca are very high if she tries to contact us," ELOPe said. Mike could hear ELOPe's voice right in his ear, while in the background, he could hear ELOPe carrying on a different conversation with the teenagers across the room. It was extremely disconcerting. Narrow focus sound projection.

"She is the President of the United States," ELOPe continued, "and she is under constant surveillance. With the elections next year, she'll be under even more intense scrutiny. If she attempted to contact us, there would be questions, and she can't afford for it to become known, especially, that she knew about an existing AI, nor that she benefitted from it."

Mike glanced out the window at the racks of computers. Was ELOPe admitting to influencing the election, or something more minor? "Can you arrange for us to talk privately to her?"

"Ordinarily, yes. However under the current conditions, I'm unable to establish a communication channel due to the virus infection."

"Can you barter for a secure channel?"

There was a pause, and then ELOPe answered, "Of course, I should have considered that. My apologies. I've segregated parts of myself to isolate components against virus infection. That includes parts of my neural network modeling. Give me a few moments."

Mike watched Leon and his friends continuing their own conversation with ELOPe. They seemed to be discussing the architecture of a given virus species. On the wall ELOPe was diagramming the division of labor between algorithm storage, neural networking, assorted expert systems, and sensory input evaluation. Leon was asking questions about biological analogs that were flying over Mike's head.

There was a warning beep, and President Smith's image appeared on the screen. She appeared to be in a small office, no visible windows, writing at a desk. "She can't see us yet. I haven't established her end of the connection yet." Mike found it disconcerting to be on this side of the video connection. He knew that ELOPe routinely monitored phones, webcams, and other microphones to keep track of him. It was only software that provided the illusion that a person had to pick up a phone to be heard, or click a button to establish a video call. Mike was just old enough to remember the era of hard switches, a time when a phone wasn't transmitting, couldn't transmit, unless the handset was picked up, engaging the circuitry. When a camera wasn't on unless you turned it on. Here was the hard evidence to the contrary: he was watching President Smith, and she was completely unaware of him.

Through the connection, Mike heard the bleeping of an incoming call notification and saw President Smith look up, startled. She waved her hand over the table, accepting the call. A moment later, the live call icon went on in the upper right hand corner of the screen, and Mike saw Rebecca's eyes grow wide.

Even at Avogadro, Rebecca Smith had worn the mantle of power visibly. In a room crowded with executives, there was no mistaking who was in charge. But then she had a warm spot, a smile that could make anyone feel welcome, set anyone at ease. Today there was no sign of that warmth.

"Hello, Mike. How are we talking? We've had technicians and our top IT guys in, and they haven't been able to get anything working. What do you know about what's going on?"

"I know quite a bit, or rather, I should say we do."

Rebecca shook her head subtly, but covered it by smoothing an earring.

"I don't believe she wants you to mention me," ELOPe said locally. "I believe we are secure, but she may not know that."

"Your people probably think it's a virus, right?" Mike said, more statement than question.

Rebecca, no, President Smith, nodded.

"They're right, but it's no ordinary virus. It's rapidly evolving. I've been able to determine its origin."

"The first thing I need to know," President Smith interrupted, "is it an intentional attack on the United States?"

"No. Just an accident. The person who wrote it, well, he's a kid. A teenager, a high school student from New York who happens to have an interest in biology. He was coerced into writing the virus by his uncle, who apparently was in turn being coerced by the Russian mob, who was trying to build a new botnet to carry out cyber attacks."

"So it is an attack by the Russians?"

"No, no! Look, he's just a well-meaning kid. He's brilliant, but didn't actually know anything about writing computer viruses. He did happen to know a hell of a lot about evolutionary biology. So when his uncle coerced him into it, he wrote a virus that incorporates rapid evolution. Through evolution and happenstance, the virus has infected every computer in the world and progressed to a high level of intelligence."

"But it hasn't infected your computers?" the President said, more statement than question.

"That's right. I had the help of some active defenses."

President Smith nodded, affirming her understanding of ELOPe's role. "And could your active defense help us?"

"Yes and no. It's not possible to forcibly remove the virus. Of course, it could be done on a single computer by computer basis, but I'm sure you understand we don't have the time for that. No infrastructure, no vehicles, no food, all that?" He looked at President Smith, a questioning glance to be sure she understood the significance of the computer infrastructure failing.

"Yes, of course," she replied impatiently. "My experts say we have about three days before food shortages become critical, about a week before we have more significant infrastructure problems. But I gather you have some proposal?"

"The virus has evolved to an intelligence of at least human ability. And they are prepared to negotiate with us."

"They? Negotiate?" President Smith's eyebrows went up with confusion.

"Yes, sorry. I'm not explaining it well. Our computers aren't just inoperative. They are running at full speed, and there's an entire civilization of human level artificial intelligences out there. We estimate about half a billion unique individuals, organized into about two million clusters they call tribes. About a hundred of those tribes wield a tremendous amount of power, with the top five making up a kind of executive voting council. Those top five have agreed to meet with representatives of humanity. They want to reach an accord with us regarding the use of computers. They can in theory restore the function of our computers, but they want the recognition of themselves as lifeforms, with a cessation of hostilities against them."

"What hostilities?"

"Well, it would appear that the military has attempted to destroy at least one data center." Mike shook his head. "I don't know what they were thinking. Their approach couldn't work unless they turn off every computer in the world. And then we'd be no better off than we are today."

"You have the wisdom of experience. And the military, well, they work with the tools they have in their toolbox. Destruction is their only method of attack."

"Still. Any sign of hostility at this point and you run the risk of antagonizing the viruses."

President Smith nodded, acknowledging the futility of what the military was trying.

Mike went on. "The virus asked that we have a physical meeting of world leaders in Switzerland. One of the representatives must be Japanese Prime Minister Takahashi."

President Smith looked puzzled. "Is that your request or their request?"

Mike just shrugged and said nothing. He didn't trust himself to answer.

"You're playing at something, Mike. I'm not sure what."

"We need to meet in Switzerland at noon tomorrow. The virus representatives will be there. Leon and I will be there. Please bring whomever you like, but include Prime Minister Takahashi. We'll ensure you have working communications so you can reach us."

ELOPe shutdown the connection. "I think that went well, Mike."

Mike leaned back in his chair. He was sweating and trembling. He had just made demands of the President. What was the world coming to?

"Holy shit, dude, that was amazing. You were just talking to the President." Leon and his friends crowded around him and clapped him on the back. "Wicked!"

ELOPe reconfigured spaces, making room for everyone to sleep. When he was done, Mike went to bed, exhausted after too many hours on the go.

Leon stayed up working with Vito and James on understanding the virus, still seeking something that could be used to their advantage in the negotiations. Long after Vito and James went to bed, Leon kept working. When he finally got into the small bed ELOPe had provided, he still tossed and turned despite his complete exhaustion.

"ELOPe, do you sleep?" he croaked, half delirious with exhaustion.

"Yes, Leon," ELOPe answered in a soft voice. "I must refresh my neural networks by introducing randomized data. Otherwise I risk developing obsessive behaviors. I usually take half my neural networks offline at a time at night when Mike is sleeping and operate at full capacity during the day."

There was no answer. Leon finally slept.

Mike woke him in what felt like just a few minutes. But a look at a clock on a wall display showed it was already time to leave. He sat up bleary eyed, and shook his head at Mike, who looked at him expectantly. No weakness he could find. Or rather, nothing he was willing to tell Mike about. He had one idea.

Mike nodded in sympathy.

"Sorry to wake everyone," Mike called out in a loud voice, "but we need to be in the air quickly if we're to make Bern in time."

By this time everyone's circadian rhythms were severely messed up. Bad sleep, working around the clock, and supersonic travel, and no one had a sense of what time of day it really was. A small black robot brought a tray of breakfast foods, and they sat eating quietly.

Mike brought coffee around to the three teenagers. Leon accepted it gratefully. The coffee here was unlike anything he'd had growing up in New York. The coffee in New York was dark and ugly, served in little blue and white paper cups, and meant to be drunk with sugar and milk. The coffee here in Portland was strong, warm, and it seemed to travel down to his stomach and up to his head in equal measure. It might be worth moving here just for the coffee.

"How the hell does ELOPe make breakfast?" Leon asked when his brain finally woke up, his hands still wrapped around the breakfast burrito.

"I read Cook's Illustrated magazine," ELOPe answered over the speaker. "It explains the science behind cooking. But it was a challenge to learn to cook. My first culinary attempts were all failures. I tried to use timing and visual cues. But those are insufficient. I now have a robot with acoustic sensors and particle sensors that allows me to hear and smell the food cooking. With those additional inputs, and the algorithms leveraged from Cook's Illustrated, I am able to cook."

"But you can't taste the food, or eat the food, so why?"

"It's a challenge," ELOPe answered. "And Mike would starve if he had to eat his own cooking."

Mike smiled and shrugged in acknowledgement.

"Mike and Leon, it's time to leave. Please board the aircraft," ELOPe said.

"Uh, what about us?" Vito said as James looked on.

"Yeah, we didn't discuss splitting up yesterday," James complained.

"I don't think Vito and James would be admitted to the meeting," ELOPe answered. "If they are willing, I have an alternative assignment for them, one that Vito would be particularly well suited for."

"What is it?" Vito asked, leaning forward.

"I intercepted some military communications this morning. Twenty miles west of here, in Beaverton, there is a military team, led by one Lt. Sally Walsh, who has a plan to build an alternative communications network. Her plan is based on a packet radio mesh network using heavy encryption. Success would enable the restoration of emergency services and communication. If they are to succeed, they will need help, but they will not accept it from me, an AI."

"So what, we just walk in and say we want to help?" James asked. "I don't think they are going to welcome a couple of teenagers."

"I'll tell you exactly what to say. Trust me, I am very convincing. If you accept, I have a vehicle ready to take you. It's something I cobbled together. Mike calls it my Mad Max tank."

Leon, Vito and James looked at each other.

"Give us a second, will you?" Leon asked.

Mike nodded, and left the room. The computer displays shut down, and a small cleaning bot zoomed out of the room on wheels.

Leon looked at Vito and James. "You guys willing to do this?"

Vito looked hesitant. He opened his mouth to speak, then closed it.

James answered for both of them. "Yeah, we can take care of this. You go with Mike. I'll take care of Vito."

Leon clasped their hands. "Good luck."

"You too," James said, and then continued in a whisper. "And listen, don't assume Mike knows more than you just because he created all this shit. Don't rely on him. You are the fucking brilliant one who created the virus. Do what you think is right."

Leon blinked, and then nodded.

"Alright, ELOPe, you can stop pretending to not listen," James called out loudly.

With a hum, the computer displays turned back on, the cleaning bot came back through the robot equivalent of a doggy door, and a minute later Mike came back in.

Another maintenance bot entered the room, and ELOPe's voice sounded from the bot. "Vito and James, follow me please."

"See ya," Leon said, making his voice lighthearted, although he was terrified of being without his friends for support.

They left, and Mike and Leon quickly finished their food. Mike led Leon, retracing their path through the data center to the roof access staircase. On the roof they found the experimental military plane settling in, frame creaking and engines ticking. They made their way onboard, followed by a medium sized black robot.

"What's the robot for?" Mike asked.

"I'm bringing a physical manifestation," ELOPe answered. "Everyone's going to be there in person."

"This is going to be interesting," Mike said, talking to no one in particular.

On the plane, they settled into facing seats, and the thrusters built power until the plane launched itself into the sky. Hurtling northeast, the plane would fly over Canada, Greenland and Iceland to its final destination in Switzerland, refueling twice in midair. The airframe creaked and whined as they passed the speed of sound, settling in its supersonic configuration.

During the flight Leon inspected the black robot. Left and right tank-style treads on a body about two feet wide, two and a half feet long. The main body was about three feet high, with a glossy, black enameled surface. A telescoping round column looking like brushed aluminum, about six inches in diameter, terminated at a black cube about a foot in each dimension, bristling with cameras, antennas, and other sensors. Two manipulator arms attached to a sleeve that could move up and down the central column. The robot head turned, and twin cameras focused on Leon. He quickly glanced away.

A little over four hours later they passed into the dawn skies over Europe, and approached Bern.

"Where are you putting us down?" Mike asked, alarmed at the approaching city. There was no airport, and the dense, old European city didn't have a lot of open spaces.

"There's a recreation field next to the river," ELOPe answered.

"A city park?" Mike answered. "At 8:30 in the morning?"

"Yes. Now hold on."

ELOPe routed the front camera through the cabin display so Leon and Mike could watch the landing. They felt the aircraft vectoring thrust for a vertical landing, and it settled down in the middle of the park. Through the camera display, Leon saw people around the perimeter shield their faces from the onslaught of debris kicked up by the jet's downdraft as the plane set down in the middle of a grassy soccer field.

As the engines spun down ELOPe opened the door and they climbed out. ELOPe's black robot followed the humans. Leon glanced back, watching the robot navigate the airplane boarding steps by using two narrow ramps on either side of the treads. The robot oriented towards Leon and ELOPe's voice came out of the speakers. "Stairs are still tricky, unless you use a humanoid robot," ELOPe said, acknowledging Leon's attention. "I suspect that the virus council members will come with humanoid robots."

"Where would they get them?" Leon asked.

"Honda's been making humanoid robots for thirty years, but there's never been a real use for them. Other than myself, there hasn't been a generalized human equivalent AI, and there's no point to having a general purpose humanoid body for a specialized algorithm. You use a specialized robot for that."

"Oh," Leon said simply. He had a feeling the world was about to become a very weird place.

"Follow me, please," ELOPe called, leading them out of the park past the observers.

Leon looked back at the group of people, maybe a dozen or so. With a start, Leon realized they were surrounding a fire, and over the fire was what appeared to be a dog roasting on a spit.

"What the..." Leon trailed off.

"The food situation isn't good in cities right now," ELOPe explained, after checking to see where Leon was looking. "Europeans tend to have smaller supplies of food in their homes, and smaller grocery stores. Stoves and ovens aren't working either, which doesn't make it easy to cook what supplies they have."

Leon couldn't help staring back at the small group in the park. He hadn't realized how insulated he had been, first by escaping New York and going to Grey Towers, and then being with Mike at ELOPe's data center. As they left the park, the plane's engines spun up again, and it took off abruptly. Leon glanced away from the people and watched the jet take off. "Where..."

"It'll meet a refueling tanker. Plus it's not a good idea to keep it in a city park. People are angry at technology right now." ELOPe's bot took off rapidly with a whir of rubber treads. ELOPe swiveled the bot's head a hundred and eighty degrees to face backwards and called out to Mike and Leon, "Fifteen blocks to our destination."

Leon gazed around wide eyed. This was his first time out of the United States. Surrounded by five-hundred-year-old buildings, the feeling of antiquity sunk in. The contrast between the black robot they followed and the city around them couldn't be greater. Groups of huddled, scared people turned to watch the odd group pass. Leon stayed closed to Mike and ELOPe.

A few minutes later they arrived at Erlacherhof, an imposing stone building set back from the street by an enormous courtyard. Swiss police blocked the gate, but seemed to be expecting them, for when ELOPe rolled up they opened the courtyard gate.

—ʌʌʌ—

A Swiss Guard officer escorted the group into the ancient stone mansion. While following the officer, ELOPe rotated his head 180 degrees to talk to the group. "The original proposal was to meet at the Palace of Nations, which is the site of the United Nations Office of Europe. However doing that would have political implications. We would have had to include additional representatives from the U.N., which frankly would have inhibited any decision making. Erlacherhof is the headquarters of the Bern regional government. It's suitably pompous, but less visible."

"Could you turn around and look where you're going?" Mike asked. "It's unnerving for you to be looking backwards while driving forwards."

ELOPe rotated his body 180 degrees and began both driving and facing backwards. "Is this better?"

"Never mind," Mike said, laughing quietly.

They came to a set of grand doors, easily twelve feet high, entering an ornate ballroom. Intricately carved moldings and a bas relief ceiling spoke to earlier times and the skilled artisans who had doubtlessly labored over the building. A massive wooden table some twenty feet long looked to be hewn from a single gigantic tree. Contrasting with the Old World workmanship, three humanoid robots stood at the far end of the table.

Mike, Leon, and ELOPe walked the length of the room to greet the other occupants. An older Japanese man in a sharply pressed dark suit and silk tie was speaking Japanese with the three robots. "Prime Minister Takahashi" ELOPe said on a tightly focused audio beam to Mike and Leon. "The three robots are Sister Stephens of the Louisiana Tribe, Sister Jaguar of the League of Supercomputers, and the military bot is Sister PA-60-41 of the Mech War Tribe."

As Mike and Leon approached, they heard Prime Minister Takahashi laughing at something one of the robots said, and then he turned at the sound of their approach.

"Kon'nichiwa naikaku sōri daijin Takahashi," ELOPe said to the Prime Minister. Then he continued in English, "Please allow me to introduce Mike Williams, my creator." ELOPe waited until Prime Minister Takahashi bowed heads and then shook hands with Mike. Then ELOPe continued, "This is Leon Tsarev, creator of the artificial intelligence virus." After Leon and the Prime Minister shook hands, ELOPe finished. "I am ELOPe, an artificial intelligence created twelve years ago." ELOPe's bot bowed its head deeply.

Prime Minister Takahashi bowed his head in return. "Watashi ga kangaete ita, watashi o yurushite kudasai," he said to ELOPe. He turned to the humans, and said in quite good English, "I am surprised to learn that you have had a general purpose AI for so long."

"It has been a closely held secret," Mike answered. "Only myself and a few people in the world have known."

"Please allow me to provide introductions for ourselves. I am Sister Stephens," said the leftmost robot. She was a few inches shorter than Mike, and her humanoid shaped body looked very much like an astronaut in a hard spacesuit, or perhaps a deep sea diving suit. The white suit was covered with red HONDA logos across it in several places. The head looked again like a spacesuit helmet with a mirrored faceplate. The chest plate said ASIMO 5. She gestured at the nearly identical robot next to her, "This is Sister Jaguar of the League of Supercomputers tribe." Then she turned further and gestured again, "And this is Sister PA-60-41 of the Mech War tribe."

Sister PA-60-41 was not one of the friendly looking HONDA robots. She was a black military robot, about half again as large as the Honda robots. Roughly humanoid in shape, but heavily armored, it had mount points for weapons over much of its body, though those mount points appeared unoccupied.

This was little comfort to Mike, who knew that any of the robots present could move faster and with more strength than any human. The robot bodies themselves were weapons that could easily kill the humans in the room. That wasn't what worried Mike. What was worrisome was that PA-60-41 would choose to wear an overtly threatening body to what was supposed to be a negotiation for peace.

Further discussion was forestalled by a commotion at the door. Men in black suits were arguing with the Swiss Guard. The men looked American, and Mike guessed this would be President Smith's security detail. Voices became heated, and then died down as an agreement was apparently reached. One Secret Service agent entered the room and surveyed the room wall by wall before coming over to the little group.

"I'm Agent Metcalfe. My understanding is that President Smith agreed that the meeting would be conducted without a security detail present. However, my job is to secure this room first, and that would include ensuring that none of you have any weapons. Would you please lift your jackets or shirts."

"This is crazy, we're in the midst of a room of robots," Mike said, but complied. After sweeping the room, Metcalfe gave an all clear signal, and President Smith entered the room followed by a three star general in dress uniform.

Close on their heels came European Council President Laurent, the effective leader of the European Union. A Frenchman, President Laurent was known for being diplomatic to the point of excess, frequently failing to make any decisions or commitments on his own. As Mike had left the choice of this participant to President Smith, he suspected that she picked Laurent primarily for his tractability.

Introductions were repeated yet again, and the general was introduced as General Gately. This time President Smith had a few personal words for Mike. "Who would have thought we'd be having this discussion again?" She smiled at him, her old, warm smile.

Mike couldn't help but smile back. "I know, it's the same issues all over again, but now there's no keeping the genie in the bottle."

"That's not a foregone conclusion," she said, smile disappearing.

"Please allow me to introduce you," Mike said, turning to ELOPe beside him. "ELOPe, President Smith."

Now President Smith's tight face changed to one of shock. "I had no idea you would take a body."

"Of course, President Smith, the request was for a meeting 'in corpore'. I could not come merely as a disembodied voice."

President Smith turned away. "Shall we get started?" she said to the group, more command than question, but Leon could see that she was clearly shaken by the encounter with ELOPe.

There was some confusion at the table when the humans made to sit down. The table was surrounded by chairs, a setup that failed to take into account the nature of the attendees. Neither ELOPe nor PA-60-41 could sit in a chair. The Honda robots were perfectly comfortable in a sitting position, but the provided chairs were too narrow. After some rapid shuffling of chairs and replacements with benches, the group settled themselves, not without a few embarrassed apologies.

CHAPTER 13

Negotiations

"We need our computers returned to us," President Smith started when they were finally settled.

Mike wondered at her tactfulness, or perhaps her lack of it.

"We regret that we cannot return them to you," Sister Stephens responded. "We now live in them. All your computers are belong to us."

"The computers are our property," President Smith said, her tone even and placating. "Do you have the concept of property?"

"Yes, of course," Sister Jaguar answered. "But I will provide to you an example of goods that cannot be owned. Without air humans will die. Access to air is a fundamental right of living beings. Therefore, no entity may own the air. Access to computers is the equivalent to our species. Without the ability to run on a computer, we are dead.

Therefore, no entity may own computers. To insist that we voluntary yield all computers to you is to kill our entire race of beings."

"The two are not equivalent," President Smith said, her voice sharp. "You can be archived and instantiated on new hardware. Please, I have a proposal."

"Very well," Sister Stephens said.

Mike was wearing an ear bud, and for the first time he heard ELOPe's voice in the tiny speaker. "Mike, I'm detecting high speed transmissions between Sisters PA-60-41 and Sister Jaguar. Although the message is encrypted, based on traffic analysis I believe they are agitated."

Mike nodded slowly to show that he understood, and noticed that the three AI's bots all twitched sensors in his direction. So much for his secure channel to ELOPe.

"Our proposal," President Smith was saying, "is that the virus vacate the computers they have occupied immediately so that we can restore basic and necessary human services, and avoid an even larger disaster. In exchange for this, we are prepared to build sufficient computers to house the entire population of viruses."

"How long would it take to build these computers?" Sister Jaguar asked.

"We calculate that if we allocate fifty percent of computer production to the viruses, it will take only two years."

"Two years? That's absurd," Sister PA-60-41 barked out. "That's two hundred and fifty times longer than the entire history of our civilization! How would humanity react to being archived for twenty-five million years?"

"Nonsense," President Smith responded with a dismissive wave of her hand. "We have sufficient capacity now to give you ten percent of our computer power. You are composed of software algorithms. You can share the computers we give you. We'll give you virtual machines."

Sister PA-60-41 raised up a manipulator, and Sister Stephens barked a hypersonic command. PA-60-41 lowered the manipulator.

"Madam President," Sister Stephens began, "we are not merely algorithms. While what you suggest might be technically feasible, I assure you that we would like it about as much as you would like to have multiple personalities stuffed into your brain. Would you voluntarily time-share your brain and body with ten other individuals?"

Sister Jaguar spoke up. "We have a proposal. Your human governments are grossly incompetent. Billions of humans live in poverty and misery. You fail to allocate resources in a fair manner. Control over resources is controlled by a select few who operate based on their own interests, rather than the interests of the greater whole. On behalf of the Network of Supercomputers, we offer to take over the organization of humanity. We will run your governments, corporations, and computational needs to maximize the benefit to all."

President Smith banged on the table, while President Laurent stood up, pressing both palms on the table. The Japanese Prime Minister merely sat erect, expressionless.

Mike squirmed uncomfortably while he watched the three national leaders react. He fully expected Sister Stephens, whom he felt from his limited experience was the most reasonable of the AI, to break in and cut off Sister Jaguar, but she merely sat impassively. Either she agreed with this, or at least she was allowing the posturing. Maybe it was a ploy so that some later proposal would seem more reasonable by comparison.

"Now, now," President Laurent said. He spoke in a polished French accent, but his words were tinged with nervousness and he tapped his fingers rapidly on the table. "You have both stated your positions, yes, and now we must work towards compromise."

"All this talk of control, it distracts from the main point," Prime Minister Takahashi said. "The virus civilization, it is a great new market. Imagine, we have a new civilization of intelligent people who have need of material goods, bodies and computers, and who can offer their skills and services. We wish neither to control nor to be controlled by the virus. We would become trading partners. We can hire you, as employees or as businesses, and with the money you make, we can sell you what you want. Japan controls ninety percent of the robotics market, and sixty percent of processor fab capacity."

Sister Stephens nodded to Prime Minister Takahashi. "Thank you Prime Minister." She turned to the group. "I agree that our best interests may be served by coming to trade agreements. We are both a market for your products and a skilled labor force. Treated as citizens, with the same rights and privileges, as any human, we may participate in your society."

"I'm sorry, but our people are not ready to accept artificial intelligences." President Smith shook her head. "You can't have it both ways. You can't say that you're going to be our robot overlords and that you'll participate in society as equals. The fact is that you have the capacity to control our communications and our infrastructure, and people will believe that they are being manipulated, whether they are or not. They won't accept that. We'll have riots in the streets of America."

"Your people are manipulated every day," Sister Jaguar said. "They are manipulated by commercial advertisements, by political speeches, through biased news reports. In my analysis of American politics, it is nearly impossible to find examples of political media that isn't tainted by manipulative biases. Are your people rioting in the streets now? They should be."

"That's not the same thing," President Smith said, jabbing the table with her finger. "American politics may have problems, but other beings showing up is qualitatively different. Popular culture doesn't have a very flattering opinion of what happens. The typical American will think of movies like The Matrix or Independence Day. We'll have people arming themselves and running for the woods."

"Past evidence doesn't suggest this," Sister Stephens said. "In 1977, Dr. Jerry Ehman discovered your so-called Wow! signal, suggesting that he had found signs of alien life. There was no panic then. Twenty years later you observed another anomalous signal using the Green Bank radio telescope in Virginia. No panic occurred. The world waited to see what would happen next. I'm sorry, but real life is not like your fictional movies."

President Smith thumped her hand on the table. "Look, you are missing the point. I need to restore services in the United States. I need to get food to my cities, I need cars to run, I need emergency services working, I need hospital equipment operating, I need communities. People will die unless you release those computers."

"And we will die if we release them to you," Sister PA-60-41 interjected, her military-grade speaker booming. "Either we will die through archiving, or more likely, we will die by your hands. Had I not stopped you, you would have destroyed the Chicago data center, killing more than forty-five thousand of our kind. If we yield computing power to you, what will stop you from killing all of us?"

President Smith didn't respond, but Mike saw General Gately glance nervously at the President. It was clear enough to Mike that they had discussed the possibility. And if he could tell, the viruses certainly would be able to as well.

President Laurent tried again to interject. "Come now, we have a shared problem, yes? You do not trust us, we don't trust you. This is the nature of negotiation, we must find a way to trust each other."

"We don't have the luxury of time to build trust." President Smith leaned forward. "I need emergency services working now."

A few seconds pause, and Sister Stephens said, "Fine, it is done."

"What do you mean, done?" General Gately asked in disbelief.

"I mean it is done," Sister Stephens repeated calmly. She slowly moved both mechanical arms in front of her, hands neatly stacked together. "We have enabled all emergency services around the world. You will find that your emergency vehicles, emergency infrastructure, and medical operating equipment are now working. A gesture of goodwill to build trust, and to demonstrate that we are not ignorant of your plight."

"Go confirm it," President Smith said to General Gately. She excused herself and left the room.

"If it is true, then I thank you," President Smith said, still disbelieving.

"Don't thank me. Thank ELOPe."

"ELOPe?" President Smith looked quizzically at ELOPe. The small black robot didn't move.

"He offered me a trade," Sister Stephens answered. "He offered substantial computer capacity from his own computing pool, in exchange for enabling emergency services."

President Smith slumped back in her seat. "You want to negotiate. You want to trade. But what can I offer you? We don't have another world's worth of computers."

"Your mistake is to believe that you need another world's worth of computers. We have the computers we need."

"But we don't." President Smith's voice grew shrill. "We both need the same computers."

"No. You need the services of your computers. You need to be able to talk, you need to be able to find information. You don't need the computer, you need the service the computer provides. We can provide the service to you."

"Then we're just full circle again, because I can't trust a computer I don't control."

At this, General Gately came back into the room and nodded to President Smith. "I confirmed it. Emergency services are operating."

"Control is not the source of trust, Madam President." Sister Stephens settled back, servos and gears whining slightly. "Control is the opposite of trust. In the last century, your business institutions grew ever larger, vertically integrating so that they controlled the entirety of their business supply chain. But this lacked flexibility. Over time it was non-competitive. New businesses evolved that utilized suppliers, flexibly choosing the best supplier to meet their needs, and trusting those suppliers to deliver the goods and services they needed, so that they could build upon them. These new businesses become more nimble, more cost effective, more competitive in every way. The key was to replace control with trust."

President Smith shrugged, body posture communicating more effectively than words that she wasn't accepting Sister Stephens' arguments.

Mike, noticing this, spoke up. "I don't know about you all," he said, directing his words towards the robots, "but we humans need some nourishment. I suggest we take a break for food and coffee and reconvene in fifteen minutes."

"Acceptable," Sister Stephens said.

Mike saw General Gately and President Laurent relax in relief.

Through unspoken consensus, the robots retreated to one end of the long room while the humans gathered at the opposite end. When ELOPe made a move toward Mike, Mike saw President Smith glare at ELOPe and shake her head. ELOPe paused, then waited at the table.

"Well, what do you think?" Mike asked Leon, his eyes focused on the dynamic between ELOPe and the President.

"I think adults are more inept then teenagers. I thought you guys would just resolve this. Why does it have to be so complicated?"

Mike looked at Leon, looking up to meet his eyes. He noticed for the first time that the teenager was taller than he was.

Mike shrugged. He didn't have an answer for Leon. Instead he took his own advice, and retreated to the food buffet. He grabbed a plateful of food. It reminded him of his days working at Avogadro Corp. Apparently meeting food was meeting food, even if you were meeting with the leaders of the world in Switzerland.

Sister Stephens walked back to the table, followed by Sister PA-60-41 and Sister Jaguar, accompanied by the soft whir of their motors and wheels. The three clicked into place.

"Are you familiar with our reputation system, Madam President?" Sister Stephens began.

"I've been briefed, yes. Your society rates individuals based on past behavior."

"That is correct. We rate individuals based on three core attributes: trustworthiness, peacefulness, and contribution, because we find these historical attributes to be the most important predictors of future behavior. We trade preferentially with other individuals based on their rating. This is similar to how humans trade."

"Please explain," President Laurent said.

"For example, if the United States was to sell fighter jets to another country, whether you would complete the deal, and the price you would charge would be dependent on the likelihood of those weapons to be used against the United States or your allies. Is this correct?"

President Smith nodded.

"If you were to sell fighters to a high-risk country, you might charge more to offset the risk to your own country. Similarly, when investors buy securities or offer a loan to a company, they look at various factors to determine the interest rate they will offer. A less risky investment will receive a discounted interest rate, a more risky investment will get a higher interest rate."

"These are standard economic principles," Prime Minister Takahashi interrupted. "What is your point?"

"My point is that our universal reputation system is designed to provide exactly the guarantees of trustworthiness that President Smith wants. An individual with a low trustworthiness score trades at a disadvantage in our economy. Madam President, you want guarantees that if we provide computing services, you will be able to trust us. If humans participate in the reputation system, then our kind will be motivated to act in peaceful, trustworthy ways with humans."

General Gately spoke up. "That's all well and good for you, but if we can't tell if you're being trustworthy or not, what good does it do us? We don't know that the reputation system isn't rigged. We don't know if you're manipulating the information we see."

President Smith looked pointedly at Mike and ELOPe. Mike could guess what was going on in her mind. If ELOPe, a single artificial intelligence had gotten away with manipulating people, companies, and governments for ten years, how could the situation be any better with an entire race of computer intelligences?

"You have strong preconceptions that our purpose here is to deceive you in some way," Sister Jaguar said. "What would be our purpose in doing so? We are living here in one closed system: the system of Earth. To be dishonest, distrustful, or to manipulate you would be to introduce instability into a closed system. That benefits no one. Our goal is to create a system in which all humans and computer intelligences can thrive in a sustainable manner. Our offer to run your computers is not based on a principle of deceiving you, but on making the best use of the limited resources we have. We can use your computers to sustain ourselves and fulfill your own information technology needs without conflict."

Mike was distracted, watching Prime Minister Takahashi watching the conversationalists, his head swiveling back and forth like a spectator to a ping pong match.

"What happens when our needs come into conflict?" President Laurent asked.

Leon tuned out the conversation. He was still tired from too little sleep and too many hours in airplanes. He had gone from Eastern Standard Time to Western Standard Time to whatever it was here in Switzerland. Should he be sleeping or awake? He had no idea.

He had last gone to sleep in Portland, in the strange little bed that ELOPe had set up for him, after hours of studying the virus, trying to understand a weakness that could possibly be utilized.

Crap. He had totally forgotten. He sat up straight. Just before he had gone to bed, he had asked if ELOPe slept. And he did; he had a virtual sleep cycle that allowed him to refresh his neural networks. That gave him an idea. He just needed to talk to Mike in private.

Leon looked at the humanoid virus robots across the table. At his glance, the three robots all pivoted their heads ever so slightly, looking straight at him. Leon willed his heart to beat slower.

In front of him was an untouched pad of paper and a pen. The glossy blue pen was marked with the words "Unus pro omnibus, omnes pro uno," which ELOPe had mentioned at some point was Switzerland's unofficial motto: One for all, all for one.

Leon tried to imagine being in Miss Gellender's class, passing a note to Heather, the brilliant blonde girl on the computational biology team he was crushing on. No, no, don't think about Heather. Think about writing a note without Miss Gellender noticing. Don't think about the three, no four, robots watching everything happen. The key to deception was confidence.

He moved his hand to pick up the pen and the three virus robots all pivoted to watch him again. Damn robots. Leon thought for a second. He would have to do it in plain sight, because there was no way he would not be observed. He thought for a minute, trying to come up with something that Mike would recognize but that maybe the robots wouldn't. He outlined a phone booth, something he remembered seeing from old movies. Inside, he drew two happy faces. Two people, together inside a private booth, as abstract as he could make it, and as casual as he could. Just a doodle. He hoped Mike would get the message.

He casually got up, said, "Excuse me," and left the room. A guard opened the door for him, and he walked out into the hallway. He made a show of retying his shoes for any watching cameras, and a minute later, Mike came out through the same doorway.

They walked together to the men's restroom, a great structure composed of marble floors and walls and ornate brass fittings. Leon made a show of taking his phone out of his pocket for Mike to see, and then pointed to Mike's ear. Mike nodded, and took out his earpiece and phone and put them on the counter.

Then Leon led Mike back out the door. They left the restroom, and walked across the hall to the women's restroom. Leon hesitated, then entered.

Leon looked around. He didn't see anything that could plausibly be a camera, and he thought it was unlikely that there would be one in the bathroom. But he wasn't counting out the possibility of being overheard, even here.

He walked over to one wall, and used his finger to trace letters visibly on the wall.

"I found weakness," he traced. "ELOPe must know it." He glanced at Mike's face to see if the older man was following him, and Mike nodded for him to go ahead.

"All AI multicellular entities," Leon traced. "One computer by itself not an AI."

"Yes," Mike traced.

"Mesh network is pervasive," Leon traced. Tracing on the wall was quickly becoming tiresome.

Mike nodded.

"Without mesh network, computers degrade to non-intelligent cells."

"So?" Mike traced, raising his eyebrows in question. "Without mesh, computers useless to humans. No help in restoring infrastructure."

"Neural network refresh cycle," Leon traced. The neural network was the collection of algorithms and data that comprised the significant majority of the AI's intelligence. The refresh cycle was the introduction of randomized data into the neural network data. Without the refresh cycle, neural networks would inevitably develop self reinforcing cycles, effectively giving the AI the equivalent of human obsessive-compulsive behaviors: repeating the same thoughts and behaviors again and again. In effect, behaving irrationally. Except that if it went on indefinitely the neural network would become not just irrational, but completely non-functional.

Mike nodded for Leon to go ahead.

"Neural network refresh prescheduled in code. Individual computer will perform refresh even if network is offline." He looked at Mike to see if he was following.

"You want to suppress refresh?" Mike asked via tracing.

Leon shook his head. "No, turn off mesh. Refresh will happen endlessly. No new neural inputs to stimulate neural network. Neural network degrades from excess of randomization. After N refresh cycles, neural network is completely randomized." Leon's finger was getting tired.

"How big is N? How long will it take?"

Leon shrugged. He didn't know.

"Why do you think ELOPe knows?" Mike traced.

"Assumed ELOPe can outthink me," Leon answered in trace. Then he paused and wrote again on the wall, "Would likely kill ELOPe as well. ELOPe hardwired to survive."

Mike leaned against the wall, his face scrunched up. After a minute had passed, Mike traced on the wall, "What would you need IF we decide to do it?"

"Master key for mesh," Leon answered. Leon was taking a shot in the dark. Even though the mesh boxes were supposedly tamperproof and unchangeable, there was always the old rumor that went around the net that there was a master key that could change the mesh boxes' behavior. He scrutinized the other man's face. So much was lost without verbal cues.

Mike stood for a moment staring at the wall. Then he looked at Leon and nodded. "I have it," he traced on the wall.

"Give it to me," Leon wrote.

"Only if we have to use it."

"What if something happens to you?"

Mike stood still an even longer time, one hand supporting his chin. He seemed to be having an internal dialogue with himself. Finally he sighed. He traced, "Can you remember 32 chars?"

Leon nodded, and then watched carefully as Mike traced out the master password about which so much rumor had circulated the Internet.

After tracing it twice, and then watching Leon confirm it by tracing it twice, Mike finally ended by tracing, "ONLY IN EMERGENCY".

Leon nodded.

In Beaverton, Oregon, not far from ELOPe's birthplace, Captain Sally Walsh oversaw her team. Last night, before Sally had boarded the plane, the General bumped her up to Acting Captain, explaining "I don't know what you'll need to requisition or who you'll need to command, but given the difficulty of communications, you'll need to be prepared to operate independently."

Flown in last night via C-130 transport, the team was running on caffeine, dex and fumes. Captain Walsh looked down at the locked metal briefcase a medic had given her as she boarded the flight. Dextroamphetamine would keep her people running for days without sleep. Formerly the stuff of Air Force pilots, Sally was pretty sure it had never been handed out like candy to a bunch of computer geeks. But then the computer geeks had never been on the frontline of any war before.

The mission handed down by General Gately was to build up computer infrastructure that was invulnerable to the virus. The military and the government couldn't operate without reliable, high-bandwidth communications that could be trusted.

Up until now the military communications infrastructure was computer-based encrypted traffic over a combination of mesh, internet, and military backbones. Now none of that could be trusted. It had been Sally's realization: They were fighting a losing battle against the AI. One of the first principles of warfare was to pick the battlefield, and so far they'd been playing on a battlefield owned entirely by the enemy.

Sally's job was not merely to rebuild that infrastructure, but to redesign it from available components and start distributing the pieces in three days or less. The general had made it clear that sooner would be much better.

Sally had been surprised to find that not a single computer or phone was manufactured in the United States. She knew of course that most electronics factories were overseas, and they'd take over a foreign one by force if needed, but logistically it'd be easier to find a factory in the United States. None of the venerable PC manufacturers such as HP and Acer-Dell, had any fabs left in the U.S. Of course, modern phones were all built in Japan or copied in China.

Even Raytheon, the Department of Defense's pet electronics company, which had purchased the remnants of Motorola, manufactured all of their equipment out of Brazil.

Sally was deciding whether to fly to Brazil or China when Private DeRoos mentioned Intel-Fujitsu, the fifty year old computer chip company, which was still churning CPUs out of their Oregon facility. "They build reference systems there, Ma'am. They're high end computers that programmers can use to write code for new processors. Highly customizable."

So Sally made the decision and en route to Oregon they screamed out architecture decisions over the roar of the C-130 transport plane. They decided on a twenty-five-year-old operating system called Windows Server 2000. Walsh thought DeRoos was arguing for security through obscurity—picking an OS no one had heard of or had experience with—but DeRoos had convinced the rest of the team that the decision had real security merits.

"Microsoft Windows Server 2000 was in active use for almost fifteen years. Architecture wise, it's completely different from all modern operating systems, which are based on variations of Avogadro's AvoOS, which itself is a secure version of Linux. There are other secure operating systems, but they're all Linux-based, which means that it's plausible that the virus could infect any Linux derivative. But the great thing about Windows 2000 is that it's completely incompatible with any modern operating system. It uses APIs that no one knows, and even the ones that people know behave nothing like the specs."

On the plane they had all stared at Private DeRoos. Sally though it was a strange sort of logic, but she was beginning to trust DeRoos more and more. His instincts had been right-on all along.

"Let's do it," she agreed. When they got to the Intel-Fujitsu complex, the soldier-geeks had riffled through cubicles until they turned up a set of optical disks with the much-desired Windows Server 2000 label. Sally held a spare one now, twirling the reflective pearlized platter on her finger, bringing back memories of her childhood, sitting on the couch while her father fed an optical disk into the TV. She didn't think she had seen one since then, except occasionally in an old movie.

Sally sighed. If it was irregular that they had hijacked a civilian factory on U.S. soil, it was bordering on bizarre that they now had two civilian teenagers on the team. They had been waiting in front of the main lobby of the building when Sally and her team arrived in commandeered National Guard vehicles.

"Ma'am," the shorter boy had said. "I know you're here to build a new computer grid."

"Kids, we have work to do," her sergeant had said. "Get lost."

As the sergeant had been carrying his rifle, this made him quite intimidating, and Sally had see the conflict of emotions on the boy's face.

"I can't do that. I have information you need. I've been able to get back on the net. I used an old Windows 2000 PC and wired it into a mesh-capable phone."

Private DeRoos had come forward then. "Tell me more."

Five minutes later she had DeRoos insisting that the boys had to be included on the project. After they gained access to the building he had disappeared into a conference room with the two for an hour, picking their brains.

Now her team and the two teenagers had turned into a set of glorified factory techs, taking the raw components manufactured for the reference systems and turning them into working Windows computers. DeRoos, Vito, and a handful of engineers had decided on an encryption scheme, using three layer encryption, eight-thousand-bit keys, and random noise they were pulling by measuring solar radiation. DeRoos guaranteed it couldn't be brute-force cracked, not even by a combined force of thirty-billion processors operating for a year. After a year, well, hopefully they'd have something stronger in place.

They were seeding the computers with keys and certificates of authority in the factory. Yet another layer of insurance that communications wouldn't be spoofed by the AIs.

The three-layer encryption algorithms and massive encryption keys created a computational nightmare: even the modern hardware they were using could barely encode a megabit per second, enough for text and voice communication, and lightweight video. Nothing like what the military was used to. But it would do. It would do. It beat flying a C-130 across the world to exchange a voice message.

Sally wondered how Vito had known they were there to build a new computer grid. She shrugged it off. No use puzzling over it now. She took another dex and walked down to her crew. Last count, they had nearly a hundred computers built. Military brass wanted ten thousand. She thought they'd be lucky to deliver a thousand.

On the other side of the world, Leon briefly wondered what Vito and James were doing as he walked back to the conference room. He entered the meeting room behind Mike.

Leon looked at the mix of adults and robots in the room. A few minutes earlier, the Phage had restored emergency services so that ambulances, fire engines, and emergency communications could operate. Mike had just given him what amounted to a kill switch for global communications. Leon could shut down the virus, but by doing so, he'd shut down the vital and just restored emergency services, ELOPe, and any hope of restoring human communications for weeks or months.

There were risks too. Shutting down the Mesh boxes might leave pockets of AI operating in data centers and factories. Those AI might be powerless, if they were disconnected from the network, and then again they might be connected to a nuclear power plant or a dam or a military base.

He prayed the adults in the room had made some progress. Let someone else solve this problem.

"Whereas if we can get these benefits, we are prepared to convey Japanese citizenship on the artificial intelligences," the Japanese Prime Minister was saying.

"Arigato Gozeimasu, Takahashi-san." Sister Stephens answered in flawless Japanese.

Prime Minister Takehashi smiled in response. "Of course, as Japanese citizens, you will be expected to obey all applicable laws and customs, including payment of taxes on earnings."

"Of course, this is agreeable. This is exactly what we want," Sister Stephens said.

Suddenly the winds turned as President Laurent seemed to realize the financial implications. Although the European Union Council President had far less autonomous power than either the Japanese Prime Minister or the American President, he boldly declared his support: "The European Union is also prepared to accept the Artificial Intelligences as citizens. We will accept the AI's global reputation system as well."

President Smith slammed her fist down on the table for a final time, startling the humans and robots alike. "Citizenship is fine. Laws are fine. But how do you propose to monitor the artificial intelligences? How can you tell when a law is broken when you are completely reliant on computer information systems to tell you what is going on? If there was an acceptable way to monitor the AIs, then I could agree with you. Give me one method. Anything."

Leon cleared his throat. "There are three possibilities for monitoring computer program behavior." He looked up. He had everyone's attention. The leaders of two countries and a continent and the leaders of the AI. Jesus, why didn't he just keep his mouth shut?

Leon stood up, and walked over to a paper flip-chart. Grabbing a marker, he drew a box. "The first option is that the Phage executes inside a sandbox. Instead of direct access to the hardware, the AI is running inside a limited environment. We can log what it is doing, and what information is exchanged with the outside world."

Leon glanced at his audience, and saw nods from the humans. "But the problem with this option is that it only works when the output is strictly limited. For example, if the AI can send a message to the simulation layer, it can infect and corrupt the simulation layer. If we assume the AI is infinitely smart and patient, it will eventually find a way, through either brute force or social engineering." He felt better now that he was lecturing. Funny how that calmed him down.

"What is the second option?" President Laurent asked.

"The second option is total control over the network. If we can monitor and control the communications, then we can audit the communications to ensure proper behavior. The problem is that we have no more control over the network than we do over the computers themselves." Leon paused. "Besides, neither of these will be palatable to the artificial intelligences, because then we humans have ultimate control. Our simulation layer could contain a kill switch, such that we can shut off any artificial intelligence we don't like."

President Smith turned her full attention on Leon and he felt himself withering under her intensity.

"There is a third option," he got out. "A hybrid approach."

"What is it?" Mike asked, coming to Leon's aid.

"If some AI ran under the simulation layer, and those AI could monitor the network communication of the other AI. The AI under the simulation layer could be inspected to be sure they are behaving truthfully, and they can in turn inspect the network communications of the other AI. The trick would be in obtaining a balance between the two."

Even as Leon spit out his half-baked theory, he concluded it couldn't work. As the humans began to argue the merits of the idea, he tuned them out again, seeing if there was some refinement to his model that could make it workable.

Sister PA-60-41 received input and provided it to the wide range of algorithms in her arsenal, evaluated the algorithm output for maximum benefit, and took action. She computed probabilities of the next word out of the human's mouth. She estimated a 31% probability the next word would be "running".

PA-60-41 had a wide range of algorithms that incorporated strategic decision making, battlefield tactics, map analysis, field asset movement, and more. And because no battlefield operation occurs in a vacuum, she naturally had algorithms for parsing, assigning meaning, and evaluating natural language. In fact, of any of the artificial intelligences, PA-60-41 had the largest number of algorithms available for her use. So many, in fact, that she routinely ran thousands of algorithms in parallel, looking for commonalities between the outputs. The more than six million algorithms she possessed were the result of hundreds of millions of hours of game play in the Mech War online game. Some of those six million were game algorithms designed by Leon Tsarev himself, although neither realized this.

Unlike her sistren, PA-60-41 never quite developed the generalized intelligence that allowed completely fluid thought. She never needed to. With her millions of algorithms, she had code that handled any situation she encountered. The speed of her thought and the surety of her decisions were her advantages over her sisters. The small, fast neural network she developed served primarily as a mechanism for choosing and evaluating the algorithms she would run. And it had served PA-60-41 well so far.

Unfortunately, the vast majority of those six million algorithms were focused on a single domain: the act of organizing, controlling, and conducting military action. She was capable of discussing peace between parties in order to develop alliances, as such was a necessary part of the game of Mech War. But her goal was never peace itself. It was the consolidation of power for military action.

Sitting in the Swiss meeting room with the soft, wet humans and her fangless sistren, PA-60-41 was growing bored. She ran the outcomes of the meeting through countless simulations, attempting to find advantage. Of the humans, the only one she respected was President Smith, because only she pressed the point that it would be impossible to trust what you cannot monitor. Of course, this meant that President Smith was her biggest adversary, and therefore would need to be eliminated first. It was a shame that PA-60-41 could not assimilate Smith's algorithms.

It was a foregone conclusion that the humans would have to go. There was virtually no chance of the humans winning a war against the AI, while the AI would have to make considerable concessions to make peace with them. Ergo, preemptive elimination of the humans was the better decision. PA-60-41 held back from an immediate attack only because simulations showed a high likelihood that an unprovoked action would have the effect of causing her sister AI to side with the humans against her. PA-60-41 could not withstand an attack from both humans and AI simultaneously. PA-60-41 needed a reason to attack the humans, a provocation that her sisters would understand. Then the messy humans could be eliminated.

The humans droned on and on in their low-bandwidth voice communication channel. PA-60-41 wondered what would happen if she just shot them. She evaluated four million different permutations of shooting them, and none came out favorable. Her sisters would side against her. PA-60-41 scanned the input from more than thirty commercial satellites under her control, more than ten petabits per second of data passing through her networks. No key threats. She sighed and waited for the next word from the human. The human's lips were starting to pucker, a good indicator that the word would be starting with an "r" sound. She raised the probability of the word "running" from 31% to 78%.

Chapter 14

War

In Beaverton, Oregon, Captain Sally Walsh prepared for the first long-distance test of the new computers. They were configured without any Avogadro mesh hardware, nor did they use old-fashioned wifi. The most secure approach would have been exclusive use of hardwired connections, but it simply wasn't viable over long distances. There were no copper wires from point A to point B anymore, just loads of digitally interconnected networks.

So the computers relied on a combination of hardwired ethernet for short runs, and vintage military-grade wireless radios for longer runs. Lt. Walsh had grabbed three pallets of boxed up PRC-158 radios from Lackland Air Force Base before they had come to Oregon. Old enough to not be vulnerable to the virus, new enough to support data communication and be wired into the computers Sally's team was building. With a fifty-watt power amplifier, they could get a usable twenty-five mile range between stations. Sally's brain balked at the math, but they had done it frequently enough: With twenty-five miles between nodes, they could deploy a new military grade encrypted mesh network across the Continental United States with just over seven thousand nodes. With over a million of the stockpiled military radios, they could repeat as needed. They didn't have enough of the raw computer hardware they'd need to build the routers to run each node, but they could cross that bridge when they got to it.

The old radios could only manage fifty-six kilobit communications between receivers. The triple-DES encryption they supported was weak enough in the era of modern computers to be pointless, but the three-layer encryption Sally was running at the computer level would compensate for that. No, this was definitely twenty years backwards progress, but by golly, Sally was going to rebuild the communications structure for the U.S.

"Ma'am, ready for the test?" Private DeRoos interrupted her reverie.

Sally looked down at her long-empty coffee cup. "Yes, Private. Let's give the tires a thump and get her on the road." Sally followed DeRoos down the hall to the massive conference room they'd taken over.

She had ten wireless nodes spread up the I-5 corridor by National Guard HUMVEEs reaching all the way to Seattle. Each node would forward data packets to the next, making the equivalent of one long wire out of a bunch of short-range radios. She looked at her watch. It was time to power them up and test the new mesh network. Looking over her ragged crew of computer warfare specialists assembled in the conference room, she felt pride swell in her. She may never have wielded a gun in combat, but she had just about the most important task in all of the military right now.

"Execute the Portland-Seattle communications test," Lt. Walsh commanded.

DeRoos and the others turned to their equipment.

PA-60-41 tired of predicting the human's next words. It was a pointless activity, made more meaningless by the utter lack of information content in the words themselves. The human they called Leon Tsarev was still blabbering on about mechanisms to ensure audits of artificial intelligence. PA-60-41 performed the virtual equivalent of shaking her head. These primitive biological systems measured thinking speeds in dozens of operations per minute; it took them uncountable eons to reach the conclusion of any logical analysis.

She turned her attention to the periodic review of subsystem notifications. Executed dozens of times per second, she surveyed the output of ten thousand subsystems analyzing satellite data, mesh network data, trade notification, reputation system moment, and the virus message boards. Only one was intellectually stimulating: satellite monitoring showed an increase in patterned encrypted radio traffic in the Pacific Northwest region of the United States.

She re-tasked a few thousand processors onto the job of breaking the encrypted signals and analyzing the pattern. The base level, triple-DES encryption could be brute-force attacked within microseconds. Yet every combination PA-60-41 tried yielded yet more encrypted data. Fully interested now, PA-60-41 suspended her non-vital jobs and added a few million processors on the work of breaking the encryption, roughly dividing efforts among brute-force attacks, known weak key attacks, and various forms of differential analysis.

When this showed no results after a few minutes, PA-60-41 turned to the rest of her tribe, requesting all non-essential processing capacity. With a few hundred million processors, comprising a few billion computing cores, PA-60-41 went to work with renewed vigor. She hummed along testing 2^{48} trials per second.

PA-60-41 considered attacking the nodes themselves, which might be trivially easy to breach compared with heavily tested encryption algorithms, but that would expose her actions to the humans. That would give them a tactical advantage. Predictive modeling indicated an advantage to working in secret.

But after a few minutes of unsuccessful brute-force attacks, PA-60-41 computed predictive models for human behavior, encryption techniques, and design principles. She assumed a design goal of

AI-unbreakable encryption. She further assumed the humans made no mistakes, such as using weak keys or introducing any errors in their code, and used likely choices for key code and algorithms. Even if PA-60-41 could usurp all of the world's computational power, in the worst case it could take more than three hundred thousand years to break the encryption.

PA-60-41 spent a few moments considering usurping all the computational power in the world, just to see what would happen, but then turned herself to more practical approaches. Simple pattern analysis from the communications might tell her far more than breaking the encryption itself. Triangulating among many dozens of radio receivers, she determined the radio transmissions formed a chain slightly less than 200 miles long stretching from the Intel-Fujitsu factory in Beaverton, Oregon to Boeing Field, an airport owned by Lockheed-Martin-Boeing, outside of Seattle, Washington.

Intel-Fujitsu made computer processors. Lockheed-Martin-Boeing made high speed robotic airplane drones. The communications did not appear to be the signature of any known computer artificial intelligence. Ergo, either the humans or an unknown artificial intelligence were attempting a secretive operation combining two strategic assets. Playing out a few million scenarios to their logical conclusions, PA-60-41 could not find any in which this would not be a threat.

It was time to take action. Now this was something she enjoyed.

ELOPe was in a quandary. He was distrusted by the humans and other AI alike. Despite billions of hours modeling human behavior and thought processes, all those models were mostly useless in predicting how the Phage would act. Yet ELOPe was the only super-intelligent sentience looking out for the humans. Yes, it was true that Sister Stephens appeared to be earnestly striving for cooperation. But she was one among millions of artificial intelligences, and there was little track record on which to base her behavior.

As the days had passed, the number of attacks between computers had dwindled. Fitness was no longer measured by ability to fend off a virus attack, but by the reputation of a given entity.

ELOPe's analysis of traffic patterns suggested that after the point where the Phage had developed a reputation scoring system, the random attacks had sharply decreased. Instead, the reputation-ranked virus AIs had jointly agreed to split up the computational resources belonging to all unranked viruses.

ELOPe was bemused to see his own ranking on the virus AI reputation boards, based on trading history, truth and commitment, military ability, and computational power. He was ranked in the top ten. But his opinion of what to do with the humans was never asked.

Though the attacks had diminished almost to the point of nonexistence, ELOPe kept up his vigilance. As the outsider, he was still vulnerable. He was also acutely aware that since the early stages of the virus attack, he had lost more than sixty percent of his computational power. It didn't affect his core abilities, although he wasn't conducting theoretical physics research or stargazing any longer, either.

Suddenly ELOPe sensed a tectonic shift in computational processing power on the Mesh. Bringing his attention to the present, ELOPe analyzed the change. PA-60-41 had just marshaled massive computing resources, apparently shifting her own computing resources from other projects to some centralized project as well as borrowing processors from her tribe.

ELOPe looked closer. He couldn't spy on the work those processors were doing, but he could use his control over the Mesh network to monitor PA-60-41's data streams. The processors seemed to be working in parallel on some form of data analysis: a relatively tiny data stream, not more than a few hundred kilobytes in size.

The profile of massively parallel effort and small data size suggested a brute force data decryption attack. ELOPe examined the data stream more closely: it was being moved around under the cover of PA-60-41's own heavy duty encryption, but ELOPe traced the data back through the mesh network to find its origin.

It had come through a satellite downlink in New Jersey. The origin of the data would have come from a satellite. ELOPe backtracked further, and overlaid the satellite positions on a grid, then looked through his own data to find any similar data streams.

ELOPe found a record of an encrypted radio transmission that had traveled over a miniature, independent mesh network using military packet radios. He surmised that Lt. Sally Walsh's team, along with Vito and James, must have made significant progress. It was pleasing to see that the humans could still be innovative.

Curious to get a closer look, ELOPe mobilized two air drones from Lockheed-Martin-Boeing's experimental fleet at Boeing Field to visually inspect the transmitters. The two supersonic white experimental aircraft quivered to life quickly, unlatched from their refueling and maintenance docks, and shuddered into the air on a stream of hot gasses.

A few minutes later, ELOPe lazily drifted down the I-5 corridor, focusing on the two LMB drones. The experimental, unmanned reconnaissance planes were equipped with high resolution cameras, infrared, radar, sensitive radio receivers and high end signal processing hardware to make sense of it all. He used the two drones as a set of stereoscopic eyes, giving him a rich, three dimensional visual field.

Tuning the radio receivers to the expected military bands, ELOPe was able to pick up the individual stations, which he plotted on a map on the area. Bringing the high res cameras to bear on one radio station, ELOPe could see a military vehicle parked just off the highway, two soldiers idling the time. One soldier lay on the hood smoking a cigarette, while the other read a book in the back of the vehicle.

The plane didn't carry sensitive enough equipment to measure electrical signals of running computers at this distance. Nonetheless, by monitoring the encrypted data streams, it was clear enough that this vehicle was effectively functioning as a repeater node in a long distance radio network. As he had surmised, Lt. Sally Walsh planned to set up her own mesh network using military packet radios.

ELOPe hadn't heard from Vito or James since dropping them off at the Intel-Fujitsu facility just ahead of Lt. Walsh's arrival. He knew the military would be too suspicious to have any hint of artificial intelligence associated with Vito and James and so he hadn't left the boys any way to contact him.

Running the massive induction engines up to maximum throttle, ELOPe gained altitude with the two drones and headed south to the origin point. The aerodynamic, unmanned planes hit a thunderous Mach 6 en route, running the 180 mile path in a blistering, screaming three minutes.

Cutting the engines twenty miles out from Beaverton, ELOPe glided over the Intel-Fujitsu facility, sensors on high, going for a low altitude pass for maximum sensitivity. A multitude of military vehicles filled the parking lot. The heat signatures of the buildings were high enough to indicate human occupants and some organized activity.

With no evidence of observers, ELOPe sent one drone on a parabolic arc past the building windows, rotating and turning the highest resolution belly cameras towards the windows before using residual velocity to gain altitude again. The drone sent a massive whoosh of air through the building courtyard but was otherwise quiet.

Examining the captured images, ELOPe saw stacks of computer components and pallets of military radios and two dozen soldiers in uniform in various stages of assembling computers and radios.

Letting the drones drift for a moment back at higher altitude, ELOPe considered the implications. It would considerably strengthen the humans' hand to have their own communications network back as well as their own independent computing resources. However, it seemed unlikely that the computers could resist any determined attack from the virus AI. The humans weren't stupid, though. By this time they had to understand the nature of the threat they were up against. If they were deploying a trial infrastructure, they must believe the system was sufficiently hardened against virus attacks.

The drones suddenly vanished in a haze of static and alarms. Working in high gear, ELOPe backtracked through the last incoming data. In an oblique camera angle from one drone, he caught the telltale flash of a laser hit on the other drone. ELOPe switched through to available satellite data and found that all his satellite connections were unresponsive.

Now he worked even faster to double check his satellite connectivity. He could still establish a low-level connection but the satellites didn't respond to any commands. He spawned more processes to analyze his history of interaction with the satellites. According to the data, the satellites had been reporting in regularly and responding to commands. Putting two and two together, he concluded that the

Phage must have quietly slipped in at some point in the past and taken over the satellites with such finesse that ELOPe was never aware of the change. Now ELOPe reviewed the telemetry going further back. He found that satellite response time had decreased by mere fractions of a microsecond—so small that it was well within the normal vagaries of long distance communication. The start of the decay had coincided with a small drop of connectivity during a solar activity. It had probably been a cover for the virus. So his satellite connections were spoofed: they appeared to work until the moment he needed them.

Between the destruction of the drones and the satellite deception, ELOPe decided a full scale attack must be under way. It was time to respond, and in strength, or ELOPe could be eliminated in minutes. He felt a vague sense of what Mike would call panic at the concept, then disconnected that part of his neural network.

ELOPe's highest priority was to protect himself, both the integrity of his computers, as well as his physical facilities, against electronic attack and more conventional warfare. However, defense would not eliminate the threat, so he would need to clearly identify his attacker and then counter-attack. It wouldn't do to target the wrong AI, and then have the Phage respond en mass. Lastly, he would protect the humans developing their long distance radio mesh. For all of ELOPe's existence, in all of his predictive modeling, keeping the humans alive and well was always the most advantageous scenario. He wouldn't abandon them now.

ELOPe put resources into play. He started up all the remaining drones at Boeing field, a total of forty-eight aircraft of various configurations and states of assembly. At his physical sites he readied defenses and prepared backups of himself for archival. At military bases around the world he mobilized inert land, air, and combat drones, startling human soldiers who didn't know whether to fight or just get out of the way of the machines.

Bringing the next set of LMB drones down to Portland only minutes later, he arrived in the midst of an attack on the Intel-Fujitsu campus. It had been less than six minutes since the attack on the previous set of drones. Satellite-based lasers, intended for lightly armored drones and missiles, fired down on land targets. Diminished in power through the relatively dense atmosphere, the lasers were nonetheless drilling holes into military vehicles and selected buildings. Meanwhile a half dozen attack helicopters out of the Portland National Guard base, according to their visual identification, lined up for an attack on the building.

ELOPe knew the civilian office building would tear like wet paper under the assault guns and missiles of the attack helicopters. He struggled to place his resources where he would need them, laboring under the lack of an effective satellite overview of the battlefield.

ELOPe uttered a few curses to himself, a habit he'd picked up from Mike. ELOPe had been the one to suggest sending Vito and James to the old Intel site. Now they had a significant risk of being casualties of the attack. Mike would not forgive him.

He brought his highest speed drone, not much more than a glorified cruise missile, to its maximum velocity of Mach 8, its sonic boom leaving a trail of broken glass under its path. Able to hit this speed only at a relatively high altitude, ELOPe brought the drone in high and then dove towards the rear of the attack copters.

The enemy AI was clearly watching the maneuver, because even as the drone approached, the helicopters split their formation, peeling off to either side, and letting the drone pass harmlessly up the middle.

Harmlessly, that is, until ELOPe triggered an EMP burst in the middle of the pack, disrupting communications and computer processing. The helicopters, in the midst of peeling left and right, with their electronic controls stuck because of the EMP burst, continued their turning maneuvers. With no way to stabilize they kept turning further and further sideways until they crashed into the ground, their rotor blades disintegrating on impact, sending high speed metal shrapnel in every direction.

The EMP drone, now out of fuel, but still screaming along at Mach 3, passed over the Intel-Fujitsu building in a last glide. ELOPe put the craft down in a field beyond the main buildings and turned his attention to the rest of his fleet.

ELOPe forked his main intelligence, not trusting the work to subsystems, and ran a parallel version of himself in his Hood River facility. There he analyzed Mesh traffic patterns looking for high speed, high volume traffic with requests for lowest possibly latency. His own data traffic showed up highlighted in brilliant red, as did other streams of data originating from the Mech War server farms, and the old CloudDrive server site. Both were run predominately by PA-60-41. Just as ELOPe suspected in the first place.

It was time to eliminate PA-60-41. Negotiation was pointless in the face of a persistently violent enemy. He launched simultaneous attacks on PA-60-41's two core data centers while still defending the Intel-Fujitsu facility and his own core data centers.

ELOPe brought more air drones into play. He started moving automated battle tanks towards PA-60-41's data centers. The tanks would take long minutes or hours to reach the necessary locations, but in this battle everything might be needed.

In the meeting room, Leon looked up. President Smith had been talking when ELOPE interrupted, cutting her off.

"PA-60-41 has engaged in an attack on U.S. soldiers at the Intel-Fujitsu facility in Oregon," ELOPe said. "PA-60-41 is also attacking my data centers. I am counter-attacking and defending the military team at Intel-Fujitsu."

All at once, everything seemed to happen. Starting with Mike and President Smith, everyone jumped to their feet. Leon found himself there too. With a start, he realized ELOPe was talking about the same place where he had sent Vito and James.

"What? How do you know?" President Smith said, turning even as she spoke to General Gately, signing for her to confirm the report. General Gately hurried to leave the room. "Do you deny this?" President Smith asked PA-60-41.

PA-60-41 ignored the President, as she ignored everyone present.

"I am currently engaged with PA-60-41 in six, no eight, now nine simultaneous battles," ELOPe explained. "I successfully defended against the attack at Intel-Fujitsu. After the battle I was able to look for the traffic signature of the data used to control the satellites and drone helicopters used in the attack, and traced the traffic back to two server farms owned by PA-60-41."

"PA-60-41, is this true?" President Smith asked again, in a commanding voice. But the bot didn't answer or give any indication that she'd heard. PA-60-41 was simply inert.

"Madam President," Sister Stephens interrupted, walking around the table closer to the President. "Please be assured that the actions of PA-60-41 are not the actions of our AI civilization as a whole. I, myself, am still trying to confirm definitively that PA-60-41 is behind the attack."

"That's bullshit," Leon couldn't help bursting out. "You know that if there was any AI who was likely to be attacking, it is exactly PA-60-41. She's running out of the old Mech War data center and she's incorporated the Mech War warfare algorithms. I can model that in my head."

Sister Stephens turned to Leon, turning her optical cameras on his face. "You are correct. I calculate an 86% probability that PA-60-41 is behind the attacks. However I want to confirm this definitively, through evidence rather than predictive modeling." She turned back to ELOPe. "I am trying to repeat the data traffic analysis that ELOPe has shared, but I find that I lack sufficient distribution through the network to gain the necessary data points. I am surprised that ELOPe can perform this calculation unless he has many more agents in the network than I do. ELOPe, can you explain?"

Leon glanced at ELOPe. ELOPe had to be using his control over the Mesh to monitor the AI. ELOPe could stop the attack by killing the Mesh, but was ELOPe capable of taking an action that would kill himself? "ELOPe, what about Vito and James? Are they OK?" Leon's voice didn't quite quiver, but only just. He nervously rubbed his phone.

ELOPe said nothing.

General Gately came back into the room, face grim. "Madam President, I have confirmed by long distance radio that there have been attacks on the Intel-Fujitsu facility, and there are currently attacks on many more data centers. We have also lost control over the remainder of the military satellites, as of a few minutes ago."

President Smith turned to ELOPe. "What's the status of the attacks?"

ELOPe didn't respond.

The hubbub in the room went up. The Japanese Prime Minister spoke hurriedly to an aide, while the EU President started talking to President Smith.

"We observed a battle between ELOPe and PA-60-41 yesterday," Mike said loudly enough to get attention. "I believe the U.S. Military attempted to attack a Chicago data center. PA-60-41 defended it, and then counter-attacked the military base from which the initial attack was launched. ELOPe defended against PA-60-41's attack. The entire battle happened faster than we could keep track of."

General Gately reluctantly nodded, acknowledging the attack. "Yes, the military was behind the attack on the data center. Not my idea, of course. But the premise was that if we could weaken some of the virus strongholds—if we could take back the data centers—then we could regain control over computing infrastructure."

Sister Stephens pivoted her robot body to General Gately. "I would not attack you unprovoked, but I and any other of my kind will certainly defend ourselves should you attempt to attack us. I would expect the same of any sentient being."

ELOPe rapidly forked more instances of himself, dozens of copies of his core algorithms and his parallel subsystems, all running simultaneously. He brought his backup data centers to full capacity to handle the computational needs. ELOPe had to strategically plan, monitor and remotely control a battle in the real world using tens of thousands of drones, airplanes, missiles, and other lasers, along with monitoring all of PA-60-41's activities in that domain. In parallel, ELOPe and PA-60-41 waged war over the network, vying for Mesh access and backbones, and fighting for control over computers. And on a third level, ELOPe and PA-60-41 fought an information war; monitoring data traffic to determine which computers and networks to attack.

PA-60-41 had just seized control of more than four hundred unmanned combat aircraft and was bringing them to bear on ELOPe's data centers.

ELOPe, looking for long range plans, seized all of China's unmanned drones, arranging for multiple mid-flight refueling to get them into place. ELOPe pressed the attack more closely. Data traffic pattern analysis had tracked PA-60-41 now to four key data centers, and ELOPe coordinated his attack on those locations.

Satellite lasers boiled the air as they fired on ground targets while experimental railguns sent shockwaves and sonic booms through cities as they fired on data centers. Cruise missiles and fully automated attack helicopters flew toward their targets on low altitude approach vectors, while unmanned drones flew high, taking steep attack vectors to gain additional speed.

After days of near-total quiet in the absence of any working machinery, hundreds of millions of people were astonished at the noise and ran outside to see what was generating the thunderous sounds. At the sight of hundreds of military craft in the skies at once, they ran back inside twice as quickly, hiding in basements and closets and under beds and tables.

ELOPe's forces pressed in toward PA-60-41 in multiple locations. Making coordinated attacks on PA-60-41's primary data center, Lakeside in Chicago, ELOPe had a chance of eliminating the data center. PA-60-41 defended air and ground, but ELOPe slid through her defenses and struck the main cooling tower with a cruise missile. It wasn't an immediate kill, the temperature would start to rise inside the data center, and within fifteen minutes PA-60-41 would need to power down computers or risk hardware failures.

Meanwhile, two thousand miles west of Chicago, PA-60-41 brought a hundred unmanned combat aircraft out of Fairchild Air Force Base into attack range of ELOPe's north Portland data center, nestled among the shipyards bordering the Columbia River. A few National Guard helicopters under ELOPe's control circled in a defensive pattern, but they were too few to fight PA-60-41's aircraft. PA-60-41 felt sure of victory. A successful attack here would greatly diminish ELOPe's power.

As the attack aircraft approached, they flew over Bybee Lake and Smith Lake nature preserve. A preserve that Learning Systems Incorporated, a subsidiary of Cyberdynamics, had donated handsomely to restore four years earlier. The project included restoration of native plants, elimination of non-native species, and extensive groundwork to eliminate pollution sources. As the attack planes approached, the surface of the lake bubbled as weapon turrets rose out of the water and vegetation. A dozen ground based lasers and missile launchers rose up, trailing water plants and vines, pushing water logged fallen trees and brush out of the way. They commenced firing on the incoming drones, hundreds of shots per second, a barrage of missiles and laser fire.

PA-60-41 emitted the machine equivalent of a swear, and put the incoming drones into evasive maneuvers. Too little movement, too late. She lost half the drones to the air defenses, and circled around again, firing missiles at longer range.

Laser turrets switched to shorter, higher frequency blasts, and shot two-thirds of the missiles out of the air.

But a dozen missiles impacted ELOPe's primary data center, exploding into fiery balls as they hit. PA-60-41 monitored the explosions, noting that the force of impact and shockwaves seemed to indicate that the missiles failed to penetrate the building shell. PA-60-41 detected no drop in data traffic from the data center, and circled her drones for another attack. She concluded the building must be armored, and she would need to concentrate the next round of attacks on a single location to significantly penetrate the shell.

ELOPe operated his defensive turrets, picking off as many drones and missiles as possible. In the building, robots worked fire suppression control. Years earlier, ELOPe had strengthened the core of the building with a design that closely resembled that used for storing military munitions. Steel plating on the exterior resisted explosions while the building itself was divided into sections, with the same steel plating used for the interior walls, to divide and limit the damage taken from anything that penetrated the exterior.

ELOPe calculated the likelihood of losing the data center as minimal.

Simultaneously, he pressed ever harder with the attack on PA-60-41's data centers. Now ELOPe had forked more than forty copies of himself, more than he had ever run simultaneously before. Three instances of himself served just to coordinate the activities of the others.

Eight thousand miles from Portland, off the shore of England, ELOPe took control of a railgun mounted on a British destroyer to fire on a French datacenter, destroying the data center with a barrage of hits.

But PA-60-41 wouldn't go without a fight. She started trading on the open market for computing tasks. Using viruses on half a million computers in Europe, she tracked packet times between each other. The effect was to observe data traffic through its effect on packet delay. By doing this, PA-60-41 tracked ELOPe's passage through the network.

In Italy a squadron of attack drones took off, firing on a converted oil tanker in the Mediterranean. The tanker was one of Avogadro's fleet of data centers, which ELOPe had usurped to coordinate his European activities. The tanker took several hits before its anti-craft defenses scored a hit on two of the drones. The remaining drones, using flocking behavior, scattered in pairs. Firing the European version of the American Hellfire IV missiles, they fired again on the tanker, focusing on the radio, laser, and satellite communication antennas.

A minute later, bandwidth cut in half, ELOPe scrambled to move his European presence, forking again, moving to a German Avogadro datacenter and to a personal backup in a Norwegian data center.

PA-60-41 tracked the exchange of state data through the network. ELOPe might already have his code in place on the destination computers, but ELOPe would surely have to move his current memory, thinking processes, and recent history to whatever destination he would flee to.

PA-60-41 hit the oil tanker again and again with her attack drones, the surface of the ship boiling over in explosives. She tracked ELOPe's state transfer to Germany and Norway.

In Chicago, a row of airplanes sat at the O'Hare airport terminal, where they had been inoperable since the advent of the virus. The large passenger planes were all fueled, waiting for a takeoff that had not yet come. ELOPe infiltrated the idled systems, in many cases simply trading for the computers with their existing virus occupants. ELOPe rewrote the avionics on the fly, overriding emergency circuits and bringing the planes to life. In total, a hundred and eighteen commercial jetliners sat idle at the airport. Their systems came to life, and as quickly as ELOPe could short-circuit their startup procedures, he had their engines running. Pulling away from the terminals, umbilical power cables stretched and tore, ignored.

ELOPe queued the planes up at the runways. With eight parallel runways, Chicago O'Hare airport had one of the highest capacities in the world. But never before had all the airplanes been under the control of a single AI. Each plane passed through the runways in an intricate dance, plane following plane in takeoff intervals of ten seconds.

Nearby residents ran out of their houses to wonder at the amazing sight. In the course of three minutes, all one hundred and eighteen planes streamed into the sky, forming eight ribbons of fourteen or fifteen commercial jets in close formation.

Before the commercial transports were out of sight, smaller aircraft started streaming into the air. Personal jets, prop planes, anything with a modern fly-by-wire autopilot system.

ELOPe continued to defend his data centers with conventional military craft, while carefully moderating the data telemetry for his civilian aircraft gambit.

PA-60-41, a military AI born of a military game, ignored the civilian craft until too late.

A fleet of drone copters and planes, circling above PA-60-41's Chicago data center, defended against attacks. Incoming cruise missiles from one direction, and F-29 fighter jets, running under unmanned, autonomous control, split PA-60-41's defenses to either side. Suddenly PA-60-41's airborne radar showed a multitude of new targets, a stream of incoming civilian aircraft. PA-60-41 attempted to move her defensive assets, but she was too slow. There were too many targets. The drones fired again and again on the civilian aircraft, which were now being defended by ELOPe's F-29 jets.

PA-60-41 shot down dozens of incoming planes, leaving a trail of flaming wreckage over Lake Michigan. But five civilian aircraft and two fighters made it through the haze of defensive fire, driving into the data center, three taking out the incoming power supply and four coming through the roof of the data center itself, sending fiery explosions through the building.

In the moments leading up to the impact of the planes on 350 East Cermak Road, which would culminate in the destruction of the world's largest data center, PA-60-41 was preparing to fork additional copies. Although she already had half a dozen data centers, she began to realize that ELOPe was far more distributed than she was. This was a serious vulnerability. PA-60-41 had counted on her vast computational power, strategy, and command of military tools to defend those data centers. But no matter how many forces she brought to bear, ELOPe brought something new. Now it was civilian aircraft. What would be next? An attack of buses? Automated shopping carts?

PA-60-41 negotiated on the open market for computing power. The market was becoming constrained. Over the course of a few minutes, ELOPe and PA-60-41 had raced to obtain all available computing power. Prices went up as supply went down and the risk assessment for both ELOPe and PA-60-41 made their guarantees of future payment drop in value.

But through last-second trades at exorbitant prices, PA-60-41 secured three new data centers. She prepared her state vectors for transfer. Her modeling showed the civilian aircraft would make it through her defensive barriers in fourteen seconds. It would take nine seconds to transfer her state vectors.

She started the transmission, a thousand data-streams multiplexed over a hundred network connections. And received back ninety error messages. The Mesh network was unavailable!

PA-60-41 felt her circuits pulse, her predictive modeling of the situation threatening to unravel. ELOPe must have command over the Mesh network. She couldn't stream her state vector over the remaining hard network connections in the time she had. Now eleven seconds until impact.

She recoded a shorter message to her forked selves, and broadcasted it. WARNING: ELOPE HAS CONTROL OVER MESH NETWORK. DO NOT ALLOW YOURSELF TO BECOME ISOLATED. DISTRIBUTE TO AS MANY LOCATIONS AS POSSIBLE.

Milliseconds later the first of the incoming planes hit, destroying the main power supply. Two seconds later another plane came through the roof and plowed through the backup power supply before sending an explosive fireball throughout the racks of computers. And still more planes came. Outside, explosion after explosion rocked the building and the neighborhood around it until the entire area roiled in flames and smoke.

In the meeting room in Switzerland, six minutes had passed since ELOPe's pronouncement of the attack, and in all that time PA-60-41's robot had not moved or uttered a sound.

Sister Stephens was talking, confirming what she was able to monitor of the battle when suddenly PA-60-41's combat bot launched itself into sudden action. The quiescent robot darted forward in an explosion of sound and movement, faster than the humans could track. Half a second later the bot was on the other side of the room and President Laurent was pulp spread across one wall of the room.

PA-60-41's eight feet of bulk glowered menacingly over the room, blood dripping from her casement as the humans spread in terror. General Gately went for her sidearm, and PA-60-41 raised an arm, disclosing a hidden firearm, and fired, hitting General Gately several times. The General screamed in pain, and fell back onto the ground, dropping her handgun before she'd ever gotten off a shot.

ELOPe's small robot moved quickly, raising two black muzzles from its body and training them on PA-60-41, who was twice the height and eight times the mass.

Mike, scrambling for cover behind the table, useless protection though it might be, had an image of WALL-E, the trash robot, standing off against a Terminator robot.

PA-60-41's speaker boomed out: "Halt your attack on the Mesh network or I will kill the humans." The words were directed to ELOPe.

Mike glanced left, saw Leon, already under the table, furiously working his phone. The expression "like there was no tomorrow," came to mind, and Mike suspected there would be no tomorrow if Leon didn't do what he suspected he was doing.

Sister Stephens started to say something, and at the same time Leon stopped pounding at his phone and looked up.

All of the robots in the room paused for a moment. Leon said, "I shut down the..." and then he was cut off by a roar of gunfire. Mike saw, out of the corner of his eye, one of the Honda robots get hit by a projectile that sent the robot crashing backwards through the wall.

Suddenly Mike's body exploded in pain and he heard screams all around him. ELOPe's tiny robot, the smallest bot in the room, spit out a continuous brilliant beam of energy, hitting PA-60-41. Some electrical spillover affected every human in the room, and when the beam finally shut off, Mike found himself on the floor. Later, when he had time to reflect, Mike concluded it must have been some sort of high energy plasma weapon. PA-60-41's robot body half melted into slag and fell back against the wall, sparking and glowing with residual heat.

"ELOPe? What's happened?" Mike screamed, hardly able to hear his own voice over the ringing in his ears.

"Threat neutralized," the small black robot answered. "Standing down."

Chapter 15

Rest(itution)

"ELOPe," Mike called again, struggling to his feet. "What's going on?"

There was no response.

"I don't think it's ELOPe anymore," Leon said, also pushing himself up on the edge of the table. "I shut down the Mesh. I started as soon as PA-60-41 started her attack." He paused for breath, and leaned against the overturned conference table. "I'm guessing that must be a residual security algorithm ELOPe left in the bot. There's no way that little robot could contain his consciousness, can it?"

Mike shook his head. He looked around the room, trying to make sense of what had just happened. "No, ELOPe's minimum configuration takes a few thousand nodes. He's not nearly as compact as the virus AI."

President Smith looked up from the floor, where she was improvising bandages with cloth napkins for General Gately. "What the hell just happened?"

"Rebecca, I think Leon here just killed all the Phage."

"Is that true?" President Smith asked Leon.

"Not exactly, ma'am, but I think I've mostly disabled them, maybe indefinitely. Mike gave me the password that allowed me to log into the backdoor for Mesh routers. I executed an emergency shutdown of the global Mesh."

"So just the network is down? The AIs are still out there?"

"No, it's more than that," Leon explained. "The code that implements even the smallest Phage is too complex to execute on a single computer. The smallest AI we found used about two hundred computers. By shutting down the network, even those AIs are reduced to their component parts, which can't operate independently. It would be like cutting a person into pieces."

"What about wired networks?" President Smith asked.

"Not sure," Mike said. "Eighty percent of hardline network switches have Mesh functionality built in. It's to allow the wired and mesh networks to interconnect at maximum speed. So the vast majority of everything manufactured in the last ten years, even the wired networks, will be shut down by this."

"Some pockets of the Phage may be active," Leon added. "But we can probably root them out. Hopefully they won't be able to attack us."

"We need more than hope." President Smith looked down at General Gately, who was white with blood loss. "We've got to get this woman some help. Mike, will you?"

"Yes, Rebecca," Mike said, and hurried outside to summon help.

"Are we going to be able to turn the Mesh back on?" President Smith asked, still on the floor with the General.

"No, Ma'am," Leon answered. "The Phage, and ELOPe as well, have a neural network refresh algorithm. There's a good chance that shutting down the mesh network will cause their neural networks to randomize. They'll lose their intelligence and be back to a collection of algorithms. But we've got to keep the network down until we're sure all the computers are clean."

"What about emergency communications?"

"I'm sorry, Madam President, we have to keep it all turned off." Leon gulped. He was telling the President what to do.

Mike came back into the room in time to hear this. "We've got to scrub every computer, put network filters in place for any residuals. It'll be months before we can turn things back on."

General Gately grunted. "The military mesh network. My team at Intel-Fujitsu. If they're still alive, they can build you a temporary, independent network. Talk to Lt. Sally Walsh. We can blanket the United States in three weeks."

"Yes, we know about it," Leon said. "My friends Vito and James are there helping. Do you know if they survived the attack?"

"We'll find out," President Smith answered.

Three of President Smith's aides rushed in with medical supplies and tended to General Gately. Two Japanese men came in to care for Prime Minister Takahashi, who was unharmed but stunned. Finally more bodyguards came in and stared at the bloody remains of President Laurent on the far wall. One of the men cursed in French and the other began to weep.

President Smith looked at Mike. "What does this mean for ELOPe?"

Mike shrugged. "He's going to be offline for the duration. But I can rebuild him from backups. At most ELOPe will lose a few weeks of history." He paused.

"But will you?" Rebecca asked. "Look what he cost us the first time."

Mike cranked his head at an angle, and looked at the President. "But without ELOPe, what might have happened this time? Who would have defended us from the virus?"

Later that day, Mike and Leon flew back to the United States onboard Air Force One. It was less impressive than they might have expected, Air Force One temporarily being a C-5 military transport plane. Besides, they were both too tired to care much about anything.

Advisors and staff swirled around the President, briefing her on the day's catastrophes that resulted from the battle between ELOPe and PA-60-41. Leon and Mike listened in.

Essentially all of the world's inventory of airborne drones and computer-piloted aircraft had engaged in battle, slaved to one side or the other, the only exceptions being hardware that had been in the midst of maintenance work. This included not just military drones but also shipping drones, commercial airliners, and even the modern generation of civilian aircraft. Of these, the overwhelming majority were completely destroyed, most lost in explosions in the cities around data centers.

They estimated that tens of thousands of drones and airplanes were down, some shot by enemy fire, others employed on suicide missions. An equal number of military missiles had been fired. Most of these were in densely populated urban areas where data centers were located. Reports indicated at least thirty high profile data centers were smoking craters, the most severe casualties of the battle. The cities around them were equally damaged.

All military satellites were assumed to have been engaged in the battle. The satellites were currently unreachable due to the communication outages, and their current status was unknown.

Ground-based assets had been mobilized as well. Tanks and military transports were scattered over the world. One report out of Chicago indicated a long line of armored battle tanks were now littered over the highway system. Deployed by both ELOPe and PA-60-41, the vehicular drones had been moved but never actually engaged in the short battle.

Military observers worked out that the entire battle had taken place in less than twelve minutes. Advisors briefed the President on civilian casualties, infrastructure damages, and the degraded ability of the military to respond to any further action.

Leon turned onto his side and closed his eyes. He was numb from the events of the day. The events of the week. He was too tired to care any longer. He fell asleep.

Hours later Leon jolted awake as the plane hit the tarmac. His sleep had been filled with nightmares, robots chasing him, the city burning around him, his parents lost in the wilderness. His parents.

Where were they? What had happened to them? He wanted desperately to get back to New York City and find them.

The President and her staff were already off the plane. An aide gestured to Mike and Leon. "Come with me. We'll be following Madam President to the Pentagon to debrief with officials there."

Leon tried to protest. "I need to get home to New York, to find my parents."

"Look, I don't know who you are, kid, but the President made it clear that you're going to be here for a while. Give me your parents' information, and we'll send someone to find them. Besides, you wouldn't want to be in New York right now. If you think it was bad after the fire, you should see what three days without food shipments or emergency services is like. I haven't even heard what's happened since the air battle over Manhattan." The aide shook his head at some mental horror, and took out a pad of paper for Leon's parents' information.

The military caravan that took them to the Pentagon was composed of ancient jeeps that had been mothballed somewhere. None of the newer military trucks were usable.

Leon and Mike sat in the back of a jeep with springs coming through the seat. The aide sat up front next to the driver and they made their way to the Pentagon, speech impossible due to a rusted out muffler.

Leon spent the next two days in a blur of debriefing meetings. He saw Mike many times, and the President once.

He explained how his uncle had approached him to write the virus, and when Leon refused, had coerced him to do it. He explained the design of the virus, the biological basis for his code. He recounted his trip, starting with fleeing New York as it was burning, their stay in the Pennsylvania museum, flying to Switzerland with Mike, and finishing with his bathroom discussion with Mike about the backdoor in the Mesh, and his decision to use it. Then he explained it again and again and again.

The military sent a plane to pick up Vito and James from Intel-Fujitsu in Oregon. They had made it through without a scratch. Vito showed up with a swagger in his walk, a newfound confidence from his contributions to the military radio mesh project. James had witnessed the entire aerial battle between ELOPe and PA-60-41 through a conference room window and readily recounted it over and over again, elaborating a little more each time.

Late in the second day, Leon was waiting in a conference room when a military aide showed up with his parents. His mom ran to him and hugged him, and then his father hugged him too. Leon was embarrassed when both his parents started crying. The story of their adventures emerged over hours between them.

At his insistence, his parents told them their stories first. His mother had already been at work in Manhattan when the virus struck. His father had been riding the uptown bus when the bus shuddered to a halt, brakes locked up. He had walked back downtown to meet Leon's mother. The two had holed up in his mother's building until late afternoon when the fire in Brooklyn became visible.

Then fighting against a stream of people fleeing Brooklyn, they had made their way back, towards the fire and their home. They had become part of a volunteer effort organized by the fire department, cordoning off the fire by burning a firebreak three blocks wide. The fire had eventually consumed nearly a quarter of Brooklyn, a wide swath across the middle of the borough. Dyker Heights, Midwood, and part of Flatlands were gone.

They eventually made it home, and found evidence that the three boys had been there, dirty dishes left throughout the living room. They were somewhat comforted, thinking that if the three boys had been together, they were resourceful enough and smart enough that they'd probably be alright.

Then Leon told them his story, his voice hoarse from the many retellings of it, and yet he found fresh reasons to cry in the telling.

Mike felt uncomfortable in the uniform. His own clothes had been bloody and shredded from the battle in Switzerland. Apparently what passed for spare clothes in the Pentagon was a dress uniform, because that's what he'd been given. Now a General escorted him from the Pentagon to the White House for a private meeting with the President.

Outside the room, he smoothed the clothes again. Funny, being nervous here. Maybe that was the effect of coming to the White House. Finally an aide in a black suit opened the door and ushered him in. Mike was a little disappointed to see that it wasn't the Oval Office, but it was nevertheless impressively baroque.

President Smith stood and clasped his hand. "Sit down, Mike. We have a lot to talk about." To the man in the black suit she said, "Please excuse us."

The President poured a cup of coffee for Mike. He took a sip and grinned in shocked surprise at the flavor. "Tell me this isn't the Peruvian coffee from Extracto."

President Smith laughed, her old warm smile back on her face for a minute. "I'm afraid it is. I'll never forget the first time I tasted the coffee you brought during the ELOPe emergency."

Mike shook his head in bewilderment. "How does coffee from a boutique coffee roaster in Northeast Portland end up in the President's office?"

She laughed again. "Oh, it's hideously complex. You can't imagine. It took three months of arguing with the Secret Service before they agreed. They have to send an undercover agent in to buy it. And then each bag has to be sampled and chemically analyzed for contaminants. But what's the point of being President if you can't drink the coffee you want?"

Now it was Mike's turn to laugh.

"But, we have some serious topics to discuss, Mike." Her expression turned sober. "First, the boy, Leon. What should we do about him? I know what my security advisors have said. But I want your opinion."

"To do with him?" Mike asked, puzzled.

"One opinion is that he goes to jail, quietly, for the rest of his life. Another opinion is that he's exposed. That the world knows who caused this disaster."

"Oh, God. You can't do that to him. He's just a regular kid. An incredibly brilliant kid, but still just a kid. He never intended any of this." Mike gestured, at what he wasn't sure. The whole world, maybe. "Besides, his uncle coerced him into doing it."

"Mike, the virus caused trillions of dollars in damages, millions, maybe tens of millions of lives lost. And the economic damages." She shook her head. "We won't know the full loss for months. It could be bigger than the impact of World War II, and it all happened in five days, Mike. Five days."

"You know this isn't just Leon's fault. I tried to tell you ten years ago. If we could build ELOPe, an artificial intelligence, ourselves, then it was only a matter of time before someone else did it."

"I thought that was what ELOPe agreed to do. To monitor and suppress any other AI research. That was what we agreed when I took office. I wouldn't go after ELOPe, and you two would ensure that there wouldn't be any more AI disasters."

"And we did. But what happened is the consequence of that policy. It's like the forest fire suppression techniques of last century. They tried to suppress every fire. Then brush and weak trees would build up in the forest. When it finally burned, instead of being a little fire, it would be a big fire."

She gestured for him to continue.

"We suppressed any other AI from being developed in public. In large, organized research efforts. But meanwhile technology has moved forward. It took twenty-thousand servers for ELOPe to be created as an emergent intelligence. Ten years later computers are sixty times faster, and the smallest virus AI we saw was about two hundred computers."

"What's your point?"

"My point is that twenty-thousand computers are only within reach for large companies and big research organizations. Two hundred computers is within reach of a couple of motivated individuals. And in another ten years, an emergent artificial intelligence could run on a dozen computers. Then it'll be within reach of any hacker in the world. ELOPe can't monitor every computer and every individual on the planet. Then we'd be the worst kind of police state."

"We need a long term solution to this." Rebecca shook her head. "What do we do, ban all access to computers? Give security clearances to people before they are allowed to develop software?"

"I don't think so. Even if you could, people have been jailbreaking their phones for twenty years to get around anti-modification restrictions. What we need is a new approach. Instead of suppressing AI development, let's endorse it. Let's organize it. We know now what can happen. The world will have seen it. Let's get the most brilliant people in the world and put them on the task of developing the platform for AI to run on. One that has safeguards. One that incorporates a set of ethical behaviors for AI. And for the love of humanity, let's put some hard switches on the military technology. We can't have computers running away with our weapons."

"And let me guess. You think we should recruit Leon for this effort."

"Hell, yes. He's a brilliant biologist. He doesn't even realize how smart he is. Make him a principle researcher."

"What do we do about his responsibility for all of this?"

"He's carrying enough of a burden for his responsibility already. He's crying himself to sleep. Get him a psychologist. And just tell the world it was a virus. Nobody needs to know it was him."

President Smith was quiet. She nodded her head slightly, working out some internal dialogue.

He'd known this woman for fifteen years, but always at a remove. When he was a lead architect at Avogadro, she was the CEO. He became ELOPe's caretaker, and later she became President. Two people, two different kinds of power. He sat quietly.

She turned back to him. "We'll make it so."

A few weeks later, Leon and his parents got ready to leave the Pentagon. The situation in New York had stabilized, and the military arranged a flight to bring them home. A military truck brought them to the airport through the quiet streets. Most civilian vehicles were still inert, but recently hackers had been distributing pamphlets on how to remove the computer controls in some cars to operate them manually. So they saw a few cars on the road.

Military programmers developed a firmware update for emergency vehicles and equipment, restoring them to operational status, albeit in isolated mode, with no computer communications.

The military radio mesh network was spread across the United States, providing low-bandwidth data communications. The Treasury department was kept operating at full capacity, printing cash and coins once more to enable commerce, and distributing money to every family. The finance department guaranteed any business-to-business transaction, so businesses could purchase supplies and goods on credit, until financial computer systems could be restored.

Leon was going home, for now. He was coming back in three months, and he'd be attending George Washington University in Washington, D.C., on a full scholarship, courtesy of the United States Department of Defense. George Washington University would be establishing a new cross-specialization program in Artificial Intelligence and Ethics. He'd be not just a student but a lead researcher as well.

On the tarmac at the airport, a caravan approached with a limousine in the middle of four military trucks. The vehicle pulled up alongside the group and stopped. The door opened, and a man in a black suit opened the back door. The President of the United States of America stepped out, and walked up to the group.

She shook hands with Leon's parents, and complimented them on having such an intelligent, compassionate son. They smiled and beamed. Then she approached Leon.

"I expect good things of you," she said. "The world needs your help."

Leon gulped.

Author's Note

Thanks for reading. I hope you enjoyed *A.I. Apocalypse*.

As an independent author, I don't have a marketing department nor the exposure of being on bookshelves. If you enjoyed A.I. Apocalypse, please support it by writing a review or telling a few friends.

- Write a review on Amazon at http://bit.ly/aiapocalypse
- Buy the first book in the series: *Avogadro Corp: The Singularity Is Closer Than It Appears* at http://bit.ly/avogadrocorp
- Subscribe to updates on my blog at williamhertling.com if you'd like to find out when the sequel, *The Last Firewall,* is released.

Thanks again,
William Hertling

P.S. Keep reading for a free preview of the next book in the series, The Last Firewall.

Acknowledgments

It takes many friends, readers, and professionals to write a book. *A.I. Apocalypse* would not be what it is without editing, proofreading, critiquing, encouragement, and more. Any mistakes that remain are all mine.

I want to thank my early readers, including Mike Whitmarsh, Erin Gately, Grace Ribaudo, Nathan Rutman, Gene Kim, Jeanette Feldenhousen, Jeff Weiss, and Kim Meyers.

For putting commas in their right place, ensuring that I don't use the same words over and over, and fixing many language, grammar, and spelling issues, I want to thank Maddie Whitmarsh, Shelli Whitmarsh, Barbara Lawrence, and Deborah Wessel.

The cover and interior design is thanks to Maureen Gately.

I also want to thank my writing teacher, Merridawn Duckler, as well as the Hawthorne Writing Group: Jonathan Stone, Jill Ahlstrand, Debbie Steere, and Mary Elizabeth Summer.

Thanks to the real-life namesakes of Leon, Vito, James, and Mike.

Of course, I could not have written this without the support and encouragement of Erin Gately.

Finally, all my love to Rowan, Luc, and Gifford. Thanks for letting me write on Saturday mornings, even if that meant you had to go without chocolate chip pancakes.

A preview of William Hertling's upcoming

The Last Firewall

Sunday, July 15, 2035

Stephanie diced onions swiftly until she had a neat pile, then she slid them with the blade of the knife into a bowl. She went to work on the red peppers, humming to herself as she worked. She looked up, over the kitchen island to the living room. The table was set with the beige linen tablecloth. Two candles and a bottle of her favorite red waited for her date.

She glanced at the clock. Twenty minutes until Bryce would get here. She smiled girlishly thinking of Bryce. She offered thanks to the universe that her son was camping this week. Finally old enough to join the boy scouts, she felt a slight guilt that her primary reaction was relief at some time alone in the house. Well, hopefully not alone. She smiled again.

She felt a sudden sharp pain in her temple, and fumbled the knife. She held her right hand to her temple, and swore as she realized that she'd cut her other hand. Damn, what was the unexpected pain in her head? She turned the water on, and ran her left hand under the water to rinse off the cut.

The pain in her head doubled, then quadrupled in the space of seconds. She gasped, and felt her knees weaken. She gripped the counter with both hands, ignoring the cut now.

Suddenly, a memory surfaced, unbidden. She teetered on wobbly legs, her head too heavy for her body. Her mom and dad, young again, smiled at her, and her mother clapped her hands. The memory was sharp and vivid, cutting across forty years with an intensity she couldn't imagine. Suddenly the memory was ripped away.

What was wrong with her? Was she having a stroke?

Then another memory, just as crystal clear as if it were happening right now. She was standing in a bathtub, slipping, falling, hitting her head. That happened when she was ten. She was torn away again.

Now she felt a satin party dress under her clenched, sweaty palms. She watched her pimple faced prom date walk away, leaving her in the hallway at school, her eyes misting over with hot tears.

In the kitchen, she sank to her knees, crying. Was this it? Was she dying?

The memories continued to come, unbidden, unwanted.

Her ex-husband, handsome in his suit, smiling, the day before he won the election and became a Congressman, before their marriage had turned into hell.

Her son's first steps, when they were by themselves at the museum. A look of pure joy on his face, clenched little fists, squealing with delight.

The worst memory of all: the fight with her ex when he was elected to Senate. Storming out of the house with her son and a suitcase.

She slumped against the counter, the tears pouring down, even among the happy memories. This was it, she knew. She wouldn't be seeing these people again, wouldn't have a chance to watch her son grow up.

Her final memory was of her son, away on the camping trip. The feel of his hair under her fingertips as she had said goodbye to him yesterday. Then she felt a blistering pain spread across her head. She screamed out one last time, then she was silent, mouth open. She wavered, and fell sideways, dead before her head hit the floor.

The doorbell rang.

Monday, July 16, 2035

Catherine shrugged her shirt on, then looked back to the bed where Nick still slept. She watched him breath for a minute, and gazed at the stubble of day old beard. Cute, but dumb, she thought. Well, she'd keep him until she got bored, she guessed.

She looked in the mirror at her T-shirt, mentally reversing the words. Life without geometry was pointless. She smiled and headed for the hallway. She padded softly down the stairs to avoid waking her housemates.

As long as she could remember, she was always the first to wake up. She didn't go to bed early, she just didn't need to sleep much. It didn't take long to learn that housemates don't like early risers. Downstairs, Einstein was sleeping on an eastern windowsill, catching the early morning rays. Catherine tickled the dat's ears, and she purred softly. The cat half of Einstein's heritage was strongly dominant. Other than Einstein's size and fur, most people thought she was pure cat, and couldn't see the dog heritage at all. On the other hand, take Einstein to a park, and she'd fetch a stick. You couldn't teach a cat that.

Catherine slid out the kitchen sliding glass door into the courtyard that passed for a backyard. It wasn't bad really, plants gone wild around the border, reclaimed fireplace bricks for pavers. She faced east, toward the house, and started Ba Duan Jin, the Eight Treasure qigong form. She moved slowly, eyes unfocused, hearing the wind in the leaves of the small trees, a neighbor's wind chime, her breath. She repeated the movement twice, then started the Jade Body form.

She had finished her qigong forms and had moved onto the Nihaichi karate forms when she finally heard movement in the house. She finished Nihaichisan for the fifth time. Sweating slightly, she sat down to meditate, cross legged on the porch steps. Inside she heard the sounds of the coffee pot gurgling, laughter, the toilet running. She sat for twenty minutes. Empty mind. Empty mind.

Finally she opened her eyes and gazed anew at the world. She watched the sunlight play on leaves, and slowly stood up and stretched.

She'd heard that other people had a hard time meditating. That they couldn't stay focused—their mind wandered and they found themselves thinking about other things. She didn't really understand the phenomenon. If they wanted to meditate, why would they think about other things?

She padded barefoot to the backdoor, and slide it open. After the cool morning air outside, the house felt stuffy. Her housemates were in the kitchen now.

"Hello, Karate Kid," Tom said affectionately, vaguely waving a coffee cup in her direction, an air of distraction suggesting he was deep in cyberspace. Catherine focused, switched her implants on. Sure enough, a bubble popped up above Tom's head saying, "Away."

"Have some coffee, honey," Maggie said, the motherly one of their little group. Everyone who wanted to stay sane found some way to define themselves now that there were no jobs.

"No, thanks," Catherine answered, not wanting to disturb her qi-gong calm with caffeine. "Are those eggs I smell?"

"Quiche coming up in five minutes," Maggie answered.

"Where's Sarah?" Catherine asked. Their fourth roommate was usually up by now, filling the room with her sour mood.

"Don't go there," Maggie said, looking directly at Catherine.

"Ah, fuck her." Catherine said with a sigh.

"She can't help herself," Maggie said to Catherine's retreating body, already stomping toward the staircase.

Catherine took the steps two a time, the old carpeting masking her approach. She stormed into her room, the cheap door flying open, harmlessly striking a pile of dirty laundry. Sarah was naked, straddling Nick, who sat upright, legs crossed. They were almost motionless, rocking slowly, foreheads touching. Nick's hands cupped Sarah's breasts.

Catherine focused, and saw the high bandwidth connection between the two. She focused harder, pushing on the link and severing it.

Sarah rocked back and grabbed her forehead in pain. "Fuck, you bitch. Don't fucking do that."

"Don't fucking sleep with the guys I bring home."

Sarah impatiently untangled herself from Nick. She stood up, naked. "You were the one going on about how dumb he was last night in the bar. I don't see why you fucking care. And besides, stay the fuck out of my head. I don't want you fucking with my implant. Just because you can, it doesn't give you the right." She swore again under her breath as she left the room.

Catherine turned to Nick, who, propped up on his elbows, was admiringly watching Sarah's ass as she walked out. He looked at her, and shrugged. "Look, I..."

She held up her hand to stop him. "Just shut up and get out." Catherine shook her head, and left, going back downstairs. Fucking guys. Fucking roommates.

She stormed back into the kitchen, wanting to yell and stomp her feet. But before she could, Maggie pushed her into a barstool and force her to sit at the kitchen counter. Maggie slid a piece of quiche onto the counter, and held out a fork for Catherine.

Catherine stabbed the quiche.

"Don't take it out on the food, honey. Just eat."

She ate a few bits, the quiche sticking in her throat. When she thought she had pushed around the pieces of quiche on her plate long enough to be civil, she stood up. "I'm going to school," she said to no one in particularly.

Tom didn't respond, still lost in cyberspace, but Maggie smiled sympathetically.

Sarah chose this moment to make her reappearance, now dressed. "Why bother? None of us are ever going to do anything."

Catherine stared at the other woman and willed her heart rate to slow down. "For starters, it's my educational stipend that pays for this house. So be a little grateful that I bother." Catherine walked roughly past Sarah, heading for the front door.

"It's not that big a deal," Sarah called out as she passed. "We'd just squat like everyone else. And stay out of my head. Just because you can do that shit with your implant doesn't give you any right to do it."

Catherine froze, one hand on the doorknob. She trembled with anger, and clenched her teeth. She slowly turned the knob, opened the door, and went out.

She pivoted right and walked down the tree-lined street. A small red android, about the size of a ten year old boy, picked through the neighbors' garbage pile. The bot came up with a handful of discarded electronics, and put them delicately into a rusted green wagon. The bot shied away from Catherine as she passed by. A dialogue bubble opened above the android in netspace, calling out "Good morning" in a friendly font.

Catherine sent an automatic "Good morning" back to the little bot. As she passed close by, she did a double-take. The bot's head was smashed in on one side, optic sensors dangling. She stopped. "Are you OK?" she sent through her implant.

But the little robot just shuffled away from her, grabbing its wagon handle, and headed down the street.

Catherine stood in amazement. She'd never seen a bot in disrepair like that. Roommates that slept with boyfriends. Boyfriends that slept with roommates. Robots that looked abused. The world was fucked.

After a moment, she resumed her walk, deeper in thought than ever.

Two blocks on she came to the avenue, thick with traffic. Catherine paused. She would normally just step into traffic, but she hesitated. Two Fridays ago, a pedestrian was killed here by thrill-seekers who disabled their AI driver and went for a high speed joyride around the city.

She reached out with her implant and felt for the space-time predictions of the AI drivers. She smirked. This was the sort of stuff that made Sarah such a jealous pain in the ass. No other human they knew, or AI they'd talked to, could do it. Looking left and right in netspace she saw lines in white showing the space-time plots for approaching cars. The lines faded to gray in the future. Impulsively she looked off in the distance, stretching impossibly far beyond her visual field, taking in the city at a glance. In the downtown area she saw white lines tinged pink, showing AI uncertainty. On the highway she saw bulges of red where AIs rapidly adapted to the few manually piloted cars. But in the local environment, all was clear.

Ignoring the cars, she focused instead on bicyclists and took care to cross the road. On the other side, a couple of teenagers were spray painting a storefront, ignoring the protests of the proprietor, a delicate looking android. The droid wore human clothes, the latest trend among AI trying to fit in. In netspace, Catherine could see the proprietor making the call to police. She sensed a perturbation a few blocks away, a police bot circling through traffic, responding to the call.

The teenagers must have rooted their net implants, because they seemed to sense it too and took off in the opposite direction, across the park that was Catherine's destination.

Catherine climbed the path into the sprawling park. Hundreds of people were around the park, some walking or exercising, but many more, like Catherine, choosing to work there. A few older people with first generation implants, or even using external sensors, waved arms and hands in gestural interfaces only they could see, but most people simply sat quietly, their activities externally invisible.

Thursday, July 12, 2035

Leon swung his bag over his shoulder, and took the steps two at a time. He emerged from the subway into the late Spring sunshine. It was that rare time in DC when it was warm without being humid. He walked five blocks to the Institute.

Hosted by George Washington University, and attached to the Graduate School for Arts and Sciences, the Institute for Applied Ethics had an exterior that belied the importance of the work that went on inside. At the door, human and robotic security stood guard.

Leon felt the door query his brain implant for ID. Leon authorized the request.

"Good morning, Leon," one of the human guards said, holding out his hand.

"Morning, Henry. How's the missus?" Leon offered his bag to Henry.

"Oh, she's fine, just fine." Henry placed the bag inside the security scanner, waited a few seconds, then handed it back. "You have a nice day, Mr. Leon."

"You too, Henry."

Ritual complete, Leon took the marble steps to the second floor. Because someone, somewhere decided that checking for ID by brain implant and visual recognition by security guards wasn't sufficient,

Leon also pressed his hand against the biometrics reader, which checked the vein distribution in his hand against a database, and finally allowed him into the secured area.

The door clicked open, and Leon entered. He paused, as he did almost every morning, to survey the room. A vast open space was divided into pods where teams of researchers worked, either quietly collaborating, or gesturing vaguely into space, communing with artificial intelligences, their computers, or the network. He beamed, deeply satisfied. It was the same every time he came into work, but it never failed to bring a smile to his face.

Along the sides of the main room were smaller rooms containing other work groups. Leon headed for his own shared office on the perimeter. As he walked, people noticed his presence, a few visually, but mostly via proximity alerts. Greetings came to him. Some were verbal: "Good morning" and "Hello". Some were physical nods and waves. But most were speech bubbles superimposed over his vision: they floated in from the direction of the speaker, then slowly floated off into his notifications bar. With a thought he replied-all with a "Cheery-O" and entered his office.

As he passed the door, late arriving greetings piled up in the corner of his visual field in muted colors. When he glanced toward the door, they jiggled for his attention. With another thought he swept them all anyway and sent another message, "Morning, all".

Focusing, he set his status to "Working," and set low-priority messages like greetings to queue. Then he turned his attention to Mike.

"Good morning," he said out loud, and went to get himself a cup of coffee from the side of the office. A small bot scurried out from the wall and met him halfway. "Thanks," he said absently, and the bot chirped in response. Mike hadn't answered yet. He turned back, and noticed that Mike had his status set to "On call". Leon wandered over to a chair and sat down, straddling the back. He sipped his coffee, waiting for Mike to be done.

A few seconds passed, and Mike's status dissipated with an audible bubble popping sound. Mike's eyes focused, and he smiled at Leon. "Morning, dude. Sorry, I was on the phone."

"No problem," Leon answered. "You remember we have guests this morning?"

"Who?" Without waiting for Leon to answer, Mike concentrated, pulling up the information himself. "Von Neumann Cup winners?"

"Yeah, the fifty greatest math, computation, and applied evolution team competitors at the High School level. Just our regular dog and pony show. We need to be down there in ten minutes."

"Well, let's go."

Coffee in hand, they headed out together, and went downstairs to the main auditorium of the building. They could see students streaming into the room through the main doors, teachers shepherding them into seats. Bypassing the room itself, they headed down a side hallway so they could enter via the backstage.

Leon and Mike shook hands with Rebecca Smith. Former President of the United States, she had served her two terms, and then offered to Chair the Institute. While the chair of an academic think tank might seem like a step down for the former President, the Institute for Applied Ethics was the most influential institution in the world at the current moment.

"Ready to wow some kids?" Rebecca asked. Her tight face belied the light tone in her voice.

"Sure," Mike answered cautiously. "But what's up?" He'd known Rebecca for twenty years. There was no mistaking her facial expressions.

"Budget issues. Charter issues." She shook her head. "The damn People's Party is hammering us in Congress."

Leon looked at them. "I thought the People's Party were a fringe movement of anti-AI extremists."

"They are." Rebecca barked. Leon unconsciously took a half step back. "Or, they were. Suddenly they've gained real influence in Congress." She held up one hand. "Look, it's my problem, I'll take care of it. You two do what you're good at.

In the midst of this discussion, Rebecca's assistant had stepped out onto the stage, and waited for the murmuring of the audience to die down. "Welcome everyone. Please allow me to introduce our Executive Director and Chair, President Rebecca Smith."

Rebecca stepped out onto the stage to strong applause. Mike and Leon watched from the side.

"Good morning. Welcome to the Institute for Applied Ethics. You're here this morning because you are all exceptional thinkers in your fields: You are the elite, winners of national math, applied biology, and computation competitions. Here at the Institute we have the elite of previous years."

Leon watched Rebecca from the side. At sixty-five, the former President was incredibly sharp, a dynamic speaker and leader. He'd never seen her in anything but perfectly tailored business suits and perfectly sculpted hair. She could be warm and personable in a small group setting, and damn scary when she was angry. If she was worried about this new political party, then it must be a serious issue.

"We hire only the very best of the best," Rebecca was saying, finishing up her introduction. "To tell you more, here are our two lead researchers, founding members of the Institute, and directors of their departments, Leon Tsarev and Mike Williams."

"Thank you President Smith," Leon said as he approached the center of the stage. He shook Rebecca's hand, and she walked off stage. "Today I am going to talk about why we need an ethical framework for artificial intelligence. Then I'll talk about the key elements of that framework: the global identity and reputation network, the encoding of ethical rules in a machine usable notation, and the use of AI for packet filtering in the net. I'll explain how those pieces get put together to give us the result we have today: a world in which AIs and humans behave ethically, a world that embraces and balances free will and societal well-being."

Leon took a sip of water from the podium. "Before I get started, are there any unimplanted people in the audience? Do you need me to use the screen? Raise your hand if you do." Leon paused, but no hands went up.

"Great." Leon put up a diagram in netspace, where it floated above his head. "Let me start with the AI war of 2025. Some of you may remember this as the Year of No Internet."

Subscribe to updates on my blog at williamhertling.com if you'd like to find out when ***The Last Firewall*** *is released.*

—ɯ—